RACH

TWO-TIME RITA® AWARD-WINNING

"With humor and eloquent prose,
Gibson brings substance and depth to
this loving, modern romance."
Publishers Weekly (*starred review*) on
True Love and Other Disasters

"Gibson does it again! This is a really fun,
straight-up romance with witty dialogue, grown-up
characters and a story readers can relate to . . .
This book will keep you up way too late—you'll be
having too much fun reading it to put it down."
Romantic Times Book Review on *Rescue Me*

CANDIS TERRY
"A fun and refreshing voice in
contemporary romance."
New York Times bestselling author Rachel Gibson

". . . This stirring tribute to those who serve their
country is one readers won't soon forget."
Library Journal (*starred review*) on a Memorial Day
anthology including *Home Sweet Home* by Candis Terry

JENNIFER BERNARD
"[S]exy and funny."
Publishers Weekly on *The Fireman Who Loved Me*

"Sexy, sassy, often hilarious, and touching . . ."
Library Journal on *The Fireman Who Loved Me*

Also by Jennifer Bernard

Rachel GIBSON

CRAZY
SWEET
FINE

(Contains previously published material)

Candis TERRY

Jennifer BERNARD

red

AVON

AVON RED
An Imprint of HarperCollins*Publishers*
10 East 53rd Street
New York, New York 10022-5299

CRAZY ON YOU. Copyright © 2012 by Rachel Gibson.
HOME SWEET HOME. Copyright © 2012 by Candis Terry.
ONE FINE FIREMAN. Copyright © 2012 by Jennifer Bernard.
Excerpt from *Run to You* copyright © 2013 by Rachel Gibson
Excerpt from *Anything But Sweet* copyright © 2013 by Candis Terry
Excerpt from *Sex and the Single Fireman* copyright © 2013 by Jennifer Bernard
ISBN 978-0-06-227725-1
www.avonromance.com

First Avon Red mass market printing: April 2013

Avon Trademark Reg. U.S. Pat. Off. and in Other Countries, Marca Registrada, Hecho en U.S.A.
HarperCollins® is a registered trademark of HarperCollins Publishers.

Printed in the U.S.A.

10 9 8 7 6 5 4 3 2 1

Contents

CRAZY
SWEET
FINE

Crazy On You

RACHEL GIBSON

Chapter One

Lily Darlington hated being called crazy. She'd rather someone call her a bitch—or even a stupid bitch—because she knew she was neither and never had been. Not on purpose anyway. But put the c-word in front of bitch, and Lily was likely to go all *crazy* bitch on someone's ass.

At least she had in the past, when she'd been more impulsive and let her feelings and emotions control her. When she'd gone from zero to ten in under five seconds. When she'd dumped milk on Jimmy Joe Jenkin's head in the third grade and let air out of Sarah Little's bike tires in the sixth. When she'd thought that every action deserved a reaction. When she'd been reckless and occasionally over the top—like when she drove her Ford Taurus into her ex-husband's front room.

But she hadn't done anything over the top recently. These days, she was able to control her feelings and emotions. These days she was a respectable businesswoman and mother of a ten-year-old son. She was thirty-eight, and she'd worked hard to get the *crazy* out of her life and off the front of her name.

Lily grabbed her tote and rushed out the back of Lily Belle's Salon Day Spa. Her last cut-and-color appointment had taken longer than expected, and it was already past seven. She had to drive sixty-five miles, make dinner for her son, help him with his homework, and force him into the tub. Once he was in bed, she had to put together all the gift bags for her spa event next Saturday night.

A single bulb glowed above her head as she locked the door. Cold night air touched her cheeks and a slight breeze caught the tails of her wool coat. It was late March in the Texas panhandle and still cold enough at night that her breath hung in front of her face.

From as far back as she could remember, people had called her crazy. Crazy Lily Brooks. Then she'd married that rat bastard Ronny Darlington and they'd called her Crazy Lily Darlington.

The sound of her boot heels as she walked to her Jeep Cherokee echoed off of the Dumpster. With her thumb on the keypad, she unlocked the doors and the back hatch popped up. She set her heavy tote next to boxes filled with skin and hair care products, then reached over her head and closed the door.

Okay, so maybe she'd been just a *little* crazy during her marriage, but her ex-husband had made her crazy. He'd skirted around with half the female population of Lovett, Texas. He'd lie and tell her she was imagining things. He'd been so good at sneaking around that she'd almost convinced herself that she *was* imagining things. Then he'd dumped her for Kelly the Skank. She didn't even remember Kelly's last name, but he'd moved out and left Lily behind without so much as a backward glance. He'd also left her with a pile of bills, a bare refrigerator, and a two-year-old boy.

He'd thought he could just move on. He'd thought he could get away with making a fool of her. He'd thought she'd just take it, and *that*, more than anything, had made her drive her car through his living room. She hadn't been trying to kill him or anyone else. He hadn't even been home at the time. She'd just wanted to let him know she wasn't disposable. That he couldn't just walk away without suffering like she was suffering. But he hadn't suffered. Lily ended up in the hospital with a concussion and broken leg, and he didn't give a shit about anything but his busted TV.

She shut herself inside her SUV and fired it up. The red Cherokee was the first new car she'd ever bought. Up until a year ago, she'd always bought used. But with the success of her salon and day spa, Lily was able to splurge on something that had always been a dream—one she'd never thought would actually come true. Twin headlights shone on the back of the spa as she reversed out of the parking lot and headed home—toward the small three-bedroom house right next to her mother's, in Lovett, in the little town north of Amarillo where she was born and raised.

Living next to her mother was both a curse and a blessing. A curse because Louella Brooks was retired with nothing to do but pry into everyone's business; a blessing because Louella was retired and could watch Pippen when he got out of school. And as much as her mother drove her insane, with her "yard" art and rambling stories, she was a good grandmother and it was nice not to have to worry about her son.

Lily eased onto the highway toward Lovett and switched on the radio to a country station. She'd never wanted to raise her son alone; she was raised by a single mother herself. Louella worked hard to support Lily and her older sister, Daisy, pouring coffee and slinging chicken fried steak for long hours at the Wild Coyote Diner. She wanted better for own child—Phillip Ronald Darlington, or, as everyone called him, Pippen. Lily was twenty-eight when she gave birth to him. She'd already known her three-year marriage was in trouble but held on desperately, trying hard to keep her family together to give her son something she'd never had—a daddy and a stay-at-home mom. She'd overlooked a lot for that to happen, only to watch Ronnie walk out on her and Pip in the end anyway.

At seven P.M., the traffic to Lovett was sparse to nonexistent, and as she drove her headlights flared on asphalt and sagebrush. She turned off the radio, fiddled around with her iPod, and sang along with Rascal Flatts. The posted speed limit was seventy, which really meant seventy-five. Everyone knew that, and she accelerated to a reasonable seventy-six.

For a year after her divorce, she might have gone a *bit* . . . wild. She might have been impulsive and emotional. Might have been lost; might have been fired from a few too many jobs; tossed back a few too many tequila shots and slept with a few too many men. Might have made a few rash decisions—like the Lily tattoo next to her hipbone and her breast augmentation. But it wasn't like she'd gone stripper-huge. She'd gone from a B-cup after the birth of her son to the full C she'd been before. Now she hated having spent money on a tattoo, and was also ambivalent about the money used on her boobs. If at a better place in her life, she might not have done it. If she'd had the confidence she had now, she might have spent the money on something more practical. Then again, Lily liked how she looked and didn't really regret it. At the time, Crazy Lily Darlington's new boobs had been the talk of the small town. Or, at least, of the Road Kill Bar where she'd spent too much time looking for Mr. Right, only to hook up with yet another Mr. Wrong.

Lily didn't really like to look back at that year of her life. She hadn't been the best mother, but supposed it was something she had to work out to get where she was today. Something she had to live through before she got her head straight and could think of her and Pip's future. Something to get out of her system before she went to cosmetology school, got her license, and built up a clientele.

Now seven years after she'd rolled her first perm and butchered her first head of hair, she was the owner of a salon—Lily Belle's, where other stylists, massage therapists, manicurists, and aestheticians rented chairs and rooms from her. She was finally doing good. So good she no longer used her caller ID to screen bill collectors.

She thought about everything she had yet to do that night and hoped her mother had fed Pippen dinner by now. The kid was bigger than most boys his age. He was going to be as big as his daddy, the rat bastard. Although lately, Ronnie had been paying a bit more attention to his son. He was taking him next weekend, which was nice since Louella had one of her bingo nights and Lily had her spa event.

The phone in her purse and the UConnect in the vehicle rang and she glanced at the steering wheel. The Jeep was still so new to her that she often hit the wrong buttons and ended the call instead of answering. Especially at night. She hit what she hoped was the right button. "Hello?"

"When are you going to be home?" her son asked.

"I'm on my way now."

"What's for dinner?"

She smiled and reached into her purse on the seat beside her. "Grandma didn't feed you?"

Pippen sighed. "She made spaghetti."

"Oh." Louella made notoriously bad Italian. Tex-Mex too. In fact, for a woman who'd spent her life serving food, she was a bad cook.

"I'm hiding in the bathroom."

Lily laughed and pulled out a bottle of water. "I'll make you a toasted cheese and soup," she said and unscrewed the cap. Her throat was sore and she wondered if she was coming down with something. Just one of the many hazards of working around a lot of people.

"Again?"

Now it was Lily's turn to sigh. "What do you want?" She looked over the top of the bottle as she took a long drink. She didn't have time to get sick.

"Pizza."

She smiled and lowered the bottle. "Again?"

A flash of light in her rearview mirror caught her attention. A cop car followed close behind, and she slowed and waited for him to go around her. When he didn't, she shockingly realized he was after her. "Cryin' all night," she muttered. "He can't be serious."

"What?"

"Nothing. I have to go, Pippy." She didn't want to alarm him as she slowed. "I'll be home soon," she said and ended the call. She pulled over to the shoulder of the road, and the headlights and red and blue flashers filled the Jeep as the sheriff's vehicle stopped behind her.

There might have been a time in her life when she would have freaked out. When her heart would have raced, her pulse pounded, and her mind spun, frantically wondering what she'd been caught doing now or what might be stashed in her glove compartment or console or trunk. Those days were over, and tonight all she felt was annoyed. Which she supposed meant she was a law-abiding citizen. A grown-up at thirty-eight. Even so, she was annoyed.

She shoved the Jeep into park and hit the window button in the armrest. The window slid down and she looked in the side mirror as the sheriff's door swung open. She knew most of the Potter County deputies, had gone to school with half of them or their kin. If it was Neal Flegel or Marty Dingus pulling her over, she was going to be *very* annoyed. Neal was a friend who wouldn't think twice about pulling her over just to shoot the shit, and Marty was recently divorced. She'd cut his hair for him last week, and he'd actually groaned when she'd had him in the shampoo bowl. She didn't have time for a traffic stop so Marty could ask her out again.

A wrinkle furrowed her brow as she watched the deputy, lit from behind, move toward her. He was shorter than Marty; thinner than Neal. She could see he was wearing a brown nylon jacket and a star on his chest. He had some gadgets hooked to the collar of his coat, and his belt seemed weighted down with various cop stuff. The stream of his breath hung in the headlights behind him as he approached, the steady thump-thump-thump of his cop boots closing the distance.

"I don't believe I was speeding, Officer," she said as he stopped by her door.

"Actually, you were." The red and blue lights bounced off the side of his face. She couldn't see his features clearly, but could tell he was young. "Do you have a weapon in the vehicle, Ms. Darlington?"

Ahhh. He'd already run her license plate and knew she had a permit to carry concealed. "It's beneath my seat."

He pulled out his Maglite and shone it in her lap and between her feet.

"You won't need it."

"Make sure I don't." He angled the light on her shoulder. "I need to see your driver's license, registration, and proof of insurance."

She grabbed her purse and pulled out her wallet. "You talk too fast to be from around here." She slipped out her driver license and her insurance card. "You must be new in town."

"I've been in Potter County a few weeks."

"That explains it." She reached for her registration in the glove compartment, then handed everything over. "No one gets pulled over for going five miles over the limit."

"That isn't why I pulled you over." He shined

his light on her information. "You crossed the center lane several times."

Seriously? So, she wasn't the best driver when she tried to do two things at once. That's why she got the UConnect hands-free system. "There's no one else on the road for ten miles," she pointed out. "I wasn't in any danger of a head-on."

"That doesn't make it okay to take your half out of the middle."

She looked up and into the dark shadows of his face—and to where the light touched his clean-shaven chin, square jaw, and a mouth made impressive by the shadow across the bow of his upper lip. The rest of him was hidden within the inky night, but she got the distinct impression that he was not only young, but very hot. The kind of hot that in her younger days might have made her fluff her hair. These days she felt nothing but a longing for home and her old flannel pj's. She should probably feel sad about that but didn't.

"Have you had anything to drink tonight?"

She smiled. "Just water." She remembered the last time Neal had given her a ride home from the Road Kill Bar.

"Is something funny?"

And the many times she'd run home from parties, diving into bed as her mom got up for work in the morning. "Yeah," she said and started to chuckle.

Only he didn't laugh. "I'll be right back," he said and headed to his cruiser with her info.

She leaned her head back and rolled the window up. The deputy was wasting her time, and she thought of her son and dinner. All he ever seemed to want these days was pizza, but that was Pip. He got something into his head, and had a hard time getting it back out.

So far Pippen was a good kid. True, he was only ten, but with her and Ronnie Darlington for parents, hell-raising had to be in his DNA. The only time she saw any sort of aggression was when Pip played sports. He loved sports, all kinds—even bowling. And he was very competitive, which normally wouldn't be a bad thing, but Pip was *hyper*competitive. He thought that if he was really good at sports, his daddy would come to his games. There were two problems with his scheme. Pip hadn't grown into himself, could hardly walk without tripping. He was awkward and, so far, a serial bench warmer. But even if he had been the best at everything, Ronny was too selfish to think about his son's football or basketball games.

A knock on the window drew her attention to the left and she hit the power button. "Find any outstanding warrants?" she asked, knowing the answer.

"Not today." He handed her information back through the window. "I pulled you over for inattentive driving, but I'm not going to ticket you."

She supposed she should say something. "Thanks"—she guessed –"Officer . . . ?"

"Matthews. Stay on your side of the road,

Lily. You want to be around to raise that son." He turned on his heels and walked back to his cruiser, the crunch of gravel beneath his heels.

He knew she had a son? She put the Jeep into drive and eased back onto the highway. How? Was that sort of info available when he pulled up her driver's license number? Had he checked her weight? She glanced in her rearview mirror. He was still parked on the side of the road but had turned off his flashing lights. Like most women, she listed her weight five pounds less. She didn't actually weigh 125, but wanted to. It seemed to her that once she hit thirty-five, she gained an extra five pounds that she just couldn't lose. Of course, having a ten-year-old boy who needed snacks in the house didn't help.

Within a few moments Lily had forgotten about Officer Matthews. She had other things to worry about, and ten minutes later, she hit the opener clipped to her visor, drove past the bas-ketball hoop planted next to the driveway, and continued into her garage. She was sure Pippen was next door, peering out the front window, and would be home before she set down her tote and purse.

As predicted—"Mom," he called out as he burst through the back door. "Grandma said she's coming over with her extra spaghetti." He tossed his backpack onto the kitchen table. "Hide."

Crap. She reached into her purse and pulled out her cell phone. "Hi, Ma," she said as soon as her mother picked up. "Pippen said you were bringing over spaghetti. I wish I'd known because I got some takeout from Chicken Lickin'."

"Oh, darn it. I know how much you love my spaghetti." Lily didn't know where she got that idea. "Did I tell you about your new neighbor?"

Lily rolled her eyes and unbuttoned her coat. The house on her left had been for sale for over a year. It had just sold a few weeks ago, and she wondered what had taken Louella so long to introduce herself and get the lowdown.

"It's a single fella with a cat named Pinky."

A man with a cat? Named Pinky? "Is he gay?"

"Didn't appear to be, but you remember Milton Farley."

"No." She didn't care either, but there was no stopping Louella when she had a story to tell.

"He lived over on Ponderosa and was married to Brenda Jean. They had those skinny little kids with runny noses. A few—"

Lily put her hand over the mouthpiece of the phone and whispered to her son, who'd wrapped his arms around her waist, "I'm going to hell for lying to your grandma for you."

Pippen lifted his face from the front of her shirt. He grinned and showed a mouthful of braces with blue bands. Sometimes he looked so much like his daddy it broke her heart. Golden hair, brown eyes, and long sweeping lashes. "I love you, Mama," he said, warming her heart. She would gladly go to hell for Pip. Walk through fire, kill, steal, and lie to her mother for her son. He was going to grow up strong and healthy and go to Texas A&M.

Phillip "Pippen" Darlington was going to be somebody. Somebody better than his parents.

While her mother prattled on about Milton Farley and his hidden boyfriends in Odessa, Lily bent and kissed the top of her son's head. She scratched his back through his Texas A&M sweatshirt and felt him shiver. Ronnie Darlington was a rat bastard for sure, but he'd given her a wonderful little boy. She hadn't always been the best mother, but she thanked God she'd never messed up so bad that she'd messed up her son's life.

". . . and you just know he was tricking everyone with his . . ."

Lily closed her eyes and breathed in the scent of Pippen's hair. She'd made sure that her son didn't go to school and have to hear stories about his weird mama. She knew what that was like. And she'd worked hard to make damn sure she never embarrassed him, and that he never had to hear other kids calling his mama Crazy Lily Darlington.

Chapter Two

Fingers of gray crept across Lovett, Texas, as Officer Tucker Matthews pulled his Toyota Tundra into the garage and cut the engine. Full dawn was still half an hour to the east and the temperature hovered just above freezing.

He grabbed his small duffle and the service Glock from the seat next to him. He'd just started his third week with the Potter County Sheriff's Office and was pulling his second twelve-hour night shift. He moved into the kitchen and set the duffle and pistol on the counter. Pinky meowed from the vicinity of the cat condo in the living room, then ran into the kitchen to greet him.

"Hang on, Pinkster," he said and shrugged out of his brown service coat. He hung it on a hook beside the back door, then moved to the refrigerator. The veterinarian had told him milk wasn't good for Pinky, but she loved it. He poured some two-percent into a little dish on the floor as the pure black cat with the pink nose rubbed against his leg. She purred and he scratched the top of her head. A little over a year ago, he hadn't even liked cats. He'd been living on base at Fort Bliss, ready to be discharged from the Army after ten years of service and preparing to move in with his girlfriend, Tiffany, and her cat, Pinky. Two weeks after he moved in with her, she moved out—taking his Gibson custom Les Paul guitar and leaving behind her cat.

Tucker rose and moved back across the kitchen. At that point, he'd had two choices: reenlist or do something else with his life. He loved the Army. The guys were his brothers. The commanding officers, the only real father figures he'd ever known. He'd enlisted at the age of eighteen, and the Army had been his only family. But it was time to move on. To do something besides blow shit up and take bullets. And there was nothing like a bullet to the head to make a guy realize that he actually did care if he lived or died. Until he'd felt the blood run down his face, he hadn't thought he cared. It wasn't like there was anyone but his Army buddies who gave a shit anyway.

Then he met Tiffany, and thought she cared. Some of the guys had warned him that she was an Army groupie, but he didn't listen. He'd met groupies, swam a few times in the groupie pool, but with Tiffany he'd been fooled into believing she cared about him, that she wanted more than a soldier deployed months at a time. Maybe he wanted to be fooled. In the end, he guessed she'd cared more about his guitar. At first, he was pissed. What kind of person abandoned a little cat? Leaving it with *him*? A guy who'd never had any sort of pet and didn't have a clue what to do with one? Now, he figured, Tiffany had done him a favor.

So what did a former Army gunner do once he was discharged? Enroll in the El Paso County Sheriff's Academy, of course. The six-month training program had been a piece of cake for him, and he graduated at the top of his class. Once his probationary period was over, he applied for a position in Potter County, and, a few months ago, moved to Lovett.

Sunlight spread across his backyard and into the neighbors'. He'd bought his first house a few weeks ago. His home. He was thirty, and except for the first five years of his life, when he'd lived with his grandmother, this was the first home to which he truly belonged. He wasn't an outsider. A squatter. This wasn't temporary shelter until he was shuffled off to another foster home.

He was home. He felt it in his bones and he didn't know why. He'd lived in different parts of the country of the world—but Lovett, Texas, had felt right the moment he arrived. He recognized Lily Darlington's red Jeep even before he ran her plates. For the past week, since he moved in, he'd be getting ready to hit the sack as she backed out of her driveway with her kid in the car.

Before he shined his light into her car, the impression of his neighbor was . . . single mother with big blond curls and a long, lean body. After the traffic stop, he knew she was thirty-eight, older than she looked and prettier than he'd imagined from his quick glimpses of her. And she'd clearly been annoyed that he had the audacity to pull her over. He was used to that, though. Generally people weren't happy to see the rolling lights in their rearview.

Across his yard and Lily's, separated by a short white fence, his kitchen window faced into hers. Today was Saturday. There weren't any lights on yet, but he knew that by ten that boy of hers would be outside bouncing a basketball in the driveway and keeping him awake.

He'd been out of the Army for two years but was still a very light sleeper. One small sound and he was wide awake, pinpointing the position, origin, and exact nature of the sound.

He replaced Pinky's milk, then she followed him out of the kitchen and into the living room. A remote control sat on the coffee table he'd made from a salvaged old door. He'd sanded and varnished it until it was smooth as satin.

Tucker loved working with his hands. He loved taking a piece of old wood and making it into something beautiful. He reached for the remote and turned the big screen TV to a national news channel. Pinky jumped up onto the couch beside him as he leaned over and untied his tactical boots. A deep purr rattled her chest as she squeezed her little black body between his arm and chest. With his attention on the screen across the room and the latest news out of Afghanistan, he finished with one boot and started on the other. The picture of tanks and troops in camouflage brought back memories of restlessness, violence, and boredom. Of knocking down doors, shooting anything that moved, and watching his buddies die. Adrenaline, fear closing his throat, and blood.

Pinky bumped the top of her head against his chin and he moved his head from side to side to avoid her. The things he'd seen and done in the military had certainly affected him. Had changed him, but not like some of the guys he knew. Probably because he had his share of trauma and stress before signing up. By eighteen, he'd been a pro at handling whatever life threw his way. He knew how to shut it down and let it all roll right off.

He hadn't come out of the military with PTSD like some of the guys. Oh, sure he'd been jumpy and on edge, but after a few months, he'd adjusted to civilian life. Perhaps because his whole life had been one adjustment after another.

Not anymore, though. "Jesus, Pink." The cat's purring and bumping got so annoying he picked her up and set her on the couch beside him. Of course she didn't stay and crawled right back onto his lap. He sighed and scratched her back. Somehow he'd let an eight-pound black cat with a pink nose totally run his life. He wasn't sure how that had even happened. He used to think cats were for old ladies or ugly chicks or gay men. The fact that he had a five-foot-square cat condo that he'd built himself, and a pantry stocked with cat treats, pretty much shot his old prejudice all to hell. He wasn't an old lady or ugly or gay. He did draw the line at cat outfits, though.

He stripped down to his work pants and the cold-weather base layer he wore beneath his work shirt. He made himself a large breakfast of bacon and eggs and juice. As he rinsed the dishes, he heard the first thud of the neighbor's basketball. It was eight thirty. The kid was at it earlier than usual. Tucker glanced out the window that faced the neighbor's driveway. The kid's blond hair stuck up in the back. He wore a silver Dallas Cowboys parka and a pair of red sweatpants.

When Tucker worked the night shift, he liked to be in bed before ten and up by four. He could wear earplugs, but he'd rather not. He didn't like the idea of one of his senses being dulled while he slept. He pulled on his jogging shoes and a gray hooded sweatshirt. If he talked to the kid, maybe they could work something out.

He hit the garage door opener on his way out and moved into the driveway. The cold morning chilled his hands, and his breath hung in front of his face. He moved toward the boy, across a strip of frozen grass, as the steady bounce-bounce-bounce of the ball and the sound of it hitting the backboard filled his ears.

"Hey, buddy," he said as he stopped in his neighbor's drive. "It's kind of cold to be playing so early."

"I got to be the best," he said, his breath streaming behind him as he tried for a layup and missed. The ball hit the rim and the kid caught it before it hit the ground. "I'm going to be the best at school."

Tucker stuck his hands in the pockets of his sweatshirt. "You're going to freeze your nuts off, kid."

The boy stopped and looked up at him. His clear brown eyes widened as he stuck the ball under one arm of his puffy coat. "Really?"

No. Not really. Tucker shrugged. "I wouldn't risk it. I'd wait until around three or four when it warms up."

The kid tried a jump shot that slid around the rim. "Can't. It's the weekend. I gotta practice as much as I can."

Crap. Tucker bent down and grabbed the ball as it rolled by his foot. He supposed he could threaten to give the kid some sort of citation or scare him with the threat of arrest. But Tucker didn't believe in empty threats or abusing his power over the powerless. He knew what that felt like. And telling the kid he was going to freeze his nuts off, didn't count. That could really happen here in the Texas panhandle. Especially when the wind started blowing. "What's your name?"

"Phillip Darlington, but everyone calls me Pippen."

Tucker stuck out his free hand. "Tucker Matthews. How old are you Pippen?"

"Ten."

Tucker was no expert, but the kid seemed tall for his age.

"My grandma says you named your cat Pinky. That's a weird name."

This from a kid named Pippen? Tucker bounced the ball a few times. "Who's your grandma?"

"Louella Brooks. She lives on the other side of me and my mom." He pointed behind him with his thumb.

Ah. The older lady who talked nonstop and had given him a pecan pie. "We have a problem."

"We do?" He sniffed and wiped the back of his hand across his red nose.

"Yeah. I've got to sleep and you bouncing this ball is keeping me awake."

"Put a pillow over your head." He tilted his chin to one side. "Or you could turn on the TV. My mom has to sleep with the TV on sometimes."

Neither was an option. "I've got a better idea. We play a game of H-O-R-S-E. If I win, you wait until three to play. If you win, I'll put a pillow over my head."

Phillip shook his head. "You're a grown-up. That's not fair."

Damn. "I'll spot you the first three letters."

The kid looked at his fingers and counted. "I only have to make two baskets?"

"Yep." Tucker wasn't worried. He'd been watching the kid for a couple of days and he sucked. He tossed the kid the ball. "I'll even let you go first."

"Okay." Pippen caught the ball and moved to an invisible free-throw line. His breath hung in front of his face, his eyes narrowed, and he bounced the ball in front of him. He got into an awkward free-throw stance, shot, and totally wafted it. The ball missed the backboard and Tucker tried not to smile as he ran into his own driveway to retrieve it. He dribbled back and did a left-handed layup. "That's an H," he said and tossed the ball to Pippen. The boy tried his luck at a layup and missed.

Tucker hit a jump shot at the center key. "O."

"Wow." Pippen shook his head. "You're good."

He'd played a lot of b-ball on his downtime in the military, and it didn't hurt that the kid's hoop was lowered to about eight feet and there was no one playing defense.

The kid moved to the spot where Tucker had stood. Once again his eyes narrowed and he bounced the ball in front of him. He lined up the shot and Tucker sighed.

"Keep your elbows pointed straight," he heard himself coach. God, he couldn't believe he was giving the kid pointers. He wasn't even sure he liked kids. He'd never really been around any since he'd been one himself, and most of those had been like him. Throwaways.

Pippen held the ball right in front of his face and pointed his elbows at the net.

"No." Tucker moved behind the kid, lowered

the ball a few inches, and moved his cold hands to the correct position. "Keep the ball lined up, bend your knees, and shoot."

"Pippen!"

Both Tucker and the boy spun around at the same time. Lily Darlington stood behind them, wrapped up in a red wool coat and wearing white bunny slippers. Crisp morning light caught in her blond hair curled up in big Texas-size rollers. The chilled air caught in his lungs and turned her cheeks pink. She was pretty, even if her ice blue gaze cut Tucker to shreds. She stared at him as she spoke to her child. "I called your name twice."

"Sorry." The kid dribbled the ball. "I was practicing my shots."

"Go eat your breakfast. Your waffles are getting cold."

"I have to practice."

"Basketball season is over until next year."

"That's why I have to practice. To get better."

"You have to go eat. Right now."

Pippen gave a long suffering sigh and tossed the ball to Tucker. "You can play if you want."

He didn't, but he caught the ball. "Thanks. See ya around, Pippen."

As the kid stormed past his mother, she reached out and grabbed him. She hugged him close and kissed the top of his head. "You don't have to be the best at everything, Pip." She pulled back and looked into his eyes. "I love you bigger than the sun and stars."

"I know."

"Forever and ever. Always." She moved her palms to his cheek. "You're a good boy"—she smiled into his upturned face—"with dirty hands. Wash them when you go inside."

Tucker looked at her slim hands on the boy's cheeks and temples, cupping his ears. Her nails were red and her skin looked soft. A thin blue vein lined her wrist and disappeared beneath the cuff of her red wool coat. The chilly air in his lungs burned. "Go inside or you'll freeze your ears off."

"My nuts."

Uh-oh.

"What?"

"I'll freeze my nuts off." He glanced behind his shoulder and laughed. "Tucker said it's so cold out here I'll freeze my nuts off."

Her gaze cut to his and one brow rose up her forehead. "Charming." She ran her fingers through her son's short hair. "Go eat before your waffles are as cold as your . . . ears." The kid took off and she folded her arms across her chest. The curlers in her hair should have made her look ridiculous. They didn't. They made him want to watch her take them out. It was silly, and he dribbled he ball instead of thinking about her hair. "You must be the new neighbor."

"Tucker Matthews." He stuck the ball under one arm and offered his free hand. She looked at it for several heartbeats then shook it. Her skin was as warm and soft as it looked; he wondered what her palm would feel like on the side of his face. Then he wondered why he was wondering about her at all.

"Lily Darlington." Her blue eyes stared into his, and she obviously didn't recognize him from the night before. She took her hand back and slid it into her pocket. "I'm sure you're perfectly nice, but I'm very protective and I don't let just any man around my son."

That was wise, he supposed. "Are you worried about me doing something to your kid?"

She shook her head. "Not worried. Just letting you know that I protect Pip."

Then maybe she shouldn't have named him Pip because that was just a guaranteed ass-kicking. Then again, this was Texas. The rule for names in Texas was different from the rest of the country. A guy named Guppy couldn't exactly beat the crap out of a Pip. "I'm not going to hurt your kid." He folded his arms and rocked back on his heels.

"Just so we're clear, if you even think about hurting one hair on his head, I'll kill you and not lose a wink of sleep over it."

For some perverse reason, the threat made him like her. "You don't even know me."

"I know that you're playing basketball with a ten-year-old at nine o'clock in the morning," she said, her accent thick with warning. "It's about thirty-two degrees, and you're talking about your freezing nuts with my son. That's not exactly normal behavior for an adult man."

Since she obviously lived alone, he had to wonder if she knew anything about normal behavior for an adult man. "I'm playing basketball and freezing my nuts off so I can get some sleep. I just got off work and your kid's basketball keeps me awake. I thought if I played a game of H-O-R-S-E, he'd cut me a break." That was close enough to the truth.

She blinked. "Oh." She tilted her head to one side and a wrinkle pulled her brows as if she were suddenly trying to place him in her memory. "You work the night shift at the meat packing plant? I worked there for a few weeks about five years ago."

"No." He dribbled the ball a few times and waited.

"Hmm." Her brow smoothed and she turned to go. "I've got to see to Pip. It was nice to meet you, Mr. Matthews."

"We met last night."

She turned back and once again her brows were drawn.

"I pulled you over for inattentive driving."

Her lips parted. "That was you?"

"Yeah." He shook his head. "You're a shitty driver, Lily."

"You're a sheriff?"

"Deputy."

"That explains the tragic pants."

He looked down at his dark brown trousers with the beige stipe up the outside legs. "You don't think they're hot."

She shook her head. "Sorry."

He tossed her the ball and she caught it. "Tell Pippen that if he cuts me a break tomorrow morning, I'll teach him how to slam dunk tomorrow afternoon around four."

"I'll tell him."

"You're not afraid I'm a pervert?"

"Pippen knows he can't leave the yard without telling me or his grandma." She shrugged. "And you already know I'm licensed to carry concealed. I've got a Beretta 9mm subcompact." She stuck the ball under one arm. "Just so you know."

"Nice." He managed not to laugh. "But are you bragging or threatening a law officer?"

"Pippen's daddy isn't really in the picture. I'm all he's got and it's my job to make sure he's safe and happy."

"He's lucky to have you."

"I'm lucky to have him."

Tucker watched her go, then turned and walked back to his house. Only one person in his entire life had made sure he was safe. His grandmother Betty. If he thought hard, he could recall the touch of her soft hand on his head and back. But Betty had died three days after Tucker turned five.

He moved into his kitchen and pulled his sweatshirt over his head. His mother had split when he was a baby and he had no memory of her. Just photographs. He didn't know who his father was and doubted his mother had *ever* known. She'd finally killed herself with a drug cocktail when

Tucker was three. As a kid, he'd wondered about her; wondered what his life would have been like if she hadn't been an addict. As an adult, he just felt disgust—disgust for a woman who cared more about drugs than her son.

He turned off the television on his way to his bedroom and kicked off his shoes. After Betty's death, he'd been shipped off to aunts who didn't want or care about him; and by the time he turned ten, he was turned over to the state of Michigan and shuffled through the foster care system.

He took off his pants and tossed them into the hamper he used for dry cleaning. No one had wanted to adopt a ten-year-old with his history and bad attitude. He'd spent most of the years between the ages of ten and sixteen in and out of foster homes and juvenile court, which finally landed him in a halfway house run by a retired Vietnam vet. Elias Peirce had been a no-bullshit hard-ass with strict rules. But he'd been fair. The first time Tucker had given him lip, he gave Tucker an old cane-back chair and a pack of sandpaper. "Make it as smooth as a baby's backside," he'd barked. It had taken him a week, but after his daily homework and chores were done, Tucker sanded until the chair felt like silk beneath his hands. Following the chair, he'd made a bookcase and a small table.

Tucker couldn't say that he and Elias Peirce had been as close as father and son, but he changed Tucker's life and never treated him like a throw-away kid. Elias made him work out the pent-up anger and aggression just below his skin in a constructive way.

Tucker didn't like to talk about his past—didn't really talk about his life. During the course of normal conversation, whenever anyone asked about his life, he just said he didn't have much family and changed the subject.

He thought of Lily Darlington and the way she touched Pippen. The way she looked into his eyes and touched his cheek and told him she loved him bigger than the stars. Tucker was sure his grandmother had loved him, but he was equally sure she'd never threatened to kick ass on his behalf. He'd had to kick ass on his own behalf. He'd always had to take care of himself.

He was a man now—thirty years old—and he was the man he was because of the life he'd been dealt. He knew a lot of guys who'd come back from Iraq or Afghanistan and had a hard time adjusting to life outside of the military. Not Tucker. At least not as much. He'd learned long ago how to deal with shit thrown at him. How to cope with trauma and how to let it go. Oh, he had some really dark memories, but he didn't live with them. He'd worked them out and moved on.

He stripped to his gray boxers and climbed into bed. Everything he had, he'd earned. No one had given him anything and he was a content man. He fell asleep within minutes of his head hitting the pillow, and at some point, when he was warm and comfy and deep into REM, Lily Darlington entered his dreams. She wore red silk and her hands touched his face and neck. She looked into his eyes and smiled as she cupped his cheek. "You're cold, Tucker," she said. "You need to warm up." The dream started nice and innocent but quickly turned hot and dirty. Her hands slid across his chest as she lowered her mouth to the side of his neck, and the things she whispered against his throat weren't in the least innocent.

"I want you," she whispered as her palm moved over his chest, down the side of his waist, then back up again. "Do you want me?" Her touch was soft and slow, frustrating, sliding back and forth and driving him mad.

"Yes. God, yes." He ran his fingers through her hair, bunching it in his hands as she kissed his neck and inched her hot palm lower—lower, down his stomach and belly until her fingernails scraped his skin just above the elastic of his underwear.

Her fingers slide beneath the elastic waistband and she wrapped her soft warm hand around his extremely tight erection. "You're a good boy with dirty hands."

His heart pounded in his chest as he shoved her against the wall and into her. All caveman aggression and hunger. In his dream she loved every second of it. She met every hard plunge of his hard dick with insatiable greed, shoving her hips into his, begging for more and moaning his name.

"Tucker!" she screamed in his head—and his eyes flew open. He sat up in bed, his lungs pulling oxygen into his chest and his pulse pounding in his ears.

A sliver of light sneaked beneath his blackout blinds and streaked across the dark room. The sound of his heavy breathing filled the space around him. He'd just had a wild sex dream about Lily Darlington. Obviously he'd gone without for too long, and he'd lost his mind. He didn't know her. She was a single mother. He felt like a pervert.

A pervert who needed to get laid before he lost his mind again.

Chapter Three

True to his word, that Sunday afternoon at around four P.M., Deputy Tucker Matthews knocked on Lily's front door. She opened it and stood in stunned silence, like she'd suffered a blow to the head.

"Is Pippen around?" He had a new basketball tucked under one arm and a pair of silver aviators covered his eyes—eyes that were a warm brown and creased at the corners when he was amused, like when she'd threated to shoot him the other morning.

Lily was so shocked stupid that he'd kept his word that all she could utter was "Ahhh, yeah." Her shock couldn't have anything to do with him looking so good. She'd seen him yesterday, knew he was good-looking. A scar creased his forehead from the middle of his right brow to the line of his short brown hair. This, along with his rough, masculine edges, kept him from being a pretty boy, but allowed him enough intrigue to give a girl bad thoughts about body searches. So why did she feel so rattled today? He was wearing that same hideous gray Army sweatshirt he'd had on yesterday, with frayed sleeves, a torn neck—and he looked like he'd just dragged himself out of bed. He was all rough and scruffy and definitely needed to shave. "You're here," she managed.

"I told you I would be."

Lily was five feet six inches tall and she noticed he was just a few inches taller—perhaps five ten. What he lacked in height, he made up for in pure, unadulterated hotness. So much hotness that it lit a little fire in her stomach and heated up her pulse. She held the door open for him and shocked herself further by wondering what he'd look like with that horribly ratty sweatshirt ripped off and his wrist cuffed to something. "Come in and I'll get him."

He took a step back instead. She couldn't see his eyes but color crept up his neck to his cheeks as if he'd read her mind. "Tell him I'll be in the driveway warming up," he said and turned to go.

No doubt, her inappropriate thoughts were written on her face and scared him. They scared her too. "Pippen," she called out over her shoulder, "Deputy Matthews is here for you."

He stopped a few steps down and glanced back at her. "You can call me Tucker."

No. No, she couldn't. The guy was probably all of twenty-five, and she was thinking of him shirtless and cuffed to a bedpost. It made her feel a bit pervy. Although, to be fair to herself, she'd never had such a good-looking guy show up on her porch before. Not even when she'd been twenty-five. Not even the rat bastard she'd married, Ronnie. And even though she hated to admit it now, Ronnie had been damn fine.

"I'm coming," Pippen hollered as he raced past his mother, shoving his arms into his jacket.

Lily shut the door behind her and leaned against it. Well, that had been weird and awkward. Yesterday she'd been fine. She'd seen him, seen that he looked much more like a faux cop from a *Playgirl* magazine than a real one. She'd acknowledged his good looks to herself, thought about body searches, *and* managed to speak like an intelligent woman. At least today she didn't have rollers in her hair and half her makeup on her face.

Her hair was pulled back in a ponytail, and she was wearing a white cable knit sweater, jeans, and a brown woven belt around her hips. If she'd known company would appear on her porch, she would have done her hair and put on some lipstick.

She pushed away from the door and moved across the living room to the couch. On the top of the oak coffee table and across the back of the red sofa sat little teal bags with the logo of Lily's spa embossed in white in each center. Several rolls of teal-and-white cellophane and bags of trail-size beauty products lay on the couch cushions. She moved the rolls aside and sat.

Tucker Matthews wasn't company. He was the next door neighbor who was playing basketball with Pippen in the afternoon so he could sleep in the morning. He'd given Pip his word and he'd kept it, which was more than she could say for her son's father, who didn't pay attention to trivial things like court orders and visitation and keeping his word. He worked on Ronnie-time, which usually depended on the latest slootie pants he'd hooked up with.

Yesterday, when Lily had walked outside and seen a stranger in her driveway playing ball with her son, she'd been a bit freaked out. Today she wasn't sure how she felt about it. Pip wanted a father so desperately. He loved any male attention, and would be crushed when the deputy tired of playing, took his ball and went home for good.

Lily rose from the couch and moved into her shiny white kitchen with yellow cupboards. She'd deal with that when it happened. God knew Pippen needed some testosterone around him, if only for a few hours. He spent most of his time with her and his grandmother. Occasionally, he spent time with her sister Daisy's husband, Jack, and their son, Nathan, when he was home from college. Daisy and Jack had a six-year-old daughter and another one on the way.

Lily went to the kitchen sink and leaned across as far as she could. She pushed aside a bamboo plant, a pinch pot, and one side of her daisy-print curtains. She could see just a sliver of the driveway with the basketball hoop. The ball hit the backboard and bounced off.

She could clearly hear the steady bounce of the ball and then a shot that was nothing but net. Clearly, the shot was not made by her son, who hadn't grown into himself yet.

Her cell phone on the counter rang and she glanced down at it. Ronnie. Great. He was probably calling to say he couldn't take Pippen next weekend.

"You better not be calling just to piss me off," she answered.

"Ha-ha-ha," he chuckled in that stupid Ronnie way that she used to think was so cool but now was like nails on a chalkboard. "I need to talk to Pip."

"Not if you're going to back out on next weekend, you don't."

"I'm not backin' out. I thought he might want to go see my parents in Odessa, is all."

Pip hadn't seen his grandparents in at least a year. "Seriously?"

"Yeah."

Ronnie was a deadbeat. No doubt. But Pippen thought the sun rose and sat on that rat bastard's ass. She could stand on her head and juggle cupcakes to make Pippen happy, and all his daddy had to do was pull up in his latest monster truck and Pip was in heaven.

"I'm sure he'll like that," she said as she moved

out the garage door and hit a switch on the wall. "You better not back out."

"I ain't gonna back out."

"That's what you said the last time you backed out." The door slid up and she ducked beneath it and walked out onto the driveway. Her son and the deputy stood near an imaginary free throw line. "If you do, it'll be the last time, Ronnie."

"He's my son."

"Yeah. You might try and remember that on a somewhat consistent basis." The cool air touched her face and neck, and the heels of her boots tap-tapped across the concrete. "Pip. Your daddy's on the phone." She handed her son the cell and watched his little face light up.

"Tucker's winning," Pippen said, excited as a monkey on a peanut farm as he took the phone from her. "One more basket and I'm toast."

She looked toward the man standing in the middle of the driveway slowly dribbling the ball. Sunlight reflected off the lenses of his glasses and shined in his rich brown hair. "I got your back," she told her son and moved to stand in front of the deputy.

"What are you doing?"

"Making sure you don't score while Pip's on the phone." She raised her arms over her head for added measure.

"We're playing H-O-R-S-E."

She had a vague memory of H-O-R-S-E from grammar school. It had something to do with the first player to spell horse winning. She'd never played. As a Texan and a girl, she'd played volleyball. She'd been one hell of a spiker.

"There's no man-to-man in horse."

She dropped her arms. "What?"

He said it again, only this time really slow. "There's . . . no . . . man . . . to . . . man . . . in . . . H-O-R-S-E."

She still wasn't quite sure what that meant. "Are you being condescending?"

He bounced the ball and moved a few inches closer. Close enough that she had to tip her head back to look up. Close enough that she could smell sweat and clean Texas air. "No. You told me I talk fast."

"I did?" She swallowed and felt a sudden urge to take a step back. Back to a safer distance. "When?"

"The other night when I pulled you over."

She didn't remember saying that, but it was true. "Where are you from, Deputy?"

"Originally Detroit."

"Long way from home."

"For the past eleven years, I've lived at Fort Bliss, then El Paso and Houston."

"Army?"

"Staff Sergeant, Second Battalion, Third Field Artillery."

He was in the Army and now the police force? "How long were you in the military?"

"Ten years." He slowly bounced the ball. "If you want to play man-on-man, we can."

Ten years? He had to be older than he looked.

"Or man-on-woman." One dark brow rose up his forehead and his voice got kind of low and husky. "You wanna play a little man-on-woman, Lily?"

She blinked. She wasn't sure what he meant. Was he joking or was that a real position or play or whatever in basketball? "Do I have to sweat?" She didn't like to sweat in her good clothes.

"It's not good if at least one person doesn't work up a sweat."

Okay, she was pretty sure he wasn't talking about basketball. She glanced over at Pippen standing at the edge of the driveway listening to his daddy. She looked back at Tucker, at her reflection in his glasses. If she leaned forward just a bit, she could put her face in the crook of his neck just above the torn collar of his sweatshirt. Where his skin would be cool and smell like a warm man.

"You're blushing."

In his glasses, she could see the pink creeping to her cheeks. Could feel it heating her chest. He was young and attractive, and she wasn't used to men flirting with her. At least men she hadn't known most of her life. "Are you hitting on me?"

"If you have to ask, then I'm not as smooth as I think I am."

He *was* hitting on her! "But I'm a lot older than you," she blurted.

"Eight years isn't a lot."

Eight years. He knew her age. No doubt from her driver's license. She was so flustered, she could hardly do simple math. He was thirty. That was still young, but not as young as she'd thought. Not so young that thinking about him as a faux cop in *Playgirl* was perverted. Well, not all that perverted. It wasn't illegal anyway.

"Your cheeks are getting really red."

"It's chilly out here." She turned toward the house but his hand on her arm stopped her. She looked down at his long fingers on the forearm of her white sweater. She ran her gaze up the frayed wrist of his sleeve, up his arm and shoulder to the scruffy growth on his square jaw. He had the kind of mouth that would feel good sliding across her skin.

"What are you thinking, Lily?"

She looked up into this mirrored glasses. "Pure thoughts."

A deep chuckle spilled from his lips. "That makes one of us."

For the second time in less than an hour, Deputy Tucker Matthews stunned her into silence.

"Momma!" Pippen called out as he headed toward her. "Daddy and me are going to Odessa next weekend to see Memaw and Papaw."

She tore her gaze from Tucker's face. "I know, sugar." She took her cell phone from her son. "Wo'll pack lots of road snacks."

Pippen turned to the deputy, "Is it my shot?"

He shook his head. "Sorry. I gotta go take a

shower before work." A slight smile curved his lips. "I worked up a sweat."

"Not me," Pippen told him. "I don't sweat. I'm too little. Momma doesn't sweat either."

He raised his brows above the gold frame of his sunglasses. "That's a shame. She should do something about that."

Lily's own brows knitted and her mouth parted. Was he hitting on her in front of her son? And was she so out of practice she didn't know?

Tucker laughed and looked down at the young boy in front of him. "But I have tomorrow and Tuesday off. We can finish then."

"Okay."

He shifted the ball from one arm to the other. "See ya later, Lily."

No way could she call him Tucker. He might not be as young as she'd first thought, but he still was young and hot and an outrageous flirt. He was dangerous for a single mother in a small town. A big old hunk of hot flaming danger for a woman who'd finally lived down her wild reputation. "Deputy Matthews."

Tucker stretched his arms upward and moved his head from side to side. It was 0800 in Amarillo and he was just finishing up the paperwork from the night before. He'd made two DUI arrests, issued three moving violations, and had responded to a 10-91b in Lovett. The noisy animal in question had been a fat Chihuahua named Hector. The dog's elderly owner, Velma Patterson, had cried and promised to keep the ankle-biter quiet and Tucker had let her off with a verbal warning.

"It was that horrible Nelma Buttersford who called. Wasn't it?" Ms. Patterson wept into a rumpled tissue. "She hates Hector."

"I'm not sure who called," he'd answered.

Tucker rose from the desk. That's what he liked about working in Potter County. There wasn't a lot happening on a Sunday night. Not like Harris County. He liked the slower pace that gave him time to plow through his paperwork.

No, not much happened, and he was fine with that. He'd seen a lot of action in Iraq and Afghanistan, and later after joining the department in Houston. Here, there was just enough going on to keep him interested, but not so much that it kept him up at night.

At least not yet. But it would. Bad things happened sometimes and he'd signed up for the job to deal with them. For as long as he could remember, he'd been dealing with bad things. He knew how to survive when shit went south.

He moved to the locker room and opened the locker with his name printed on cloth tape. He unbuttoned his beige and brown long-sleeved work shirt and pulled at the Velcro tabs at his shoulders and the sides of his waist. The vest weighed a little under ten pounds. Nothing compared to the body armor he'd worn in the military. He set it inside the locker and buttoned his shirt over his black tactical undershirt.

"Hey, Matthews," Deputy Neal Flegel called out as he entered the locker room. "Did you hear about the 10-32 up at Lake Meredith?"

He'd heard the call over the radio. "Yeah. What kind of idiots are out on the lake that time of night?"

Flegel opened his locker and unbuttoned his shirt. "Two idiots fishing in a leaky ten-foot aluminum boat, no life jackets, and a cooler full of Lone Star."

He knew from listening to the radio that they'd recovered one body close to shore. Another deputy, Marty Dingus, entered the locker room and he and Neal shot the shit like two old compadres. Brothers. Tucker had had a lot of compadres. Brothers in arms. Some of them he'd straight-up hated but would have died for. A sheriff's department wasn't unlike the military in that regard. They both played by big-boy rules. He was the new guy in Potter County. He'd been in this spot before, and he knew how to roll and adapt and get along for the sake of the job. He looked forward to getting to know the deputies here in his new home.

"How do you like Potter County so far?" Marty asked. "Not quite as hot as Harris County."

Tucker reached for his jacket inside his locker. Marty wasn't talking about the temperature.

"That's what I like about it." He'd been in enough "hot" places to last him a lifetime.

Neal peeled off his vest. "Did you find a place to live?"

Tucker nodded and shut his locker. "I took your advice and found a house in Lovett. On Winchester. Not far from the high school over there."

"Winchester?" Neal frowned in thought. Both deputies had been born and raised in Lovett and still lived there with their families. "Do we know anyone who lives on Winchester?" he asked Marty.

"Now?" Marty shrugged and shook his head. "When we were in school, the Larkins . . . Cutters . . . and the Brooks girls."

"That's why it sounds familiar." Neal set his vest inside his locker. "Lily Darlington lives on Winchester. She bought the house right next door to her mama."

Marty laughed. "Crazy Lily?"

Crazy Lily?

"Some of my earliest wet dreams involved Crazy Lily." Both men laughed and Tucker might have appreciated the humor if he hadn't recently had his own sex dream about Lily Darlington.

"She's my neighbor." Tucker shoved his arms into his jacket. "Why do you call her crazy?" She hadn't acted crazy around him. More like she'd driven *him* crazy in that white sweater yesterday. He'd taken one look at her tits in that sweater and all the blood in his head had drained to his pants.

"I don't think she's crazy these days," Neal said. "Not like when she used to dance on tables."

Lily danced on tables? "Professionally?"

"No. At parties in high school." Marty laughed. "Those long legs in a pair of tiny shorts and Justin's were something to see."

Jesus.

"She's not like that anymore," Neal defended her. "I think that concussion she got driving her car into Ronnie's front room back in '04 knocked some sense into her."

Jesus, Joseph, *and* Mary. "Who's Ronnie?"

"Her ex."

"And she drove her car into his front room? On purpose?"

"She always said her foot slipped on account of a migraine," Neal answered. Both men laughed and Neal continued: "She was never charged with anything, but everyone knows Crazy Lily Darlington drove her car into that house on purpose. She came real close to being 5150'd." Neal shrugged. "But she was already in the hospital for few days, so it didn't make sense."

5150? Tucker had picked up a 5150 last year in South Houston. The schizophrenic woman had locked herself in her bedroom for three days and had been eating her mattress.

"It was just a good thing Ronnie was off with his latest," Marty added.

Holy Jesus. He was having crazy sex dreams and lusting after a crazy woman. A woman who'd possibly tried to kill her ex by running her car into his house and had almost been locked up on a 5150 hold. That piece of info should be enough to shrivel his nuts, but it didn't. He thought of her and Pippen and her fierceness. He thought of her hands on his own chest, and his hands running up long legs, and he didn't know who was crazier. Him or Crazy Lily Darlington.

Chapter Four

Lily pulled the Jeep into her garage and left the door up. She'd dropped Pippen off at school and gone to Albertson's for a few groceries. She had a lot to do before Pippen got home from school.

She got out of the car and walked toward the curb. Pippen had been so excited after talking to Ronnie yesterday. The thought of going to Odessa with his daddy kept him wired all day and night, and he'd had a hard time falling asleep.

A big beige garbage can sat at the curb and she grabbed the handle to pull it into the garage. The cold plastic chilled her palm and she glanced up as Tucker's silver Tundra pulled into the drive next door. She quickly returned his wave and ducked her head as she tugged the big can into her garage. Pippen had gone on and on about Tucker too. Tucker was going to teach him to dunk and free throw, and juke. Whatever that meant.

She pushed the garbage can against the wall, moved to her Jeep, and opened the back. She'd listened to Pip until she hadn't been able to take it another minute. She'd spread her arms and said, "What am I? A stump full of spiders?"

Pip had rolled his eyes. "You're just my momma."

Yeah, just his momma, and he thought the sun rose and set on Ronnie's deadbeat ass. Lily grabbed the handles of two grocery bags and heard Tucker's boot heels just before his shadow fell across the threshold of the garage.

"I'll get those," he said.

She glanced across her shoulder at him as he stopped next to her in his brown jacket and tragic pants. Then she put her chin to her shoulder and glanced behind her. Tucker playing basketball in her driveway with Pippen was one thing—but carrying her groceries inside was another. She was a single mom in a small town that would never completely forget her wild past. None of the neighbors seemed to be home. "You can get the others," she said and hurried to the back door. "Thank you."

"No problem." He grabbed the remaining four bags and shut the back of the Jeep.

"Pip says you're going to teach him to dunk." She pushed a big button by the back step and the garage door slid closed.

"I'll try." He followed her into the kitchen and set the bags on the counter next to her "He needs to work on his dribbling first."

Lily unbuttoned her navy pea coat and hung it on a hook by the door. That morning she'd dressed in her pink yoga pants, white sports bra, and Spandex tank. Later, she planned to drag out her mat, pop in her Rodney Yee DVD, and do a little downward facing dog in her living room. She looked back at Tucker's profile. At his chin and mouth and wide shoulders. Besides her brother-in-law and nephew, Pippen was the only male who'd ever been in her house. It felt weird to have Tucker there. "Thanks again."

"Thank me with coffee." He turned to face her and reached for the zipper of his dark brown jacket. His long fingers pulled the tab downward. One slow inch at a time as his eyes took a languid journey down her body, blatantly checking her out.

She should say something clever and witty or indignant, but as always with him, she couldn't think. Clearly his testosterone was throwing off the balance in the house. Throwing her off the balance. "Won't the caffeine keep you up?"

He raised his gaze to her face, pausing for a heartbeat on her lips before he looked into her eyes. "I have today and tomorrow off."

Lord love a duck, his energy caused friction in her stomach. Fiery dangerous friction that she hadn't let herself feel for a long time. She moved to the coffee maker and filled the filter with Italian roast. With Tucker, it wasn't a matter of *letting*. It was more like a bombardment. "I'm off today too. And I have a million things to do before Saturday's spa event." It wasn't necessarily a hint for him to leave. Not yet. In a few more minutes, she'd kick him out. There'd been a time in her life when she liked playing with fire, but she was a respectable mother of a ten-year-old boy. It wasn't just her anymore.

"You work at a spa?"

One cup and she'd kick him out. Lily glanced over her shoulder at him as he walked to the little kitchen table and hung his coat on the back of a chair. Like two thin arrows, twin creases ran down his back from his shoulders to his waistband, pointing to his nice round butt in those horrible pants.

"I own a spa in Amarillo." She returned her attention to the coffee maker and filled the carafe with water, then poured it into the machine. Not just any guy could make those pants look good. She hit the On button then turned to face him. "Lily Belle Salon and Spa." He picked up an extra teal-and-white invitation from a small stack sitting on the table. "I'm having a big event Saturday. You should come by and win a facial," she joked.

"I don't even really know what that is." He set the invitation back on the table. "Belle is your middle name?"

"Yeah. My mom named my sister and me after flowers."

"It's pretty."

Behind her, the coffeepot spit to life, filling the air with coffee-scented steam. In front of her, Tucker moved across the kitchen. Matching shirt creases ran from the dark brown epaulets on his broad shoulders, slipped beneath his gold star, name bar, and breast pockets. Her gaze followed the thin lines down to his flat belly and further. "Where's your"—she pointed at her waist and then his—"cop stuff?"

"My duty belt?"

"Yeah." She looked back up into his brown eyes. "Your weapons and cuffs?"

"Secured in my truck." His gaze locked with hers and he didn't even bother to hide the interest in his eyes. It was hot and intense, flaming the friction in the pit of her stomach and scattering it across her body. "How long have you had your own spa?"

"Three years." She moved to her left and turned away from his gaze. Away from the chaos it caused, and she opened the cupboard. A collection of random mugs sat inside and she grabbed two. "Do you want cream or sugar?" One cup. Just one cup. She turned and almost hit him in the chest with the pink sparkly Deeann's Duds mug.

"Both." He took the mugs from her and set them on the counter by her hip. "But not in my coffee." He took her hands in his and slid her palms up his chest. "Touch me," he said, his voice a bold rumble beneath her hand.

She raised her gaze from their hands on his breast pockets to his eyes. Suddenly, she couldn't swallow or breathe. He was dangerous and she pulled her hands from beneath his. Cool air hit her heated palms and she closed her fingers into fists.

"Please, Lily." The silent longing in his voice whispered to the dormant longing in her soul. He lowered his face and her breath rushed out.

"What are you doing?" she murmured as his warm mouth skimmed her jaw. "I don't think this is a good idea."

"Then don't think." His warm breath spread across her skin. "I know I have a hard time thinking when I'm near you." He kissed her just beneath her ear.

"Don't say that."

"Why?"

"You don't know me."

"Let's change that." He opened his mouth on her sensitive skin. "Around you, I have a hard time doing anything but getting hard."

"Too soon. That's crude." Her head fell to one side.

"That's the truth. Do you want me to lie?"

Too fast. No. She sometimes liked crude but she knew she shouldn't. She knew she shouldn't let him kiss her throat. She should make him stop, but she couldn't.

"Put your hands on me," he said against her throat and she opened her fingers and slid her hands up to his chest and shoulders. At the touch of her palms on his bare neck, a shudder ran up his spine. "That's good." His mouth slid across her cheek to her lips.

Was this happening? Was she going to let this happen? Right there in her kitchen? Where she cooked breakfast for her son. One of his hands moved to the nape of her neck and tilted her head back with his strong fingers, coaxing her mouth with the promise of a kiss. A warm shiver ran up her spine and he lifted his head. His lips teased her, and she raised onto the balls of her feet and followed his mouth. Evidently she was going to let it happen. Right there in her kitchen where she cooked Eggos and Toaster Sticks.

Beneath the slight pressure of his lips, her mouth opened and his tongue swept inside. Hot and liquid and unraveling a ribbon of fire from her throat, down her chest to the waiting friction in the pit of her stomach.

He fit his free hand into the curve of her waist and pulled her into him. Her breasts brushed his chest and the kiss deepened. His tongue touched hers while his mouth created a warm suction that felt ripe and so delicious—the ribbon of fire in her stomach engulfed her thighs and tightened her nipples against the front of his shirt.

A deep groan vibrated his chest against her breasts. His grasp on her waist tightened, relaxed, flexed, then slid to her behind. Pleasure flushed her skin and she opened her mouth wider, kissing him deeper. She ran her hands over his shoulders and chest and neck. He untangled his fingers from her hair and slid his palm down the side of her throat and across her shoulder. While his tongue plunged into her mouth, his hand moved to her ribs. He fanned his thumb across Spandex and the side of her breast. Back and forth, driving her mad with the want of his touch. Her breasts tightened while other places in her body turned liquid with need. She melted into him even more. Against her pelvis she felt the stiff ridge of his erection and she rocked against him, loving the feel of it. The size and weight and hard length.

His hands slid to her back, his fingers brushing her bare skin above her tank top. This had to stop, but she didn't want it to. Not now. Now she wanted more. This was crazy. She was crazy. As crazy as everyone said. Crazy Lily lusting after her neighbor and she didn't seem to care. He'd ignited something in her she hadn't felt in a long time. Crazy, consuming lust.

Tucker took a stop back and grasped her shoulders. Her hands slid to down his shirt, his star cool against her palm and his breathing, heavy, harsh, lifting his chest. "Lily. I want more."

Great. She wanted more too. She took a step toward him but his grasp tightened, keeping her at arm's length. She didn't understand. If he wanted more, why was he pushing her away? "So do I," she said, although she thought it was obvious.

"I want you." He dipped his head and his heavy gaze looked into her. "All of you."

She raised a hand to her mouth and touched her wet, tingling lips. Was he talking some strange sexual position? If so, she might be okay with it. Would probably be okay with just about anything. Had probably been there and done that. Several times. But he was young and she had eight years of experience on him. That was probably his attraction to her. "What exactly do you want?" However, there was one part of her that would always remain virgin territory. She didn't judge women who went there. She just wasn't one of them.

"When I saw you today, I knew I wanted every bit of you. That I want to know all of you."

She dropped her hands to her sides. "You said that." She really didn't want to have to come right out and say it but . . . best to be up front because real ladies didn't do it in the back. "My bottom is a no landing strip."

His brows pulled together over his suddenly sharp brown eyes. "What?"

"I just thought you should know."

"Thanks for clearing that up." He frowned and took another step back. "Jesus, Lily. You thought I want anal sex?"

She shook her head, more confused by him than ever before. And he was plenty confusing. She put her hands on top of her head and blew out a breath.

"That's not only disturbing, but insulting."

"I'm disturbing?" She put one palm on her chest. "You said you wanted to know every bit of me. And that bit of me is off limits."

"I wasn't talking about your ass, for Christ

sake." He raised a hand, palm up. "I was talking about you. Your life. Your heart and soul."

Her heart and soul?

"I want more than sex."

She turned and grabbed the mugs for something to do with her hands. What could he possibly want? More than sex? All men wanted sex. Her heart and soul? She reached for the coffee carafe and poured. What did that mean?

"I've had relationships that were just about sex. I don't want that anymore. I don't want that with you."

"Relationship?" The coffee sloshed over one side of the Everything's Bigger In Texas mug and she turned to face him.

"Pushing you away was the hardest thing I've ever done." He scrubbed his face with his hands then dropped them to his sides. "I still can't believe I did it, but I don't want to start out that way."

"Start? We can't start anything. We can't have a relationship."

"Why?"

"Because."

"That's not a reason."

"Okay." She raised a hand toward him. "You're thirty and I'm thirty-eight."

"So."

"So I have a young son." She dropped her hand. "I can't just . . . just can't go around . . . with you."

"Because I'm thirty?"

She'd already lived so much down. "People will

talk." And it was nice walking into a room and not hearing whispers behind her back.

"So what?"

If he could say that, then people had never talked about him. "They'll say I'm a cougar, and that you must want someone to take care of you."

"Bullshit." He moved across the kitchen and grabbed his coat. "You're not old enough to be a cougar." He shoved his arms into the sleeves. "I have my own house and car and money. I don't need a woman to take care of me. I can take care of myself and anyone else in my life." He stormed across the kitchen but paused in the doorway long enough to say, "I tried to do the right thing today, but the next time I get my hands on you, we're not going to stop." She heard him walk through the living room and open the front door. Then, "Hello Mrs. Brooks."

Crap! Her mom.

"Deputy Matthews?" Lily raised a hand to her throat as her mouth fell open. Please God, just let her mom walk inside without stopping to ramble. "How's your cat?" Obviously God wasn't listening to Lily Darlington. Probably punishing her for putting her hands on the young neighbor.

"Pinky's good. Thanks for asking."

"Marylyle Jeffers had a black cat like yours. She had diabetes and had to have her foot cut off." No wonder Lily acted a bit imprudent sometimes. Her mother was one taco short of a combo plate. "Leg too."

"Oh I'm sorry—"

"Then she caught the pleurisy and died. Not saying it was her cat, but she did have horrible luck. Even before she was struck with—"

"Momma, you're letting out the bought air," Lily interrupted and stuck her head into the living room. She couldn't look at Tucker and pinned her gaze squarely on her mother's pile of gray hair. She was sure she was a bright red and didn't know what was more embarrassing—what she'd done with Tucker or her mother's inane rambling. "Thank you again for carrying in my groceries, Deputy Matthews."

"You're welcome. See you two ladies around."

Louella Brooks stared at the closed door, then turned her gaze to her youngest daughter. "Well."

That one word packed a wealth of meaning. Lily ducked back into the kitchen, looked at the two coffee mugs, and raised the Everything's Bigger In Texas mug to her mouth. She managed to hammer back half. It burned her tongue and throat and she set it back down as her mother entered the room.

"He certainly is a nice-looking boy."

Lily swallowed past her scalded taste buds and throat. She reached for her pink Deeann's Duds mug and turned with a slight smile on her face. "Nice too. He carried in my groceries."

A scowl settled into the wrinkles on her mother's face. "You're a single woman, Lily. You have to be careful who you let in your house."

"He's a deputy. What do you think he's going to do? Kill me?" Touch me? Kiss me? Drive me as crazy as everyone says I am?

"I wasn't talking about your physical safety."

Lily knew that. "He just carried in my groceries and had a half a cup of coffee." With her free hand, she pointed to the mug on the counter. "Then he left." And thank God too. If he hadn't stopped when he had, her mother would have used her key and strolled inside. The mere thought of her mother walking in on her and Tucker was too horrible to contemplate.

"Single gals can't be too careful when it comes to their reputations. Just the other day, the cable repairman was in Doreen Jaworski's house for three hours." She gave Lily a knowing look. "Cable repairs don't take three hours."

"Ma, Doreen is in her seventies."

"Exactly. She always did wear her clothes kind of sudden. Of course that was before she married Lynn Jaworski . . . which just goes to show, people's memories are longer than pulled taffy."

Lily closed her eyes and blew into her coffee.

"Her daughter Dorlynn didn't fall far from that tree. She—"

Lily didn't bother to stop her mother. Louella was going to talk until she ran out of words, which could take a while. Since her mother's retirement from the Wild Coyote Diner, the rambling had gotten worse. Nothing to do for it but block out her mother's voice and retreat into her own head.

Unfortunately, her head was filled with Tucker. He'd said he wanted a relationship, but he didn't know her. Didn't know her past and what everyone said about her. At least not yet. He'd no doubt change his mind once she heard about the Ronnie incident of '04.

Lily took a sip of coffee and winched as it hit her scalded tongue. But her past wasn't the biggest reason any sort of relationship was impossible. She was busy. She didn't have time. She couldn't get involved with him.

He was thirty. She hadn't even known what she'd wanted at thirty.

He might not have a problem with the age difference, but she did. People would call her a cougar. That crazy cougar, Lily Darlington. If it was just about her, she might risk it. Might show the world her middle finger. But it wasn't just her. She'd gone to school with a momma who wasn't wound too tight. Kids could be really cruel, and she couldn't do that to Pip.

Chapter Five

The rows of track lighting in Lily Belle's Salon and Day Spa sparkled like gold fire in the sequins of the owner's dress. The long-sleeved dress covered Lily from collar bone to mid-thigh, and might have been considered modest if not for the fact that it clung to the curves of her body. A body she kept thin and toned through a busy life, Rodney Yee, and the Pilates Power Gym in one of the spa's back rooms. She not only cut hair, she was the owner and face of her business, and it was important that she reflect a positive, healthy image.

Lily's blond hair was pulled into a loose, sexy bun on the left side of her head, and she stood in the middle of the spa, chatting and sipping her first glass of champagne of the night. The party was officially over in half an hour and she was looking forward to slipping her feet out of the sparkly gold pumps. The spa had given away over ten thousand dollars in products and services and signed up a lot of clients for spa packages. Given the expense of the party and giveaways, Lily figured she'd broken even, which was fine with her. Her goal had been to bring in new clients, make them happy so they'd return. And with each return visit, happy clients generally wanted to try the newest facial or latest filler.

"I need to get going," her sister, Daisy, said as she moved toward Lily. She wove her arms through her tan trench coat and pulled her blond hair from beneath the collar. Daisy was six months pregnant and a red maternity dress hugged her belly. Daisy was older, but Lily was taller. There were other little differences between the two, but they looked enough alike that there was no denying they were sisters.

"I'll walk you out."

"No need."

"I want to." Lily set her glass on a table and moved through the spa toward the front. "I'm so glad you came tonight."

"I didn't win a darn thing, though."

Lily smiled and opened the door. "Don't worry about it. I know the owner and I'll hook you up."

"Good, 'cause once this baby is born, I need some color in my hair and Botox in my forehead."

Lily folded her arms across her chest and huddled against the chill of the night. "I've been trying to talk mom into getting Dysport because she doesn't want 'poison' in her face."

Daisy laughed. "How did it go with Ronnie yesterday?"

Lily shrugged as the two moved across the

parking lot. Their heels tapping against the pavement as they walked to Daisy's new van. "Ronnie was an hour late, of course. But he did make it."

"Do we think that's progress?"

Lily shook her head and a gold hoop earring brushed her neck. "We think it's a fluke. He's dumber than a road lizard and admitted his last girlfriend took off with his big screen TV and Xbox. Once he finds a new sloozy, he'll forget about Pippen again."

"Oh, my gosh," Daisy said, disgust lowering her voice. "He still plays Xbox? At his age? What a loser."

"I know. Right?" Lily laughed. "A thirty-eight-year-old 'gamer.' He probably sits around with one hand on the controller and the other on his balls."

"Ick."

"It's just embarrassing that I ever married him."

"Well, at least Pippen takes after you." An awkward pause stretched between them before Daisy said, "You had a hard time for a while, but you came through all that. And look at you now." They stopped by the van and Daisy opened the driver's side door. "I'm really proud of you, Lil."

Her heart got all mushy. "Thanks."

"And I wanted to ask you if it would be okay if we name the baby after you."

Her mushy heart got all tingly and the backs of her eyes pinched. "Are you sure?"

"Absolutely."

"Is Jack sure?" Given her past, it might be something the baby had to live down.

"It was originally his idea, but as soon as he mentioned it, I knew I wanted to name her Lily too. It just seems right, but I wanted to make sure you weren't planning on having your own baby 'Lily' someday."

Lily laughed. "I don't even have a boyfriend." For some weird reason Tucker's face popped into her head. "And I don't see a man in my future. I don't think I have very good judgment."

"The rat bastard doesn't count. He never deserved you, and you deserve someone as great as you, Lily. Someone who looks at you and knows he's lucky."

Someone like Jack. Jack looked at Daisy like that. She hugged her sister. "You're going to make my face run." She stepped back and waved her hands in front of her eyes.

Daisy climbed into the van. "Go back inside before you catch your death."

"Drive carefully and take good care of little Lily." She took a step back as Daisy fired up the engine, then waved as her sister pulled out of the parking lot. She refolded her arms and smiled as she walked toward the front of the spa. *Little Lily.* Several years ago, she had given up the dream of finding the right man and giving Pip a sibling. She'd always wanted a happy family, and hoped for two kids and a dog, but it just wasn't in the cards for her. That was okay. Her family wasn't perfect, but they were happy.

When she opened the door to her salon, she had a big grin on her face. There had been a time when she and Daisy hadn't been very close, and now she was naming her baby girl after her. *Little Lily*.

While she'd been outside with Daisy, the rest of the clients had left and only a few employees remained. The sound of female laughter filled the front of the spa and salon as the caterers started to pack up and break tables down—laughter mixed with one deeper chuckle. Lily's feet skidded to a halt and her gaze took in the back of a familiar dark head, broad shoulders narrowing to a trim waist and nice behind. She didn't need to see a uniform or ratty sweatshirt to recognize Tucker Matthews.

"Deputy Matthews."

"Hey, Lily." He turned toward her and his brown eyes took her in with one sweeping glance. "You said to come by and get a facial."

She looked at the faces looking back at her. At the inquisitive gazes of her assistant manager, two beauticians, and aesthetician. "Deputy Matthews is my neighbor and I mentioned he should come by and *win* a facial." She turned toward him. "I didn't think you'd take me up on it."

"Yeah. I noticed there aren't any men here tonight."

A few women had dragged their husbands or

boyfriends, but they'd left as soon as the final prize had been won. She glanced at the clock on the wall above a manicure station. "The party is over in fifteen minutes. If you wanted to win a facial you're too late."

His grin told her he knew that. "You should show me around your salon. In case I need"—he glanced around—"a haircut or something."

No, she *shouldn't*. The caterer caught her attention and gave her a nod. "I have a few checks to write," she said. "Maybe one of the girls will show you."

"I will," young, perky Melinda Hartley volunteered.

Tucker lifted one brow and wrinkled the scar on his forehead.

"Excuse me." Lily moved through the salon to her office. The caterer followed her. She sat down at a desk covered in paperwork and a big open appointment book; her computer sat at one end of the desk, and behind it hung a massive ornate mirror that had once decorated a brothel in Tascosa. The caterer sat opposite, slid a red velvet chair toward Lily's big desk, and then they went over the bill. While they counted the bottles of wine and champagne that had been consumed and calculated the charges for the extra linen Lily had ordered at the last minute, her mind was elsewhere in the salon. Melinda Hartley was about twenty-five. She was pretty and a really good colorist. She was also a little conceited and loud. If Melinda was in the room, everyone knew it. Just as everyone knew all about Melinda's sex life, whether they wanted to know or not. She *was* a butt girl, and Lily had had to talk to her about appropriate workplace conversation. If it wasn't for the fact that it was hard to find a good colorist in the Texas panhandle, she would have fired Melinda months ago.

And she was out there. In the salon. Somewhere with Tucker. Probably telling him about her sex life. Tucker was a guy. He was probably loving it.

Lily wrote out the balance she owed the caterer and tore the check from her business account. She handed it across her desk and watched the caterer walk out the door. Melinda was closer to Tucker's age and didn't have a child and Lily's baggage. She shuffled the paperwork on her desk, sorting customer surveys and treatment plans. Until tonight, she hadn't seen Tucker since that morning in her kitchen five days ago. She'd heard from Pippen that the two played basketball when Pip got home from school and before Tucker got ready for work. By the time Lily made it home, Tucker was already gone, which was a good thing. He clearly wasn't good for her good intentions.

"Now, that wasn't very nice."

Lily glanced up at Tucker leaning a shoulder into the doorframe of her office. He wore a gray crew neck sweater and button-fly Levi's. His arms were crossed over his chest and he looked annoyed—annoyed and good enough to nibble up one side and down the other. "What?"

"Melinda."

She rose from her chair and moved to the front of her desk. "You didn't like her?"

He shrugged one shoulder. "Not really. She's loud and talks too much." He pushed away from where he was leaning and shut the door. "She wanted me to screw her on a massage table."

That was a bit crude and she'd get to his language in a minute. The inappropriateness of shutting the door too, but first she wanted to know . . . "Did she say that?"

"Not exactly. She was much more graphic about where she wanted it."

"Oh." Lily moved past the red chair to the center of her desk and sat on the edge. "She can say really inappropriate and offensive things. She's one of those people who doesn't have a filter, but I didn't know she'd go that far."

He shrugged. "I wasn't offended. I was in the Army for ten years, I've heard worse."

She took a breath and let it out. "Thank you for not taking her up on her offer in the massage room."

He moved toward Lily. "She isn't the woman I want to shove on a table." He stopped in front of her and she stood so she wouldn't have to stare up at him. Just a few sequins separated his chest from hers, "Isn't her panties I want to see around her ankles." He took her hand and slid it up his chest. "You're the women I want to shove on a table with your panties around your ankles."

"Tucker! Don't say things like that."

"Why not?" He buried his fingers in her loose bun on the side of her head. "It's the truth. I told you how I feel about you. I want you. I want everything about you. Getting you naked is one of the things I want." With her four-inch heels, they were close to the same height and he pressed his forehead into hers. "I know you want that too."

After the other morning, she couldn't exactly deny it, and she was too old to play coy games. "Anyone can walk in here." The fire he'd started in her veins a few days ago flared in her chest. The crazy consuming lust that absolutely could not happen here.

He shook his head and his eyes turned a shade darker. "They had their coats on and were walking outside when I came in here."

"They could come back."

"I locked the door."

"We can't do this here." She meant to sound more forceful, but the crazy, consuming lust burned her throat and toasted her pitiful resistance.

"That's what I thought until you stood up and walked toward me. You shouldn't have worn that dress."

"You're blaming my dress?" But this is Amarillo, she rationalized. Not Lovett. In a town the size of Lovett, the fact that he'd shown up tonight would have been telegraphed to half the town by now. In Amarillo, she was just another salon owner and no one cared.

"Yes, and the tight outfit you had on Monday. The way you've been in my head for the past five days and the hard-on that won't go away no matter how many times I abuse myself. I didn't think we were going to do this here, but I'm think we have to now."

"What if someone—" His mouth on hers silenced her protest. The other morning, he'd started slower, kissing her neck and throat and cheek. Easing her into it. Tonight he hit her fast with hot lust and wet pleasure. His mouth working hers, feeding and hungry. It pulled her up on her toes and smashed her against his chest, so close she could feel the pounding of his heart. Her hands slid over his arms and shoulders and the back of his head. And like the other morning, a deep shuddering groan vibrated in his chest as if he couldn't get enough of her touch. She liked knowing she did that to him. A strong beautiful man who couldn't get enough of Lily Darlington.

She kissed him back, her tongue slick with carnal implications. He pressed his erection into her pelvis and she had to lock her knees to keep from falling. She slid up his chest then back down, feeling every hard muscle and length of his harder erection.

He grasped the bottom of her sequined dress, drew it up her thighs to her waist. His hands found her bare behind and he fingered the thin lace of her thong panties. He palmed her bare backside and rubbed his denim button fly against the tiny triangle of lace covering her crotch.

He lifted his face and came up for air. "Lily," he gasped.

She looked into his eyes, dark and sleepy with lust, and reached for the bottom of his sweater. She pulled it over his head and tossed it to the wooden floor. She lowered her gaze to the brown hair on his hard, defined chest. For some reason, she'd thought his chest would be bare. But it wasn't. He was a man with a man's chest and a thin line of hair trailed down his flat abdomen, circled his navel, and darted beneath the waistband of his Levi's. A snarling bulldog was tattooed on the ball of his shoulders with the words U.S. ARMY inked beneath. RELENTLESS was tattooed in heavy black ink on the inside of his forearm, which described him perfectly: his hands, his mouth, and the lust rolling off him in heavy, relentless waves.

She bent forward and kissed his shoulder, ran her fingers across his pec and down his belly to the front of his jeans. She squeezed his erection and caressed him through the denim. Desire, hot and gripping, tightened her breasts and stomach and pulled between her legs.

"Wait." He grabbed her shoulders and turned her until her back was against his chest. He reached for the zipper on the back of her dress and slid it down. Through the old bordello mirror, she watched as he slid her dress from her shoulders.

Just before it slipped down her arms, she placed her hands on the sequins over her breasts.

"I have implants," she told him. She hadn't worn a bra because strap lines showed beneath the tight dress, and in a moment he would see the thin scars beneath each areola.

Confusion lowered his brows. "What?"

"I have breast implants. Do you have a problem with that?"

"Is that a trick question?"

She shook her head as he grasped her wrists. "Some men don't like implants."

In the mirror, he raised his gaze from her hands to her face. "A man told you that?"

She shook her head. "A few women in my chair over the years have mentioned it."

"A man would never say that unless he thought it would get him laid." He shoved her wrists to her sides. For a second, her dress caught on her hard nipples then slid down her stomach to her waist. "Lily." The breath left his lungs and brushed the side of her head. "You're beautiful."

The dress fell to the floor and she kicked it aside. She stood in front of the mirror wearing nothing but her white panties—owning a salon and spa made it easy for her to keep her pubic area waxed and trimmed into a perfect triangle hidden beneath her thong—but looking at her abdomen . . . it was flat but not as tight and toned as she'd like. She examined the palm-size yellow-and-orange lily tattoo on the inside of her hip that she'd thought was such a good idea six years ago. "Are you lying to get laid?" She tried to turn to face him, away from her image in the mirror, but his hands moved to her abdomen and he pulled her against him. The hair on his chest tickled her bare back. She felt completely wrapped up, surrounded by his relentless passion.

"I'll never lie to you, Lily." He slid one hand up and cupped her breast. Her hard nipple stabbed his warm palm and her breath caught in her lungs. "You're so beautiful and I ache to be with you."

She knew the feeling. She ached too. All over. Then he slipped his hand beneath the little triangle of her thong and touched her where she ached most.

"You're wet," he whispered next to her ear. "Push your panties down for me. Push 'em down around your ankles." He brushed this thumb across her nipple and again she had to lock her knees to keep from sliding to the floor. She did as he asked, then looked at his big hands—one covering her breast the other her crotch. He slid his fingers deeper between her thighs and she reached behind her bare bottom and slipped her own hand beneath the waistband of his jeans. She wrapped her hand around his hot thick shaft and squeezed. She reached up with her free hand and brought his mouth down to hers. She gave him a long wet kiss and her heart pounded in her chest. She loved the way he touched her. She wanted him every bit as much as he wanted her.

Tucker lifted his mouth from Lily's and looked into the deep blue of her heavily lidded eyes. He turned his attention to the mirror and watched his hands on her body . . . on the perfect patch between her legs, and his fingers lightly pinching her pink nipples. Her hand gripping his cock was driving him close to the edge. She tore at the buttons of his Levi's, and he pulled a condom from his back pocket a second before his pants slid down his legs.

"Grab the desk with your hands."

She stepped one foot out of her thong, then she bent forward and looked back over her shoulder at him. "You remember the no man's land, right?"

"I'll never do anything you're not comfortable doing." He didn't want to hurt her. He wanted to make it so good she wanted more. He pulled himself out of his boxer-briefs and rolled the condom down the shaft of his penis. "Spread your feet a little bit for me."

She did and he slid his hand over her bottom and between her legs. She was wet and ready and he parted her slick flesh. Her back arched as he positioned himself and he slid into the hot pleasure of her body. She was incredibly tight around him. Pulling him deeper and deeper until he couldn't sink any deeper.

She moaned low in her throat and whispered his name. He looked in the mirror, at him naked behind her, her beautiful face turned back, looking at him. *Mine,* he thought as he pulled out and thrust into her again. She pushed her bottom against him. Straining, wanting more. He gave it to her in long powerful thrusts. He drove inside again and again, his heart pounded *boom-boom-boom. Mine. Mine. Mine.* Over the roar in his head and ears, he heard her say his name. Telling him she wanted him. More. Harder.

"Tucker," she moaned loud enough to be heard in the next county as he felt the first tightening pulse of her orgasm. Good, he thought on some primal level. He was sure they were the only two left in the salon, but he didn't care. If there was anyone around, they'd know what the two of them were doing. Know they were together. That she belonged to him now. He'd never been a possessive man, but as her orgasm pulled his own release from deep in his belly, he knew that he wanted this to last forever.

The most intense pleasure he'd ever felt in his life rippled through his body and slammed into his heart. It spread fire across his skin, grabbed his insides, and stole his breath. He doubled over and planted his hands on the desk next to Lily's. He buried his face in the curve of her neck and closed his eyes.

As crazy as it sounded . . . as crazy as it felt . . . as crazy as it was—he'd fallen in love with her even before he'd walked into her salon earlier. He'd fallen for her that first day in her driveway.

"Jesus," he whispered. He'd never fallen so fast and hard and it scared the hell out of him. Scared him more than Taliban rounds whizzing past his nose and slamming into the granite mountain by his left ear. He'd been trained by the military what to do in combat. Trained by the sheriff's department how to take down a felon bent on escape. But this? This was new territory. There was no training. No taking cover. No fighting back. There was just Lily and how she made him feel.

Chapter Six

Monday morning, Lily pulled her Jeep into the parking lot of Crockett Elementary School and reached into the backseat. "My last appointment is at four. It's just a cut and style so I should be home around six." She stopped the SUV next to the sidewalk and handed Pippen his Angry Birds backpack. "What do you want for dinner?"

He wore his red coat zipped all the way to his chin and said into the nylon collar, "Pizza."

Of course. She leaned toward him. "Give me some sugar, sugar."

He unbuckled himself. "Tonight," he said. He'd stopped giving her sugar at school last year, but a mom could always try. "Is Tucker coming to play basketball today?"

She shrugged. "He's working, so I don't know. I haven't talked to him." Not since he'd left her house yesterday around noon. Only half an hour before Ronnie had dropped Pippen off home. Four hours early, which was so typical of Ronnie.

She hadn't been all that surprised. She was just glad she'd been alone and had taken a shower.

Pippen opened the door and slid out of the car. "Maybe he will."

"Maybe." She gave him a little wave. "Love you, Pip."

"Love you, Momma." He shut the door and she watched him run to a group of his friends hanging out near the playground equipment. She took her foot off the brake and drove out of the parking lot. Her first appointment today wasn't until noon. Her assistant manager was certainly capable of running the salon when Lily wasn't there.

She stopped at a red light and thought about the last time she'd been in the salon, having sex with Tucker in her office. Sex that had been so good she might have moaned Tucker's name a little too loud. She hoped she hadn't and that everyone had already left the building like he'd said. By the time they'd redressed and left the office, the salon had been empty. Thank God.

After she'd left the salon that night, Tucker followed her home in his truck and they'd spent the rest of the night in her bed—having sex and talking. At least she'd talked. It seemed like every time she asked him questions about himself, he changed the subject back to her or kissed her until she didn't feel like talking anymore.

She pulled her Jeep into the garage and closed the door. She couldn't exactly be angry about his lack of personal disclosure. There were certain things in her past that she wasn't going to talk about either.

The cell in her purse rang before she even got in the back door. She figured it was someone at the salon and answered without looking at the number. "This is Lily."

"This is your neighbor. Come over so I can kiss you good night."

Lily smiled. "Mom?"

Tucker chuckled and she could see his smile in her head. A smile that curved his lips and lit up his brown eyes. "Come over or I'll come over and get you."

She couldn't have that. Her mother might walk in. "Give me a few minutes." She hung up and changed out of the yoga outfit she'd worn in anticipation of working out. She had a whole different workout in mind now and changed into a pink-and-blue polka dot nighty, pink thong, and pink cowboy boots. She tied her trench coat around her waist and checked her pink lipstick in the mirror.

There were three boards missing at the back of the fence that separated her yard from Tucker's. The previous owner's Newfoundland, Griffin, had always preferred her yard to his; and no matter how many times she'd fixed the boards, Griffin knocked them down whenever he heard Pippen playing outside. Griffin had been a sweetheart of a dog—huge, but a sweetheart who'd had a real fondness for Pip. After about the fifth time of Griffin knocking down the boards, Lily had given up and left them stacked neatly on the ground.

Lily grabbed a pot of coffee on her way out the door.

Tucker had said several times that he wanted her. He wanted everything about her, but he didn't know everything about her. He didn't know her past. He didn't know that people thought she was crazy. At least, she figured if he did know, he would have mentioned it right before he took off running for the hills. She wasn't going to be the one to tell him.

She moved through her yard, slipped through the fence, and knocked on his back door. "Italian roast?" she asked and held up the pot as he answered the door.

His brows pulled over his eyes and his scar wrinkled. "How did you get back here?" He wore a beige cold-weather base layer that clung to his chest and arms like a second skin. And of course his work pants and boots.

"A few boards are missing in the fence."

He held the door open and she stepped inside. "Convenient."

The kitchen was pretty much as she recalled from the last time she'd been in the place, when the realtor had spruced up the place for an open house. Oak cabinets, white walls, new gray counter tops, and vinyl flooring with a stone pattern. A small black cat sat by the door to the garage, lapping up milk from one of two purple bowls with flowers painted around the edges. The bowls sat on a little white rug with the name PINKY written in pink at the bottom.

Lily set the carafe on the counter and reached for her belt. "My mom told me you have a cat."

"Pinky got out and I had to track her down that day I met your mother," Tucker said as he reached into a cupboard and pulled out two plain white mugs. "Pinky has no survival skills."

Lily bit the side of her lip to keep from laughing. "How did you end up with a cat with no survival skills?"

"She belonged to an old girlfriend."

"And she just gave her to you?" Lily shrugged out of her coat, hung it over a chair, and stooped down by the little cat.

"Not exactly. The girlfriend moved out and left her cat behind."

The hem of the nighty slid down her thighs as she lightly stroked the cat from the back of her head to her tail. "She abandoned her animal?" Lily couldn't imagine that. She liked cats but didn't have a pet because she wasn't home enough to take care of one. Now that Griffin was gone, Pippen was harassing her for a dog.

When Tucker didn't answer her question, she looked up over her shoulder at him. He stood in the middle of the room—two mugs of coffee in his hands, like his feet were frozen in place. "What?"

"What are you wearing?"

She stood. "A comfy nighty and my cowboy boots."

"Panties?" He held the mug toward her as his eyes slid over his body.

"No self-respecting Southern lady leaves the house without her hair in place, her makeup done, and her panties on." She took the mug from his hand and blew into it. "That sort of fast behavior could lead to a bad reputation. I went to high school with Francine Holcomb, and she left the house without wearing her undies on more than one occasion. Her reputation never did recover. 'Course, everyone knew that Francie was as loose as grits, bless her heart." She took a sip. She was nervous and had to stop before she sounded like her mother. "How was your day?"

He brought his gaze up to hers. "Better now."

For the first time since she'd stepped in his kitchen, she noticed the pinch of exhaustion at the corners of his brown eyes. "You look tired. Did something happen at work?"

He shrugged a shoulder and leaned his hip into a counter. "I responded to a call about one this morning at Rodale Jewelry store on Seventh near the highway. When I got there, a guy was trying to kick in the back door. He saw me and took off." He took a swallow of coffee. "I chased him for about half a mile before I caught him climbing inside a Dumpster behind Rick's Bait & Tackle."

Lily wrinkled her nose. "Did you have to climb into the Dumpster?"

"I grabbed his belt just as he was diving in and pulled him back out. It was real ripe too. Smelled like Rick had just thrown out some expired bait. If I'd had to jump in there and get covered with fish eggs and dead crickets, I'd have been pissed."

She couldn't imagine running in work boots and gear. She was in good shape, but probably would have passed out after a hundred feet. "Was he from around here?"

"Odessa." Tucker looked at the scratches across the back of his hand. "He was scrappy for such a skinny guy."

Lily moved toward him and took his hand in hers. "How'd this happen?"

"He didn't want to be cuffed very badly, and I scrapped it on the concrete trying to dig his arm from underneath him."

She raised his hand to her mouth and lightly kissed it. "Better?"

"Yes." He looked back into her eyes and nodded. "He tried to kick me in the balls too."

"I'm not going to kiss your hairy balls, Tucker."

He chuckled like he thought he was real funny. "Didn't hurt to mention it."

She dropped his hand and thought for a moment. "Well, maybe if you got them waxed."

He sucked in a breath through his teeth. "Do men do that?"

"Some men." He looked so horrified it was her turn to chuckle. "They wax their whole bodies. It's called manscaping."

He set his mug on the counter. "No one is going to put hot wax anywhere near my balls." He ran his hands up her arms and pulled her close.

"Don't be a baby." She set her mug on the counter next to his. "I get waxed."

"I noticed." He grinned. "I like it. It makes going down on you real nice and neat. I can see what I'm doing."

Her eyes widened and she felt color creep up her cheeks. "You looked at my . . . my crotch."

"Of course. My face was down there. I don't know why you're embarrassed. You've got a real nice . . ." He paused as if searching for the right word then gave up. "I don't like the word *crotch*. I've got a crotch. You're all high and tight and pretty down there. Like a juicy peach." His brows drew together. "Or is that one of those things I shouldn't say?"

She didn't know. She supposed it was a compliment, but it had been a while since she'd been involved with a man. She couldn't recall if they talked so free and easy in the beginning or if they saved their real thoughts for later—after they reached that comfortable stage. Or was it just Tucker? "Have you always talked this way to women?" Or maybe guys Tucker's age where just more direct.

He looked up toward the ceiling and thought a minute. "No." His gaze returned to hers. "I used to have a filthy mouth. When I was in the Army I talked a lot worse. I had to work really hard to get the f-word out of every sentence. I couldn't even ask for the ketchup without dropping it at least twice. In the military, swearing is not only a way of life, it's an art form." He slid his hands across her shoulders to her neck and his thumbs brushed her chin and jaw. "Living with a bunch of guys for months on end in a bunker in an Afghanistan outpost will turn anyone into an animal. You get shot at every day, live in dirt, and the food's shitty. Inventive swearing is just something to do to pass the time and impress the other guys."

"You must have liked it. You did it for ten years."

"I loved it right up until the second that I didn't."

"What made you decide you didn't love it anymore?" She put her palms on his flat belly and brushed her fingers across the fabric of his shirt. She knew he loved it when she ran her hands all over him. Her touch seemed to soothe even as it excited him. And she loved the feel of his hard muscles and tight skin beneath her hand and mouth.

"The last time I took rounds, I got shot five times. Four were stopped by my ballistic plates." Her fingers stopped and she raised her gaze to where he pointed at the scar on his forehead. "The fifth got me here and I decided I didn't want to be taken out that way. I'd given the Army enough. It was time to do something else. When my enlistment was up, I got out."

She stared at his forehead, horrified. "You could have died, Tucker. I bet your family was worried sick."

"I didn't die and I'm here with you." He kissed

her upturned mouth. "I like having you here when I come home. You should come over every morning."

She settled against his chest. "I can't every morning. I have to work."

"What time do you work today?"

"I have to be there by noon."

He raised the big watch on his wrist. "Then why are we out here wasting time?" He reached for her hand, led her out of the kitchen, and through the living room. She got a quick impression of wood and leather and real art on the walls—no nudie posters or dogs playing poker painted on velvet. He had a big screen TV and books. They continued down the hall and she looked in a bathroom that appeared surprisingly clean. She hadn't known what to expect, but not this. Not this grown-up house, with big-boy furniture. It just didn't fit her preconceived image of him. "Do you play Xbox?"

"I'm thirty, not thirteen." He stopped next to a bed with a real headboard. "I'm only too glad to show you I'm a grown man. Although, after our sexual three-peat the other night, I'm surprised it's even in question."

During the next few weeks, Lily snuck through the back fence several more times after she took Pippen to school. There were some women, she supposed, who would have qualms about sneaking around. That would feel uneasy or guilty or that she was doing something wrong. Lily wasn't one of them. She liked Tucker. She liked spending time with him. She was wildly attracted to him and he made her laugh. He seemed to have his head on straight and he was good to her son. He was also very good in bed, and she didn't want to stop sneaking through the fence to spend time with him.

The more time she spent with him, the more she discovered things about him. Like that Tucker recycled old wood. He made a coffee table out of an old door and a chair and his entertainment center out of wood he'd reclaimed from a demolished ranch house near Houston. She also learned that he ran five miles on a treadmill and lifted weights, which was good because he liked a big breakfast before he went to bed in the morning.

While he ate, she sipped coffee and answered questions he asked about her life. He himself gave up little about his own, though. He talked about his job and who he'd arrested and on what charge, and he talked about playing basketball with Pippen while she was at work. He talked a little about the men who'd served with him in the Army and his time in Iraq and Afghanistan. He said that after he got out of the Army, he was closed off but wasn't anymore. For a guy who didn't consider himself "closed off," he would only go so deep into his life, and when she asked about his family, he told her they were all dead. Case closed. End of story.

Conversely, he asked a lot of questions about

her family, and like him, she only went so deep. She told him about growing up in such a small town and that she'd fallen for Rat Bastard Ronnie Darlington because Ronnie owned a truck and looked good in a pair of jeans and a T-shirt. She talked about her low expectations and lower self-esteem. She talked about Ronnie leaving her with a two-year-old and a drained bank account, but didn't mention the part about driving her car into his house.

On the third Monday they both had off, she told him about the time her sister Daisy had tried to kick Ronnie in the crotch outside the Minute Mart. Of course, she didn't mention that she'd been involved in a hair-pulling fight with Kelly the Skank at the same time. Let him think Daisy, the responsible one, was the crazy sister.

They spent the next few hours in bed, and when she got up and dressed he stacked his hands behind his head and watched her.

"When are you going to come to my front door?" he asked.

She looked across her shoulder at him as she hooked her bra behind her back. "I can't do that." She'd been the subject of gossip and speculative gazes most of her life, but she hadn't given the people of Lovett anything to talk about in a long time. She planned to keep it that way. "People will talk."

"Who cares?"

She reached for her blouse and threaded

her arms though the sleeves. "I do. I'm a single mother." She pulled her hair from beneath the collar. "I have to be careful." And if and when their relationship ended, no one would know about it. She'd probably be upset. It would be awkward, but the whole town wouldn't know she'd been dumped again—this time by a younger man. She could hold her head up, and Pippen wouldn't have to live it down.

Tucker sat up and swung his feet over the side of the bed. He watched her button up the front and he stood and stepped into a pair of jeans. He loved opening his back door and seeing her there, but he wanted more. "There's a difference between being careful and thinking we need to keep a dirty secret."

She glanced up from her hands. "I don't think we're a dirty secret." A secret, yes. Dirty, no.

"Have you told your sister about me?" He arranged his junk then zipped up his pants. "Your mother? Anyone?"

Her blond hair brushed her cheeks as she shook her head. "Why is it anyone's business?"

"Because we're sneaking around like we're doing something wrong and we're not." He reached for a T-shirt and pulled it over his head. "I told you right up front I want all of you. I'm not going to treat you like you're just a piece of ass."

"I appreciate that, Tucker." She stepped into a pair of black pants. "But I have a ten-year-old son and I have to be very careful."

"I like Pippen. I'd play ball with him even if you weren't in the picture. He's a funny little kid, and I think he likes me."

"He does."

"I would never do anything to hurt him."

She looked up at him as she buttoned her pants. "Kids are cruel. I don't want our relationship to be something that Pippen has to hear about at school."

More than anyone, he knew how mean kids could be. "Duly noted." But it was more than Pippen. Tucker might be younger than Lily, but that didn't mean he'd been born yesterday. Lily wanted to keep their relationship a secret for reasons other than her son. Tucker wanted to get a megaphone and let the whole town know. This feeling was new to him. He'd been in love before, but never like this. Never fallen this hard—so hard he wanted to put his hands on her shoulders and shake her even as he wanted to pull her into his chest and keep her there forever.

This situation was new to him. She had a son. He had to be careful of Pippen's feelings, but that didn't mean he was going to hide like he was doing something wrong. As if Lily had to live like a nun and they had to sneak around like sinners. He'd be respectful, but he wasn't anyone's secret and sneaking around just wasn't his style.

Chapter Seven

"My mama worked at the Wild Coyote Diner until she retired last year," Lily said as she painted vanilla crème and butterscotch highlights into her eleven-thirty appointment's hair. For dimension, she added a caramel lowlight every third foil. With the tail of her brush, she sectioned off a thin line, wove the tail through the strands, then she slid a foil next to her client's scalp. "And my brother-in-law owns Parrish American Classics."

"I used to eat at the Wild Coyote all the time. Open-face sandwiches and pecan pie." Wrapped in a black salon cape, her client, Sadie Hollowell, looked back at her through the mirror. "What's your mama's name?"

"Louella Brooks."

"Of course, I remember her," Sadie said. And Lily remembered Sadie Hollowell. Sadie was several years younger than Lily, but everyone knew the Hollowells. They owned the JH Ranch and had run cattle in the panhandle for generations. And if there was one person the people in town loved to talk about more than Lily, it was anyone with the last name Hollowell. Sadie had moved away from Lovett for a good number of years, but she was back now taking care of her sick daddy. Being that she was the very last Hollowell, Sadie was numero uno with the Lovett gossips. You couldn't swing a cat without hitting someone who was talking about Sadie.

Just yesterday, Lily had cut Winnie Stokes's hair and heard that Sadie had left the Founder's Day celebration last Saturday with Luraleen Jink's nephew, Vince Haven. According to Winnie, Vince was the new owner of the Gas and Go and a former Navy SEAL. Supposedly, he was hotter than a pepper patch and his truck had been spotted at the Hollowell ranch house well into the wee hours of the morning. Evidently, Sadie didn't care if people gossiped about her or she would have made Vince hide his truck in the barn. Lily envied Sadie that screw-you-all attitude. Maybe if she ever moved away like Sadie, she'd have it too.

A bell above the door chimed, and through the mirror a huge bouquet of red roses entered the salon, so big it hid the delivery man. "Oh, no." He set the flowers on the front counter and one of the girls signed for them.

"Are those for you?" Sadie asked.

"I'm afraid so." Yesterday Tucker had sent stargazer lilies. His way of letting her know that he would not sneak around. He wasn't hiding.

"That's sweet."

"No, it's not. He's too young for me," she said and felt a blush creep up her neck. Everyone in the salon knew about Tucker. After he'd showed up at the spa party, and locked the door to her office, there was little doubt what Lily Darlington was doing with the young Deputy Matthews. Adding to the intrigue and gossip was the fact that she arrived late sometimes to the salon. Before Tucker, she'd always been one of the first to arrive.

She painted strands of hair, then wrapped the foil. Salons filled with female employees were just a natural hotbed of gossip, and Lily's salon was buzzing more than usual. She had to do something. Something to make it stop before it reached Lovett. But other than kicking Tucker out of her life, she didn't know what to do about it. Telling everyone to shut the hell up would only confirm it.

"How old is he?"

She sectioned off another slice of hair. "Thirty."

"That's only eight years, right?"

"Yeah, but I don't want to be a cougar." God, she hated even the thought of that word. So far the gossip had been contained to the salon here in Amarillo, but it was only a matter of time before it spread to Lovett. She shouldn't have had sex with Tucker in her office. For a woman who cared about gossip, that had clearly been a mistake. One she should regret perhaps more than she did.

"You don't look like a cougar."

She didn't feel like one either. "Thanks." She

slid a foil against Sadie's scalp. "He looks about twenty-five."

"I think he has to be young enough to be your son before it's considered a cougar-cub relationship."

"Well, I don't want to date a man eight years younger." She swiped color out of one of the bowls and continued painting Sadie's hair. No, she didn't want to date someone eight years younger, but she didn't want to stop seeing Tucker either. Just the thought of him gave her that funny, scary feeling in her stomach and made her heart hurt in her chest. Her feelings for him scared her. Scared her in a way she hadn't been scared in a long time. "But Lordy, he's hot." And smart and funny and nice. He'd built Pinky a cat condo, for goodness sakes.

"Just use him for his body."

"I tried that." She sighed, thinking about the flowers and his suggestion yesterday that they take Pippen to Showtime Pizza or bowling. He wanted more from her but that wasn't a surprise. He'd told her what he wanted from beginning. *All of you,* he'd said, but she wasn't real clear what that meant. All of her for now? Until she turned forty? "I have a ten-year-old son, and I'm trying to run my own business. I just want a peaceful, calm life and Tucker is complicated." But *was* Tucker complicated? Maybe, but more accurately, their relationship was complicated. A better word to describe Tucker was *relentless.*

"How?"

"He was in the Army and he saw a lot. He says he used to be closed off but isn't anymore." There were things he was keeping to himself. She hadn't a clue what those things were. Things that might have to do with his military experience or childhood or God knew what. "But for a man who says he isn't closed off anymore, he doesn't share a lot about himself." But neither did she.

For another hour, she wove color through Sadie's hair. They chatted about growing up in Lovett and Sadie's daddy, who'd been kicked by a horse and was currently a patient at the rehab hospital a few blocks from Lily's salon.

After she finished putting the color on Sadie's hair, she sat her under the salon dryer for twenty minutes and went to her office. She moved behind her desk and reached for the phone. "Thanks for the flowers," she said when Tucker's voicemail picked up. "They're gorgeous, but you really have to stop spending money on me."

She had an enormous pile of paperwork in front of her, invoices and business accounts to be paid. The sink in the aesthetician's room needed attention, and she called a plumber and scheduled an appointment. She finished Sadie Hollowell by trimming her straight hair and blowing it dry, giving it some texture and Texas sass.

After Sadie, her next appointment wanted a long, layered cut, preferred by most Texas women and Lily herself. The long, layered cut could be pulled back into a ponytail, loosely curled, or teased and stacked to Jesus. It was three o'clock when she finished, and she decided to grab all her paperwork and head home. It wasn't often that she could pick Pippen up after school, and she told her assistant manager she was leaving before she walked out the back door. It was almost sixty degrees and she shoved all her work into the backseat of her Jeep. As she pulled out of the parking lot, she called her mother.

"I'm off early enough to pick Pippen up from school," she said as she headed toward the highway.

"Okay. He'll like that." There was a pause and then her mother said, "He's been spending a lot of time playing basketball with that Deputy Matthews."

"Yeah, I know."

"Well, I don't know if it's such a good idea," Louella said.

"He's a nice man." With her eyes on the road, she fished around in her console for her sunglasses.

"We don't know that. We don't know him at all."

If her mother only knew how well Lily did know the deputy. Knew he was good with his hands and liked to be ridden like Buster, the coin-operated horse outside Petterson's Drug. "He plays ball with Pippen in full view of everyone in the neighborhood, Ma. Pippen likes him, and let's face it, Pip spends way too much time with women. Spending time with a man is good for him."

"Huh." There was another pause on the line and Lily expected a rambling story about so and so's son who'd been molested by the Tastee Freeze man and had grown up to be a serial killer of biblical proportions. "Okay," she said.

"Okay?" No story? No rambling tale of disaster?

"Okay. If he's good to my grandson, then that's good enough for me."

Lily shoved her glasses on her face. Well, the world must have just officially ended. It wasn't exactly a ringing endorsement from her mother, but at least she wasn't accusing him of crimes against nature.

"Yesterday, my mom told me it's okay if you play with Pippen."

Tucker's brows pulled together and he handed Lily a plate he'd just rinsed. "You told her about us?"

Lily took the plate and set it in the dishwasher. "Not exactly, but she knows that sometimes you play ball with Pip when he gets home from school."

He reached for a kitchen towel and dried his hands. "What does 'not exactly' mean?"

Lily shut the door to the dishwasher. "It means I'll tell her. Just not now."

"Why?"

"Because she'll want to know everything about you," which was just *one* reason, but not the biggest one. "And you keep things to yourself. It makes me wonder what you're not telling me." There were things she had to figure out, like her feelings for him, and if she could trust the feelings he said he had for her. And if it all went south, could she handle it? "What deep dark secrets are you keeping from me? Did something happen in the military?"

He shook his head. "Being in the military saved my life."

"Tucker!" She pushed his shoulder but he didn't budge. "You were shot five times."

"I was shot at more than that." He smiled like it was no big deal. "That was just the last time. If not for the Army, I'd be dead or doing time in prison."

Prison? She took the towel from him and slowly dried her own hands. She looked closer at his smile, and a felt a somber blanketing of her heart. "Why do you say that?"

He turned away and reached into the refrigerator. "Before I enlisted, I was going nowhere and had nothing. I'd already done several years locked up in juvenile detention and was living in a youth home." He pulled out a half gallon of milk and moved toward the back door. "They kick you out at eighteen, but I was ready to leave anyway."

He knelt and poured milk into the empty cat dish. He wouldn't look at her so she moved to him and knelt beside him. "Where was your mother?"

"Dead," he said without emotion, but he

wouldn't look at her. "Died of a drug overdose when I was a baby."

"Tucker." She put her hand on his shoulder, but he stood and moved to the refrigerator.

"Your daddy?" She rose and followed him.

"Never knew who he was. She probably didn't know either. I'm sure he was some crackhead like her."

"Who took care of you?"

"My grandmother, but she died when I was five." He put the milk inside and shut the door. "Then various aunts, but mostly the state of Michigan."

She thought of Pippen and her heart caved in her chest. "Tucker." She grabbed hold of his arm and made him look at her. "Every baby should be born into a loving family. I'm sorry you weren't. That's horrible."

"It was fucked up, to be sure." He looked at the floor. "I lived in eleven different foster homes, but they were all the same: people just taking in kids to get money from the state. They were just a stop-over to someplace else."

Honest to God, she didn't know what to say. She'd thought his secrets had something to do with . . . Well she hadn't known, but not this. Though it did explain some of his rough edges and why he might be relentless. "Why didn't you tell me?"

"People look at you differently when they find out no one wanted you as a kid. They look at you like something must be wrong with you. Like it's your fault."

She wanted to cry for this big, strong man who'd once been a lost boy, but felt she should be strong like him. The backs of her eyes stung and she blinked back her tears.

"I especially didn't want you to know."

"Why?"

"When people find out you've spent time in the juvenile jail, they look at you like you might steal the family heirlooms. No matter what else you do in your life."

She cupped his face in her hands and looked into his eyes. "I would never think that. I'm proud of you, Tucker. You should be proud of yourself. Look at you. You've overcome so much. It would have been easy and understandable if you'd gone bad, but you didn't."

"For a while I did. I stole everything I could get my hands on."

"Well, I don't have family heirlooms." She ran her hands across his shoulders, comforting him. "But maybe I should search you the next time you leave my house."

He flushed and cut his gaze to the side. "I would never steal from—"

"I'm going to like searching you too. Maybe I'll search you when you enter, just for good measure. Maybe I should search you right now."

He looked back at her, relief in his eyes. "But this is my house."

She shrugged. "I just don't think I should pass up a good opportunity to search you. Never know what I might find."

"I know what you'll find." He pulled her against his chest. "Start with the right front pocket."

She did and found him hard and ready for sex.

"Are you on birth control?" he asked, his voice going all smoky.

She thought it an odd question at this stage. "I've had an IUD for about seven years now." Ever since a pregnancy scare when Pip had been three.

"Do you trust me?"

"With what?"

"I had to have a complete medical exam before I joined the Potter County Sherriff's office. Top to bottom. I'm clean. Do you trust me?"

He was asking to have sex without a condom. To take their relationship to the next step, and she wanted it so much it scared her. If they took things slow, maybe everything would work out. "Yes. Do you trust me?"

"Yes." He took her hand and led her to his bedroom. He kissed and touched and undressed her. He made love to her whole body, and when he entered her, hot and throbbing skin to skin, she moaned and arched her back. He cupped her face in his hands and looked into her eyes as he plunged in and out of her body. "Lily," he whispered. "I love you."

Complete euphoria rushed through her blood and heated her whole body. He said he loved her and she felt it in every part of her body. The euphoric feeling stayed with her long after she left his house that morning. Long after she went to work and returned home that night. She woke with it, but when she returned home after dropping Pippen off at school, her happy euphoric bubble got shot all to hell.

She pulled her Jeep into the garage just as Tucker was getting home from work. It was garbage day and she walked out to the curb to pull her empty can inside.

Tucker being Tucker, he met her in the driveway and pulled it inside for her. She quickly shut the garage door and he followed her into the kitchen.

A smile played at the corner of her mouth. "Want coffee?"

"What are you doing tomorrow night? I have it off. I thought we could go to Ruby's. Some of the guys said Ruby's serves a good steak but to avoid the seafood."

Ruby's? Her smile fell. A restaurant in the middle of downtown Lovett—where the news that she was dating young Deputy Matthews would reach everyone by dessert. That wasn't taking things slow. What she felt was so new, she wasn't ready for that. "I have Pip."

"Can't he stay with your mom or sister for a few hours."

"That's awfully short notice, Tucker."

He folded his arms over his beige work shirt. "What about Sunday?"

"I don't know." He was pushing her. She understood him, but there was so much to think about.
Everything was happening too fast. He said he
loved her, but could she let herself love him as
much as he deserved? That crazy kind of love that
consumed and burned? She was too old and had
too much to lose to love like that again. "I have a
lot of work."

"Monday."

"How about someplace in Amarillo." That was
a nice compromise. "The restaurants are better in
Amarillo."

"No. How about Ruby's?"

"Why?"

"Because I'm tired of hiding. I want a whole life
with you. You and Pip."

"You're young. How do you even know what
you want? When I was thirty, I thought I wanted
something different than I want now."

"Quit treating me like a kid. I might be eight
years younger than you, but I've lived a lot of different lives—enough of them to know what I want
and what I don't want. I love you, Lily. I told you
that and I meant it. I want to be with you. I'm into
you one hundred percent, but if you aren't, you
need to tell me. I'm no one's secret. Either you're in
one hundred percent with me, or I'm out."

Out? A panicky little bubble lifted her stomach.
"It's been just a little over a month!"

"It's been almost two months since I fell in love

with you that first morning I saw you with curlers in your hair and bunny slippers on your feet. Knowing you love someone doesn't take time. It doesn't take ten years or ten months to figure it out. It takes looking across a driveway and feeling like you've been hit in the chest—like you can't breathe."

Out? Her head spun and the panicky bubble grew in her abdomen. Love made her impulsive and emotional and irrational. It made her panicky and crazy, and she'd worked so hard to be rational and sane. She didn't want to be crazy, but she didn't want to let him go. She was so conflicted she couldn't think, and she hated that feeling. It brought back all sorts of other feelings and memories . . . of pain and betrayal and hair-pulling fights. "I need a little more time."

He shook his head. "I'm not waiting around for the crumbs from your table. I spent my whole childhood doing that. The outsider looking in. Waiting. Wanting what would never be mine. I can't do it anymore, Lily." He folded his arms over his chest. "Are you in or out? It's that simple."

There was so much to think about. Her. Pip. What if he left her after a few months or years? Would she survive this time? Would she lose her mind again? "Why are you so stubborn about this?"

"I'm not stubborn, Lily. I just know what I want. If you don't want the same thing, if you don't want to be with me, you need to tell me now. Before I get in any deeper and start thinking I can have things that I can't."

"It's not that easy, Tucker. You can't expect me to make a decision right this very second."

"You just did."

Chapter Eight

"Are you still playing basketball with Deputy Matthews?" It had been three days since she'd seen Tucker. He hadn't even tried to contact her. She'd dialed him up twice, but he hadn't picked up or returned her call.

Pippen nodded as he snapped Legos together. "I almost beat him at H-O-R-S-E today."

She felt empty and envious—envious of her own son because he got to see Tucker. It was Saturday night. She should be relaxed and happy. Her salon was doing great, her son was fine, and she had the next two days off. Instead of relaxed, she felt edgy and ready to jumpy out of her own skin. "Do you like him?"

"Yeah, and Pinky too."

He wanted a life with her. He wanted her to jump in with both feet or not at all. "Did you go into his house?"

Pippen shook his head. "Pinky got out and ran into our backyard like Griffin used to. I took her back 'cause she's little and has no survival skills."

She thought of Tucker pouring milk into a little cat bowl. Most of the men she knew said they hated cats. Only a supremely confident man would own one named Pinky. "What would you think if we had Tucker come over for dinner sometimes?" His confidence was one of the things she liked about him.

"Can we have pizza?"

"Sure."

"And maybe he could come with us when go bowling," her son suggested and snapped some sort of wings on the Legos. "He'll probably win, though."

Probably. Both she and Pip sucked. In the past, Pippen had always nagged her to call Ronnie to go bowling with them. "What about your dad?"

Pippen shrugged. "He has a new girlfriend. So, I probably won't see him for a while."

A sad smile twisted her lips as her heart hurt for her son. Ten years old and he had Ronnie Darlington all figured out. "What if I went out on a date with Tucker? If he took me out to dinner or something. Just him and me. Would that bother you?" she asked, even though she wasn't positive that Tucker would ever speak to her again. She remembered the look in his eyes the last time she'd seen him. Sad. Final.

He snapped a few more Legos together. "No. Are you going to kiss him?"

She'd like to kiss him. "Probably."

He made a face. "Grown-ups do gross stuff. I don't want to go to high school."

High school? "Why?"

"That's when people have to start kissin'. T.J. Briscoe told me his older brother rolls around kissin' his girlfriend until his parents come home from work."

There would come a day when Pip's thinking would radically change. Thank God she had a few more years before that happened. "Well, you don't have to kiss anyone if you don't want to." Lily bit the corner of her lip to keep from smiling. "Except me."

She rose from the couch and moved into the kitchen. She looked through the window at Tucker's house. The lights were out and he was no doubt working. Hiding in one of his favorite spots, waiting for unsuspecting speeders.

For the past few days he'd been avoiding her. He'd been honest about his life. He'd told her everything because he loved her. She hadn't been quite so honest. She hadn't told him everything because . . . she hadn't wanted him to leave her.

She closed her eyes and pressed her fingers into her brows. She hadn't been open and honest because she hadn't wanted him to leave, but he'd left anyway. She hadn't wanted to date him because of his age. She'd been afraid of what people would say. He hadn't cared. He'd been bold and fearless. She used to be bold and fearless. She used to love with her whole heart, like Tucker.

She lowered her hands and looked at his empty house. Her heart got all pinchy and achy. She did love him. She'd fought it, but she loved him with her whole pinchy, achy heart. Loved him so much it crawled across her skin and brought tears to her eyes. Her head got all light and anxious. She couldn't control her feelings. They were too big—too much—but unlike her thirty-year-old self she wasn't losing it. She couldn't control loving Tucker, but she wasn't out of control. She knew exactly what she was doing when she grabbed her coat and purse.

"Pippy, I need to go somewhere."

"Where?"

She wasn't quite sure, but she had a good idea. "Just out for some air."

She called her mother and made up a lie about having forgotten something at her salon. When Louella walked in the door, Lily shoved her arms in her coat and walked out.

She jumped in her Jeep and headed to Highway 152. She wasn't crazy, she was going after what she wanted. What she'd been afraid to want for a long time.

Tucker had mentioned he liked to hang out behind the Welcome to Lovett sign, waiting for speeders. She drove past—and sure enough, a Potter County cruiser sat several feet behind the sign. She flipped a U, floored the gas pedal, and hit eighty as she passed. She was still in perfect control. Not feeling crazy at all. She glanced into the rearview mirror and saw nothing but the inky black night.

"Okay," she said, still in control and not the least crazy. She flipped another U and this time got up to ninety-six. She glanced into the rearview and smiled as the red, white, and blue lights lit up the Texas night. She pulled over and waited. She crossed her arms and stared straight ahead, waiting. Her heart thumping and her chest aching. If she wasn't careful, she might hyperventilate. A Maglite tapped her window and she hit the switch.

"Lily."

"Neal?" She stuck her head out the window and looked down the highway. "What are you doing here?"

"My job. What are you doing out here driving like your tail's on fire?"

"I'm looking for someone." If Tucker wasn't on highway 152, where was he?

"I need your driver's license, registration, and proof of insurance."

Lily gasped. "You're not giving me a ticket are you?"

"Yes, ma'am. You were doing ninety-eight."

Ninety-six, but who was counting. "I don't have time Neal," she said as she dug around in her jockey box. "Can you just mail it to me?" She found her registration and handed it over with her license and insurance card.

"No. I'll be right back."

"But . . ." She didn't have time to sit around. She glanced in her rearview mirror and watched him move to his car. She called Tucker on her UConnect but hung up when his voicemail answered. Where could he be? She didn't want to kick in the back door of a jewelry store on the off chance he'd respond. She wasn't that crazy. Yet.

Within a few minutes Neal returned. "Sign here," he said and shined his light on a ticket clipped to a board.

"I still can't believe you're giving me a ticket."

"I can't believe you sped by me twice. What the hell is wrong with you, girl?"

"I thought you were someone else." She signed the ticket and handed him back the pen.

"Who?"

He was going to find out anyway. "Deputy Matthews."

Neal rocked back on his heels and laughed. "Tucker?"

Lily didn't have a clue what was so funny. "We're dating." She raised a hand and dropped it back on the steering wheel. "Sort of."

"Poor bastard. Are you going to drive your Jeep into his house?"

"That's not funny, and I can't believe you're bringing that up." Actually she could. Neal had been one of the first responders that horrible night of infamy. And this was Lovett. No one could just let anything go.

"Tucker's at the Road Kill with some of the

guys. It's Marty's birthday and someone got him a stripper. If you go there, don't get all crazy."

She frowned. "I don't get crazy anymore."

"Then why are you out here speeding up and down the highway?"

It might not look like it, but she was in control. "I'm not crazy."

He tore off the ticket and handed it to her.

"I thought you were my friend, Neal."

"I am. That's why I wrote you a ticket for one-twenty instead of one-eighty-five like you deserve."

Lily gasped once more. "One hundred and twenty dollars?" She stuffed the ticket in her coat pocket.

"Good to see you, Lily."

"Wish I could say the same." What a jerk, but she had been raised right so she grudgingly added, "Tell Suzanne and the kids I said hey."

"Will do and slow down." Neal stepped back and Lily eased the Jeep back onto the highway. The Road Kill was about twenty minutes away and she was careful to drive the speed limit. She even drove a few miles under, but her mind raced—spinning and tumbling, and her heart felt like it was cracking. She was in love with Tucker. She took a deep breath and let it out, checking herself. She felt okay. Still not feeling crazy. Okay, maybe a tiny bit, but not enough to drive her car through someone's house *crazy*. That *was* crazy. Destructive crazy, and she wasn't that Lily anymore.

The gravel parking lot of the Road Kill was filled,

but she was able to find a spot near the front door. She'd just go in, tell Tucker she loved him, and everything would work out. It had to . . . because she didn't want to think about a life without him in it.

Honky-tonk music filtered through the cracks in the building and grew louder when she went inside. Everyone knew that the back rooms could be rented out, and she headed through the bar. A few people called out her name and she held up a hand and waved as she wove her way through the crowd. When she got to one of the back rooms, she slipped through the door as a stripper in a cop outfit cuffed Marty Dingus to a chair. From an MP3 player, Kid Rock sang about picking up a "mean little missy" in Baton Rouge. Lily's gaze scanned the room until it landed on Tucker, who stood to one side. He wore a black T-shirt and jeans and his head was cocked to one side as if he was studying the stripper's butt.

Her heart pounding in her chest, Lily walked past the shocked gazes of some of the other deputies. Tucker was transfixed on the stripper and raised a bottle of Lone Star.

"Seriously, Tucker?" She stopped next to him. "Cadillac Pussy?" She pointed to the MP3 and the music blaring from the small speakers. "You know how I feel about crude language."

His head whipped toward her and he lowered the beer. "What are you doing here, Lily?" He looked shocked but not in the least ashamed.

"Apparently, I'm hunting you down." She

turned her finger to the half-naked girl bumping and grinding. "And you're watching Marty get a lap dance."

Tucker shook his head. "She hasn't got to the lap dance part yet. That never happens until she strips to her G-string." He said it like it didn't even occur to him to be embarrassed that he knew that kind of information.

While she'd been out getting a ticket and acting a little impulsive, he'd been having a beer and watching a half-naked girl. Now . . . Now she was starting to feel a little crazy around the edges. "If you can drag yourself away from the sight of that stripper's butt, I'd like to have a few words with you. Outside?"

"Sure." He started through the small crowd of men and she slipped her hand into his. He looked back into her eyes and gave her hand a little squeeze that she felt in her heart. They moved down a short hall out the back door. A wooden deck had been built on the back of the bar, but this time of year it was empty.

Lily stopped next to a table turned on its side. She took a deep breath, past the big lump in her throat. Overhead light shined down on them, but his face gave nothing away.

She had to jump in now. All the way. "I love you, Tucker. I love you and I want to be with you." She swallowed hard and lowered her gaze to the dip in his throat. "You were honest with me and told me about your past and who you are, but I haven't told you about me." She shook her head and got the rest out in a rush of words. "Everyone thinks I'm crazy. I admit I've done a few crazy things in my past. Things that it took me a long time to live down, and I'm afraid once you know, you'll leave."

"I'm not going anywhere." He put a finger beneath her chin and raised her gaze to his. "I know who you are, Lily. I know all about you. I know you were one tick away from being 5150'd for driving your car into your ex's house. I know that you were knocked flat by him, but you pulled yourself up and made a success of yourself. You should be proud of yourself for that.

"I know that you love your son and the first time I saw you with Pippen, I saw *how much* you love him. You said you'd kill for him, and I knew that I wanted to love and be loved like that."

She blinked. "You know people call me crazy? Why didn't you say something?"

"Because it's not true. You're passionate and you love with your heart and soul, and I want that."

"What if it is true? I worked really hard not to be crazy, but I admit I'm feeling a little crazy right now. I got a speeding ticket tonight because I thought you were hiding behind the Welcome to Lovett sign."

"Whoa." He whipped he head back and forth. "What—"

"You've been ignoring me and I wanted to get your attention. So I raced up and down the highway." She pulled the ticket out of her pocket. "But it was Neal."

He tipped his head back and laughed. Long and loud, and then he gathered her against his chest. "You acted that crazy to get my attention?"

"Not *that* crazy. Just a *little* crazy."

"That's funny."

"Not really. Now Neal thinks I'm crazy again and he'll probably tell the guys you work with."

"I'm a big boy. I can handle anything as long as I have you."

"You do, Tucker, but it's not just me."

"I know, and I know I'm not Pippen's daddy. I can never be his daddy. Hell, I don't know how to be a dad, but I know that I'll never treat him mean or ignore him or leave him out. I'll never let him think he doesn't matter or disappoint him." If it was possible, her heart swelled more and she squeezed her arms around him. He pulled back and looked into her eyes. "I'd do anything for you, Lily, but I can't change my age."

"I know." She rose onto her toes and kissed the side of his neck. "I don't care."

He shivered. "You cared a lot a few days ago."

"A few days ago I was scared. I was afraid of what people would say. I was afraid of a lot of things, but you weren't. You were bold and unafraid."

"Are you kidding me? I've been scared shitless this whole time that you would never love me back."

He'd never acted scared—shitless or any other kind. "Two days ago you told me I had to get in or out." She lightly bit his ear. "I want in, Tucker. All of you. All the way." She dropped back on her heels and looked up into his face that was no longer free of expression. His smile was as big as hers.

"I want you all the way, Lily Darlington."

"People will say you're crazy."

"I don't care what people say." He pressed a quick kiss to her lips. "Just as long as I get to go crazy on you."

Home Sweet Home

CANDIS TERRY

This is dedicated to the men, women, and families of the Idaho Army National Guard at Gowen Field and the Mountain Home Air Force Base. Please accept my heartfelt thanks for your service and dedication. You keep us safe. You make us proud. God bless.

Chapter One

When you grew up in a town the size of a flea circus anonymity was impossible.

There hadn't been a chance in hell he could have slipped back in unnoticed. As an Army Ranger, Lieutenant Aiden Marshall had been to some of the most hellish corners on earth and no one had been the wiser. Except for maybe the enemy. Yet the moment he'd cranked the key in the ignition of his old pickup, it seemed the entire population of Sweet, Texas, had heard the engine catch.

Today he'd traded his fatigues for an old T-shirt and Levi's, but the dog tags pressed against his heart verified he'd be a soldier until the day they put him in the earth.

He was damned lucky he wasn't already there.

As he drove the winding road through pastures where longhorns grazed, he did not take for granted the faded yellow ribbons hugging the trunks of the large oaks that bordered the road. Those ribbons had been placed there for him and two of his best buddies. They'd all enlisted the

same day. Survived boot camp and Ranger training together. Hit the sands of Afghanistan as one.
Fought side-by-side.

He'd been the only one to make it home.

In the trenches they'd added one more friend
to their unit. One more who'd proven faithful and
trustworthy. One who'd offered comfort on dark
nights and lonely days.

One more Aiden had to leave behind.

The pressure in his chest tightened as he lifted
his hand in a wave to the group of seniors in jogging shoes waiting to cross the road. On the way
to his destination, he could not ignore the joy on
the faces of those who waved or shouted "welcome back" as he passed by. Those in his community knew none of the anguish that kept him
awake night after night. They were just happy he
had made it home.

His hometown had been hit hard by the loss
of two upstanding soldiers, men who'd been his
brothers-in-arms. Men he'd been honored to serve
with. As a survivor, he felt none of the joy and
all of the guilt. The hardest thing he'd had to face
upon his return was the visits he'd paid to those
heroes' families. Looking them in the eye and ex-
pressing his sorrow for their loss when so much
of it had been caused by his own miscalculations.
Yet they'd taken him into their arms, offering *him*
consolation he did not deserve. The thought still
took his breath away.

On Main Street, beneath the old water tower

where local businesses displayed patriotic signs and the flagpole in Town Square flew a pristine Stars and Stripes, Aiden eased his truck into the gravel lot beside Bud's Nothing Finer Diner. Over the years the good people of Sweet had tried their best to make the town appeal to tourists. The apple orchards—like the one his family owned— had blossomed into bed-and-breakfasts, art galleries, antique shops, and wine rooms. Judging by the near-empty streets, the place still had a long way to go.

In a space near the door he cut the truck's engine, leaned back in the seat, and inhaled the aroma of chicken-fried steak that floated in through the window on the warm summer breeze. Bud's Diner was little more than a yellow concrete box, but since the day Aiden had been old enough to sit at the counter, he'd enjoyed extra thick milkshakes and homemade eats that made his mouth water. Even when he'd been halfway across the world Bud's was the first place the townsfolk gathered to mourn, celebrate, or discuss local politics.

He snatched the keys from the ignition and opened the door. Through six tours and countless missions in the Middle East, his mouth had watered for a slice of home. He was about to get his wish.

The bell above the door announced his arrival to the farmers and community members who huddled inside around tables nicked and scarred by years of diners with eager appetites. Marv

Woodrow, a World War II vet, stood on feeble legs and gave him a salute. Bill McBride, a Vietnam vet, stood and gave him a one-armed hug and a fist bump. The rest also welcomed him home as he made his way to the counter. He graciously accepted their warm reception, though the soldier and friend inside of him rebelled.

Why was he still here when his friends were not?

He glanced around the diner at the wood-paneled walls and the Don't-Mess-with-Texas decor. As wonderful as the greetings had been, there was one welcome he'd looked forward to the most. Even though he wouldn't enjoy giving her the news he had to share.

Back in the kitchen a good-natured argument surfaced.

"Pick up your own danged pickles, Bud. I've got my hands full of Arlene's sweet potato fries, a buffalo burger, and Walter's patty melt."

"But the pickles are burnin' in the fryer, girl."

A feminine sigh of exasperation lifted above the lunchtime chatter and forks clanging on plates. At the sound, the tightness in Aiden's chest eased, and a rare smile pushed at the corners of his mouth. Before he could breathe, the owner of that sassy tone marched out of the kitchen.

"Here's your melt, Walter." She set an overflowing plate down in front of the old guy at the end of the counter. "Don't be surprised if that hunk of meat finds its way back to the cow before Bud gets movin' back there."

Aiden picked up the plastic-coated menu he could recite blindfolded and watched her work. Quick hands. Sweet smile. Thick honey-colored hair pulled up into a ponytail that swung across her back. A pair of jeans hugged her slender thighs. A yellow *Bud's Diner* T-shirt molded to her full breasts and small waist.

Good thing he was sitting down because his lower half was definitely standing at attention.

She swiped a towel over a newly vacated seat near the end of the counter. Catching a glimpse of a new customer from the corner of her eye, she drawled, "I'll be right with ya, darlin'."

Two seconds later she set down the towel, pulled her order pad from the pocket of her apron, and made her way toward his end of the counter.

"What can I . . ." Pencil poised, her blue eyes lifted and that beautiful, plump mouth slid into a warm smile. "You're back," she said in a slow whisper.

A quick heartbeat passed while her gaze ate him up.

Then, before he could blink, she launched herself into his arms.

From the moment she'd figured out the difference between boys and girls, Paige Walker had known what she wanted in life.

And what she wanted was Aiden Marshall.

He'd been a rough-and-tumble boy who'd escaped her amorous intentions in elementary school when she'd tried to talk him into kissing her behind the cafeteria. She'd finally caught him in high school, where *he* became the teacher and *she* the willing student in their kissing lessons. They'd been together almost every day until the darkest day in America crashed down in the nightmare no one had ever expected. The following week Aiden, Billy Marks, and Bobby Hansen enlisted in the Army.

When Aiden had left for boot camp he made her no promises. Once he'd been approved for Ranger training his infrequent letters dwindled. Over the past couple of years he'd barely sent more than a quick note or two. Though he'd told her not to, she'd promised him that she would wait.

And she had.

As his strong arms curled around her and tucked her in close, she knew all those lonely nights she'd waited with worry and fear burrowed into her heart had been worth every second.

Aiden was home.

Paige pressed her cheek against his faded T-shirt and listened to the steady heartbeat in his chest. She inhaled the fresh scent of his soap and his underlying masculine heat. With a sigh she leaned her head back and looked up at him while her fingers molded around his hard, defined biceps.

A man like Aiden was impossible to ignore, unless you had severely poor eyesight, or you just didn't care for a guy with a movie star face and a body honed for elite military missions. On top of all that he had the most amazing mouth—lips that knew how to give a girl a kiss she'd remember until one day she could kiss him again. Today he'd discarded his army fatigues and settled into a worn pair of Levi's that accented his long, muscular legs and cupped his generous package like a lover's hand. He looked so good she wanted to lay him down on the counter and feast on him like an all-you-can-eat Sunday buffet.

On a good day Aiden's short dark hair and the spark in his brown eyes could stun the breath in her lungs. She hadn't seen him in over two years—when last he'd come home to his dying father's bedside. Since then hell had broken loose. Today while he stood close enough for her to touch and hold, Paige knew in her heart Aiden Marshall was a changed man.

While she told herself it only mattered that he was safe and everything would be just fine, her fears resurfaced.

Aiden may be home.

But the smile in his eyes had vanished.

Chapter Two

After several hours and several slices of apple crumb pie à la mode, Aiden and his full stomach leaned back in the chair. He listened while Hazel and Ray Calhoun excitedly described how the senior center had contacted a new TV makeover show to try to put a better face on their small town and increase the tourism. Aiden couldn't imagine why Hollywood would ever come this far south. It only mattered that the folks in this town and other small towns across America cared enough to try to make things better. These hard-working, generous-hearted people were the reason he, Billy, and Bobby had enlisted.

A dainty hand with clean, short nails settled over his shoulder. He looked up into the blue eyes he'd dreamed of on many a lonely night. A sudden jolt struck him in the center of his chest. Paige had always had a way of doing that to him. Even now when he knew the heart had been ripped out of him and he had nothing left to give.

"If y'all are done monopolizing the lieutenant's time, I'd like to borrow him for a bit," Paige said in a teasing drawl. "But only if that's all right."

"Oh pooh." Gertie West wrinkled up her nose. "We were just getting to the good stuff."

Aiden glanced out the front window where the sun hung low in the sky. As much as he'd like to, he couldn't put off the conversation he and Paige needed to have any longer. It would be unfair to her and selfish of him.

He stood and pushed the chair back. "I really do need to get going."

"You come back tomorrow, young man," Ray Calhoun said. "We want to hear all about your adventures."

Adventures.

Not exactly what he'd call them.

Wasn't likely he'd discuss them either.

He gave the afternoon diners at the table a nod and turned toward Paige.

"Come with me." She smiled wide enough to flash those pretty white teeth. "I have something I want to show you."

"Your car or mine?"

She slipped her hand into his and tugged him toward the door. "How about for old time's sake we take your truck?"

A sensual flood of memories he thought he'd buried long ago popped up fresh like a spring daisy. "Sun's still shining." He smiled and gave her hand a squeeze. "I think the population of Sweet might take offense to you whipping off that T-shirt."

"Wouldn't be the first time." She grinned. "Now come on. We're wasting daylight."

As she tugged him through the gravel parking lot, he watched the way her hips swayed. Nothing outrageously obvious. Just a smooth motion that belied the passion lit deep in her core. He'd almost forgotten all the little idiosyncrasies she possessed. Like the way she lifted her arms toward the moon when she was on top of him, giving him the best sex of his life. Or the way she'd snuggle right against his side and drape her smooth leg over his hips. Or even the way she'd reach for him in her sleep, then sigh when she found him.

He'd carried those memories with him through boot camp. Through extensive Ranger training. Through numerous deployments to Iraq and Afghanistan. Then one day everything around him exploded. After that, he hadn't allowed himself to think of the things that had made him happy. He didn't deserve to be happy. Not when those closest to him—those he was supposed to protect—were no longer able to have happy thoughts.

Without hesitation, Paige climbed up into his truck and slid right to the middle where she'd always sat. When he moved onto the seat beside her, she grinned like someone had just handed her a present. His hand paused on the key in the ignition.

How the hell could he even consider breaking her heart?

He didn't want to.

But it had to be done.

Chapter Three

Paige tried to remain positive, though Aiden's smile had once again disappeared. She knew the hell he'd been through from the stories his brother Ben had relayed. She knew she couldn't expect him to just come home and they'd pick up where they'd left off. From the moment she'd heard the news that his duties had been served and he intended to leave the military, she'd made a vow that no matter what, she'd keep a smile on her face. For both of them. She'd see him through whatever demons he had to face. Because there had never been a doubt that she loved him with her whole heart. And nothing could ever take that away.

She leaned forward and turned up the radio while Keith Urban sang about days going by. "Hang a right on Dandelion Street."

Aiden turned his head and looked at her with those deep brown eyes that made her think of the many wonderful nights she'd spent with him looking down at her while their bodies spoke the oldest language in the universe. "You moved?"

She nodded as the truck rambled down her street. "A little over a year ago."

"You still have Cricket?" he asked of the border collie mix she'd rescued from the shelter.

"Of course. She's still got a good amount of crazy going on, but age seems to have settled her down a bit."

"Happens to the best of us, I guess."

"Pull in there." She pointed toward the long gravel driveway that invited visitors up to the gingerbread Victorian that sat behind a white picket fence.

Aiden ducked his head to get a better look through the windshield. "Isn't this your Aunt Bertie's place?"

"Was." Paige reached down and grabbed her purse from the floorboard. "Aunt Bertie developed dementia and we had to put her in assisted care. She needed the money so I bought the place. Come on. I'll show you around."

"You bought this?" He got out of the truck and looked up at the two-story house. "On a waitress's salary?"

"Shocking isn't it?" While he stood there gawking, she walked around the front of the truck, took his hand, and led him toward the front door. "Actually, I bought it on the salary I make at Bud's, plus the money I make doing taxes and accounting for a few local businesses. I make money from the apple orchard too."

"Taxes?"

"Oooh." She laughed at the sudden wrinkle between his eyes. "You look so surprised. I like that."

"I do remember you skipped out on geometry class more than once and that you never liked math."

"That was before I realized the benefits." She turned the key in the lock and pushed the door open. "I completed my bachelor's via the Internet," she explained. "I'm now the proud owner of a business administration degree. Got a gold tassel and everything."

He stepped inside the foyer, gave a slow whistle, and rocked back on the heels of his worn cowboy boots. "You're a very impressive woman, Paige Walker."

"I know." The praise made her smile. "But you'd better be careful because I have a whole bunch of *impressive* up my sleeve just waiting to be unleashed."

He didn't need to ask what she meant. He'd seen her *impressive* side before. She only hoped he'd want to see it again.

A glimmer lit up his eyes and hope warmed in her heart. She reached out, took his hand, and gave him the nickel tour of Honey Hill—named after the honeycrisp apples that grew in the orchard back between the barn and the creek. The place was way more than she needed right now. But she had big plans. Always the optimist, she'd purchased the oversized home. With *him* in mind.

Later, on the back veranda, Aiden lifted the chilled bottle of Sam Adams to his lips and drank. The beer tasted crisp and smooth. The phenomenal view of Paige's backyard offered a lush landscape accented by rows and rows of apple trees laden with ripening fruit. Curled up at his feet lay Cricket, Paige's brown-and-black-spotted border collie. While Paige had gone inside to throw together a meal for them to share, he and Cricket played fetch with a slobbered-up tennis ball. A heaving sigh lifted the dog's broad chest. Apparently he'd worn her out, as now her breathing was deep and even. Not a single brown eyebrow or white paw twitched or moved.

On impulse he reached down and combed his fingers through her soft fur. When she looked up at him with those deep brown eyes, a fist grabbed hold of his heart and squeezed. He'd always thought of himself as a man who could handle anything. But lately his losses refused to lessen their grip on his conscience.

"Need a refill?" Paige asked as she came toward the wrought-iron patio set where he sat. Her hands balanced plates of plump, juicy pieces of barbecued chicken and a mountainous glob of potato salad.

He lifted the bottle. "I'm good."

She set the plates down, and the aroma wafted up and tickled his appetite. "I don't suppose there were many beers to be found in the Middle East."

"Not really. Lots of sand to chew on, though."

She flashed a quick smile as she sat down opposite him and handed him a fork and knife. Earlier at Bud's he'd had a large helping of chicken-fried steak and several pieces of pie. Yet as the sweet honey flavor of the barbecue rolled across his tongue, he felt like a starving man.

"Good thing I cooked last night." She sipped from her wine glass. "Or this would be carrot sticks and Goldfish crackers."

"Didn't you used to eat those all the time in high school?"

"Yep. They even make them in rainbow colors now." She grinned. "You can have a different color for every meal."

He laughed. "Only *you* could make a feast out of a baked cracker."

"I can make a meal out of chocolate chip cookies too. Speaking of, did you get the packages I sent?"

"Yes. Thank you. I shared. Your oatmeal raisin cookies and the teriyaki jerky went over the best with the boys." She took a bite of chicken then looked up with a glimmer of mischief in her blue eyes. "Good thing I checked the guidelines before I sent those girly magazines."

"Yeah, totally against the rules." He chuckled. "But definitely would have been appreciated."

She reached across the table and snagged a chicken leg from the enormous portion on his plate.

"Hey. No fair stealing."

A grin flashed just before her teeth sank into the meat and tore off a chunk.

"You think you can just pick up where you left off with swiping my food? You didn't even wait this time till I wasn't looking."

"You never minded sharing and you know it."

She was right. Unlike other girls, Paige had never been shy about taking what she wanted. She'd never been shy about eating in front of him. She'd never been shy about snatching a fry from his plate or even a bite of his cheeseburger. To his delight, on many occasions over the years, she had, in fact, turned eating into an erotic adventure.

Her tongue darted out to lick away a smear of sauce from her top lip, and his body went on full alert. During his deployments he fantasized about Paige. Her passion. The softness of her skin. The firmness of her breasts beneath his hands. The slick heat as he entered her body. During those long, lonely nights she'd become his dream girl. Sitting across from her now, watching her in the flesh, brought those fantasies back with a vengeance. Along with a sizeable erection.

For a moment they ate in silence. Then Paige set her fork down on her plate and folded her hands together. Because he knew her as well as he did, he predicted what she would say before the declarations were even out of her mouth. And like so many conversations they'd had in the past, he wanted to listen to every word. Not just to hear that sweet, sexy drawl, but because whatever she had to say was important.

"Aiden? I know you have a lot going on in your mind. I know you've been through more than most could ever even imagine. I won't tell you I understand. I won't say I know how you feel."

She reached across the table and covered his hand with her own. The contrast was startling. Hers small and soft. His large and calloused. The compassion in the gesture stole his breath. He'd forgotten the power of a tender touch. A gentle moment. A quiet calm that soothed a soul.

"What I will tell you," she continued, "is that I'm here for you. If you need to talk or even if you just need to sit and gaze out into the sky without a word. I'll be right here."

The pressure in his chest squeezed until he thought he might explode. She didn't know what she was saying. He had too much to tell—most of which was ugly and tragic. She was a soft, sweet woman who didn't need to hear all the hideous details of what he'd been through.

When you open yourself up to talk, it will help the nightmares go away.

The advice of his PTSD counselor sprang up inside his head. Before he could stomp it down, Aiden looked across the flicker of the votive candle into the eyes of the woman he'd known since she was a sprite in pigtails. He knew her. Trusted her. Believed she had a spine made of steel. And though he knew he had no business pulling her into his nightmare—knew he should just say what he'd come to say—if he wanted to talk to anyone about what had happened, Paige was the one.

"You sure about that?" he asked.

She gave him a slow nod.

In that moment, something greater than the fight-or-flee instinct took over. He took a long pull from his beer while the candlelight danced in her eyes. It wouldn't change what he'd come to tell her, but maybe the time had come for him to release the claws of anguish that had dug into his soul. And the only person he could imagine sharing that information with was Paige.

Chapter Four

Like the slow release of pressure from a tea kettle, Paige listened to Aiden explain what had happened in Afghanistan. As they strolled along the bank of the creek, he told her of the local people and their small villages, many who only desired to exist and wanted to help the American soldiers. He told her of the Taliban who wanted no part in making peace. He told her nightmarish tales of men, women, and children being executed in the streets for no reason. And then he told her of the ambush. Their intel had been sketchy. The terrain rugged. And on that day he'd watched his two best friends die.

"There's not a waking moment that I don't think about those boys." He paused, ducked his head, and shook it slowly. "Boys. Hell. They were warriors. And I was honored to be their friend."

Paige pressed her hand against her chest to hold back the wail that threatened to push through. But she would not falter. Aiden trusted her to be strong. Perhaps this was the first time he'd chosen to recount his story. She would not and could not let him down.

He stopped beneath one of the more mature trees in the orchard—her favorite place to sit and think. Dream and desire. A place where she kept one of Aunt Bertie's handmade quilts wedged into a fork in the tree and the most recent romance novel she'd chosen to read tucked inside the quilt.

Aiden reached up and inspected a ripening Honeycrisp that dangled from a low branch. "And then . . . there was Rennie."

"Rennie?"

A smile pushed up the corners of his beautiful mouth, and Paige's heart stumbled.

"Renegade." He gave another slow shake of his head. "The fourth member of the three musketeers." When he looked up, his entire expression had changed from a simple smile to a full-on grin. "Intel was waiting for a break, and we had some rare down time. One night after dark, the boys and I headed into the tent for a game of cards. Billy had lost three games straight. In the midst of his complaints I heard a sound outside. When I went to check I found this . . . puppy. This little fluff of dirty golden fur wandering around outside our tent."

"A puppy?"

He nodded. "Wasn't unusual to see dogs or cats hanging around. Looking for food. Shelter. Someone to care. Needless to say, they don't view animals the same way over there as we do here."

His unspoken words sent a chill up her spine. She looked down at Cricket, who'd curled up at the base of the tree for a quick nap. Aiden didn't need to describe the neglect or abuse the animals there must suffer. And she couldn't bear to think of it.

"When I knelt down," Aiden continued, "that dirty little pup whimpered over to me. I picked him up. When he looked at me with those deep brown eyes and licked my chin, I was a goner." He laughed, and the genuine sound gave Paige hope.

"We weren't supposed to keep a pet. For a long time we hid him. Then when he got too big to hide, our commander—who'd known Rennie was there all along—just turned his head. When we had to go out in the field, someone else was willing to take care of Rennie while I was gone. He offered a lot of comfort to those of us who'd been away from home for so long. But when I'd come back, Rennie would be there. He never left my side."

A slow intake of air stuttered in his chest. "Until the day they sent me home and I had to leave him behind."

"Leave him behind?" The idea was unimaginable. "Why?"

"Not allowed."

"That's stupid."

"Pretty much."

The shadows that veiled his eyes told Paige all she needed to know. Leaving that dog behind had stripped him of anything else left in his soul.

She curled her fingers around his arm. "Isn't there something you can do?"

The broad, strong shoulders that bore the weight of so much grief lifted in a shrug. "Someone mentioned an organization that helps bring back soldier's dogs. But there are no guarantees."

"Oh, Aiden." She pulled him into her arms and embraced him. "I'm so sorry."

"I left him with my team." His hands settled lightly on her hips. "But all I can think about is him sitting there wondering why I abandoned him."

Paige's heart broke into a million pieces. Aiden was not the type of man to abandon anything or anyone. Though a poor dog alone in the middle of the desert wouldn't know that.

As water tumbled over the rocks in the creek and moved along the sand, Paige felt Aiden close himself off. Everything inside him seemed to be at war with the peaceful surroundings. As if he didn't deserve to be there. As if only a part of him stood on solid ground.

She pressed her cheek against his chest. Heard the stutter in his heart. She couldn't change what had happened. She could only offer him the chance to forget. If only for a moment.

Lifting her head, she looked up into the handsome face she'd known since before she'd learned to tie her shoes. While the moon glowed above them, a dragonfly skimmed the rippling waters, and the click click of the cicadas surrounded them as they looked into each other's eyes.

Heat and tension pulled them together, and their lips touched on a brief kiss. He pressed his forehead against hers, and Paige curled her fingers around the back of his neck.

"I missed you," she whispered. "So much."

His dark gaze moved slowly over her face. The memories of lying in his arms, kissing him, tasting him, caught like a sigh in her chest. "Touch me, Aiden."

"My hands are dirty, Paige. I don't want—"

She knew that in his mind, he could never clean them enough to wash away what he'd had to do with them in the war. She stepped back. Instead of relief in his eyes, she saw sorrow. Hunger. Whatever battle raged within him, Paige knew she could give him the one thing he'd missed for God knew how long.

Comfort.

She grasped the bottom of her shirt and pulled it over her head. Then she reached between her breasts, unlatched the plain white cotton bra, and tossed it to the ground. She took a step forward until the tips of her breasts met with the smooth, worn cotton of his shirt.

"Touch me, Aiden." She let her fingertips waltz across his strong jawline. "Let me welcome you home like I've always dreamed."

How could he resist?

Good intentions told him to pick up her clothes

and hand them back to her. Good intentions told him to walk away.

She deserved better.

Good intentions did *not* move lower in his body. Everything below his belt was running on heat, and emotion, and need. He'd loved Paige the day he'd tossed his duffel on his back and headed off to basic training. He'd loved her when his boots had hit the sands of Iraq. He'd loved her when he'd read her letters over and over—yet rarely responded.

For her sake.

He was responding now.

To her inner strength. Her optimism. Her unwillingness to give up on him.

For his sake.

Paige. The woman who'd waited for him. Even when there had been a significant chance he would never come home.

For weeks, months—hell, even years—he'd dreamed of holding her close. Touching her. Tasting her. Devouring her.

She deserved better than him.

Instead of walking away as he should, he curved his hands over her smooth shoulders, drew her close, and covered her mouth with his own. The soft touch of her lips brought him back. The womanly scent of her skin urged him to move forward and never look back. His hand slid down the curve of her spine, cupped her bottom, and brought her tight against his erection. She leaned into him, rose to the balls of her feet, and wrapped her arms around his neck with a sigh. His arms surrounded her and they came together—heart to heart. His gaze swept over her plump, moist mouth, and their lips met again. Their tongues touched and danced. And the past simply melted away. He could kiss her all day and it would never be enough.

Her fingers were cool as they slipped beneath his shirt to pull the fabric over his head. And then they stood flesh to flesh. Her body warm, ripe, and full of promise. Memories. Hope.

Desire burned inside of him as she briefly broke their embrace to grab a quilt stuck in the fork of the apple tree and spread it on the ground. And then she was back in his arms, touching him. Caressing him with heated silk that glided along his nerve endings, making his heart race, his desire spin out of control.

She unzipped his jeans and slid them down his legs. She tossed the pants into the increasing pile of clothes and kissed her way back up his thighs. Her long, delicate fingers embraced, stroked, and enticed his already throbbing erection. When she cupped him with gentle hands and took him into her mouth with a low hum of satisfaction, it was everything he could do not to buckle at his knees.

For a moment he stood there with his hands buried in the thick of her honey-gold hair, selfish with the need to feel whole again. Anxious with the desire to be one with her. To be buried deep within her warmth. To be held within her arms. He dropped to his knees, eased her back to the quilt, and followed her down. His hands molded to her full breasts, smoothed down her luscious curves. He bent his head and kissed her mouth, then he moved lower to savor the erect tips of her breasts. She tasted like sunshine, and honey, and all the good things he remembered about being alive.

When his heartbeat kicked into a frantic race, his hands made quick work of removing her jeans and tiny pink panties and adding them to the pile of clothes beneath the apple tree. Her warm, soft lips danced across his chest.

She looked up at him with a smile in her eyes. "I like your tattoo."

He gave a brief glance to the eagle in flight that covered his left bicep then leaned down and licked the small heart tattooed just above her left breast. "I like yours too."

He moved over her, their bodies pressed together, and she opened to let him in. He slid inside her and was overcome by the rush of liquid heat. He lowered his forehead to hers until he could quell the need to pump hard and find a fast release. When his mind finally got the signal, they settled into slow, languid movements that allowed him to soak in every tiny sensation that spiraled through their connected bodies.

"I'm so glad you're home," she sighed against his ear.

For the moment, he was glad too.

Before his demons returned to mess with his thoughts, he gave Paige all his attention. He made slow, sweet love to her, as if he were still the man he used to be. When they came together with a final thrust and moan, Aiden realized that he'd give anything to be the man Paige wanted him— needed him—to be.

As much as he wanted it to be true, he also realized it was impossible to resurrect the dead.

Chapter Five

Content and sated in Aiden's arms, Paige knew the exact moment his past came crashing down. His body suddenly tensed at noises that had surrounded them the entire night. Yet now, he reacted as if they were the enemy. Oh, he wasn't *showing* her any of that, but when you knew the boy before he'd become the man, it wasn't hard to see. Her only alternative became distraction.

She rolled to her side and laid her head on his shoulder. Then she took advantage of his perfect, masculine chest and let her fingers play in the soft, fine hair. "We can do that again anytime you're ready."

To her delight, he chuckled.

"I've been out of commission for so long, recovery could go either way."

"Mmmm." She leaned in and kissed him. "I'm willing to wait."

In that moment, his body tensed in a whole different way. And though she tried to drag her arm across him to hold him in place, she did not succeed. Before she could mutter the words "What are you doing?" he was up and tugging on his clothes.

Damn.

"What's the hurry?" she asked.

His hands stopped on his jeans mid-zip. He watched her through eyes filled with regret.

Damn it.

"I'm sorry, Paige."

"Don't say that." When she realized he wasn't going to come back and lie down beside her, she felt exposed and got up to dress. "There's nothing to be sorry for."

"The hell there isn't." The zipper on his jeans slid to the top, and he shook that old gray T-shirt like a flag of surrender. "I just took advantage of you."

"Are you crazy?" She yanked her T-shirt over her head. "I'm no Strawberry Shortcake, Aiden. I wanted you. You wanted me. That's consensual need. *Not* exploitation."

"I shouldn't have done that."

"You beautiful fool." A humorless laugh pushed past her lips. She looked up at him through the moonlight. "I've waited years for you to do exactly *that*."

He jammed his fingers into his short hair then dropped his hands to his lean hips. "I didn't come see you today for this, Paige."

"I know." She folded her arms across her chest as if they could hold back all the emotions. All the things she wanted to say.

"I came . . . to tell you goodbye," he said. His tone quiet. His words flat.

Her heart slammed against her ribs. "You're leaving again?"

"I don't know." He glanced behind him, then back at her. "I don't know what the hell I'm doing. I'm broken, Paige. And I'm pretty damned sure nothing can fix me."

"That's bull."

He shook his head. "The person you knew went to war and never came back. You deserve better than what I have to give."

"The man I *knew* is standing right here. Feeding me a bunch of crap I don't believe."

"Move on, Paige. Forget about me." He glanced away again, and Paige knew even he was having a hard time believing his own words. Then those dark, haunted eyes came right back to her. "I can't love you."

"Can't? Or don't?" She sucked in a lungful of air to calm the desperation churning like butter in her stomach. "Because there's a difference."

His chin dropped to his chest and he shook his head. "Too much has happened."

"Maybe so. But you're wrong, Aiden. You're still the man you used to be. Only more." Paige kept her voice calm. Yelling wouldn't get through to him. He had to arrive at conclusions on his own. No amount of whining or persuading would do a bit of good. She just had to state the facts and then give him time. She'd already given him plenty. What were a few more days, weeks, months?

"I love you, Aiden." The confession that jumped from her mouth was not a surprise to either of them. "I always have. If I have to give you up because you've fallen in love with someone else, I'll do it. I won't like it, but I'll do it. Because your happiness means everything to me." Her fingers curled into her palms. "But I will *not* give you up and let this sorrow swallow you and make you disappear. I can't do that."

She slowly shook her head and held back the wash of tears that burned in her eyes. "*You* may have given up on you. But I *never* will."

Several heartbeats passed while they stood an arm's length away from each other in a stare-down that Paige swore she would win. At their feet Cricket woke from her nap and gave a little whine as if she sensed the tension in the air. Paige stood in place, resolute that she would not bend in her belief. No matter what he said.

The pressure in her chest squeezed harder as he bent at the knees and gave Cricket a brisk rub on her head. Then he stood, stepped forward, and wrapped Paige in his arms. He held her tight. Kissed her forehead. And completely broke her heart.

"Goodbye, Paige."

Chapter Six

If you wanted to get the word out in Sweet, one method worked faster than picking up the phone. Luckily for Paige, today the Digging Divas Garden Club held their monthly meeting at Bud's Diner. In two shakes of a can of whipped cream, the message would go out faster than a speedboat on smooth water.

Paige grabbed her keys off Aunt Bertie's oak dresser and jogged down the stairs. Just like when she'd gone for her college degree or made the purchase of Honey Hill, she had a plan. So far she'd been batting a thousand. She wouldn't allow this goal to be any different. It simply meant too much.

Ten minutes later her red F–150 slid to a gravel-spewing-stop in the lot beside Bud's. She grabbed her work apron from the seat and jumped down from the truck. The lot was still half-full with late morning coffee-slurpers. In another hour the lunch crowd would converge and there would be standing room only. A perfect audience for when she sounded the alarm.

"I stayed up half the night doing Internet research," Paige said, searching the focused expressions around the crowded tables. Her heart trembled with how much they cared about the situation and how eager they were to help. "Early this morning I made a few calls to the organization and they said they would look into it. Well, they work fast. Before I left for work they called me back with the news that they can make it happen. They don't require a fee, but they do ask for donations to keep them afloat and able to help others in the same situation. I figure we need to come in around four thousand."

"Dollars?" The brim of Ethel Weber's lime green straw hat bobbled above her lavender hair.

"Hard, cold, American cash," Paige answered.

"That's nothing." Ray Calhoun lifted his old farmer's hand in a dismissive wave. "Hell, we raised ten thousand to pay for Missy Everhart's funeral when she took ill so fast."

"Can't put a dollar amount on what this will do for someone who's given so much," said Jan West, owner of Goody Gum Drops, the candy store painted like a peppermint stick in the center of town.

"Can we get it done before the Apple Butter Festival?" Paige asked the crowd gathered inside the diner.

"Three weeks?" Hazel Calhoun scoffed. "Easy Cheesy."

Bill McBride, Vietnam vet and local good guy,

stood, imposing in his leather vest and various military patches. "Consider it done." He turned to the crowd. "Right?"

The unity in the agreement that echoed across the diner sent a ribbon of warmth fluttering through Paige's heart.

Aiden may not ask for much, but the people who loved him the most were about to give him everything.

The axe arced high overhead then slammed into the rotted tree trunk. Aiden pulled his hands back, yanked a bandana from his back pocket, and swept the cloth across his forehead.

Damn the sun was hot today.

He'd promised his brother, Ben, that until he figured out what the hell to do with his life, he'd help out around the farm and orchard. At the rate he was going he didn't imagine he'd figure it out any time soon.

It had been nearly two weeks since he'd walked out of Paige's life. Two weeks since he'd slept little more than a couple of hours without dreaming of her. Two weeks in which his instincts had screamed for him to get his stupid ass back in his truck and go to her. Take her in his arms. And beg her forgiveness. He wrapped his hands around the axe handle and dislodged the wedge from the tree stump. But his instincts had been wrong before. They'd even gotten his two best friends killed. So what the hell did he know?

Not to trust himself. That was what.

"Thought you'd be long gone by now."

Mid-swing, he looked up, surprised to see Paige and her dog coming toward him. Damn. The woman managed to make a pair of jean shorts and a silky little tank top look hotter than some flimsy piece of lingerie. Her hair was pulled up into a just-out-of-bed tangle on top of her head and her smooth skin was kissed with a golden tan. While her white tennis shoes ate up the ground, her tongue darted out to lick the half-eaten cherry Popsicle in her hand. The heat rolling through his body had nothing to do with the sun above his head.

"Yeah. Me too," he said as Cricket plopped her furry dog butt in the shade of a nearby tree.

Bringing with her the scent of ripe peaches, Paige came to a stop in front of him. "So why are you still here?"

How could he explain that while he didn't quite know where he belonged, he also couldn't bear the thought of never seeing her again? That he couldn't bring himself to just pick up and walk away. A lump lodged in his throat as he thought of Rennie. He'd unwillingly walked away from the dog who'd given him companionship and loyalty. Did he really believe he could *willingly* walk away from Paige?

He shrugged and felt the sting of a sunburn on his shoulders. "Promised Ben I'd help him out."

Her red-stained tongue licked up the side of

the Popsicle while she studied him through those sharp blue eyes—which triggered an instant reaction in his jeans. Her head tilted. "Is that so?"

"Yep."

"I'm sure Ben appreciates your help."

"What are you doing here?" he asked, although he didn't mind having her in front of him with next to nothing on, licking that Popsicle like it was . . . tasty.

She smiled and tossed the remainder of the Popsicle to Cricket. Then she turned those blue eyes on him. "I've come to make you a proposition."

A layer of sweat glistened across the tops of Aiden's broad, strong shoulders. Highlighted that soaring eagle tattoo. Beaded down his chest and rippled stomach toward the waistband of his low-slung Levi's. Unlike the thugs one saw walking the streets of the big city, Aiden did not have a mile of underwear showing. Which only made Paige wonder if he had any on at all or if he'd gone commando. A blue bandana stuck out from his back pocket, and his work boots had a coating of sawdust across the toes.

A low hum vibrated low in her pelvis. There was just something about a shirtless, sweaty, hard-working man that made her want to tear off her clothes. When that hard-working man was as gorgeous and amazing as Aiden, it was a wonder she hadn't given in to the desire. It took everything she had to compose herself and stick to what she'd come here for in the first place. Which did not include gawking at him or being tempted to stick dollar bills in his shorts.

"A proposition?" A furrow crinkled between his brown eyes.

"Not *that* kind of proposition." Although it had crossed her mind. "I'm going to respect what you said the other night even though I don't agree. Are you willing to listen to my offer?"

He leaned the axe handle against the tree trunk he'd been chopping and folded his arms across that amazing, muscular, sweaty chest. "Shoot."

She hopped up on the tailgate of his truck. "When I made the decision to buy Honey Hill I knew I couldn't have that much property or responsibility without a good business plan. And . . ." She swung her legs back and forth in time with the thoughts swinging through her brain. "I might have dreamed a little too big."

"Are you afraid of losing the place?"

"Oh. No. Nothing like that." The concern on his face forced her to quit stalling. "Part of my plan is to expand the orchard. Instead of just trying to sell apples, I plan to create apple products—butter, jelly, cider. That kind of thing. I need to do more research. Crunch some more numbers. Come up with a marketing plan. And—"

"And?" Dark eyebrows shot up his forehead. "That's not enough?"

"Oh, you know me. Complete one project, come up with ten more."

"I do remember that about you."

The smile and slow glide of his eyes over her body said that wasn't all he remembered.

"And I plan to turn the house into a bed-and-breakfast."

"Wow. You are ambitious." He laughed. "But what has this got to do with me?"

"Both my sisters have their own thing going on. And I need a partner." She hopped down from the tailgate. "You interested?"

"I'm a soldier, Paige. What do I know about cider and bed-and-breakfasts?"

"You're smart. You know apples. You're handy with tools. And people love you."

He shook his head. "Not true."

"*Never* disregard the way people feel about you, Aiden. Sometimes . . . it's all you have."

His head came up and something sparked in his eyes that gave her the smallest pinch of hope.

"You don't have to give me an answer right now. Just think about it." She gave a whistle to Cricket who reluctantly got up from her cool spot beneath the tree. Paige felt the heat of Aiden's gaze on her backside as she walked toward her truck. Someday he'd trust his instincts. His gut. His heart. And he'd let life happen. Until then she'd wait. Apparently she'd become quite good at that.

"Why are you doing this, Paige?"

She turned at the sound of his deep voice, inhaled one more glimpse of that mouthwatering physique, and noted the look of complete and utter puzzlement on his face.

"We're a good team, Aiden." She lifted her hands in the air then dropped them with a slap against her thighs. "Maybe someday you'll figure that out."

Chapter Seven

A week later, Aiden stepped from the shower, wrapped a towel around his waist, and went in search of something decent to wear that didn't say camo or thread-bare cotton. Five days ago he'd been cornered in the cereal aisle of the Touch and Go Market by Gladys Lewis and Arlene Potter, president and co-president of the Sweet Apple Butter Festival committee. After they charmed him with compliments on his cereal choice— Cap'n Crunch original, not Crunch Berries—and thanked him for his service in the Army, they'd asked him to be a judge in the festival's apple butter competition. Apparently the prior year there had been a controversy due to favoritism.

How could he refuse the two little blue-hairs? Especially when, mid-sentence, Gladys turned around and smeared a glob of crimson lipstick across her mouth so she'd look pretty for a soldier like him. Or so she said. So now, when he'd rather be enjoying the festivities from where he could blend into the background, he'd be thrust in the spotlight. With respect he would listen to all the nice things people had to say, while deep inside he thought of himself as a total screw-up. He'd failed his best friends. He'd abandoned his dog. And he'd disappointed Paige.

Jesus. He was batting a thousand.

He turned his attention back to matters he could control. There were two sides of clothing choices in his closet. Military and ultra-casual. Not much in-between. He grabbed a freshly laundered button-down shirt off a hanger and jammed his legs through a pair of khakis he'd swiped from Ben's closet. A split second later he grabbed his keys, headed toward his truck, and prayed he would not be accused of favoritism if Paige had entered the contest this year.

A wide variety of SUVs, trucks, and economy cars were parked bumper-to-bumper along the curb at the Town Square—better known as the entertainment hub of Sweet. Whether it was a birthday party, a battle of the bands, or the Fourth of July picnic, it happened in the little park smack dab in the center of town. Though the latticework gazebo had seen better days and the trees were tall and ancient, the folks mingling around the grass lot filled the square with spirit and a sense of renewal.

Aiden glanced past the rainbow of canopies where vendors hawked everything from scented candles to homemade cinnamon rolls to handmade animal puppets. Over the brims of sun-

deflecting Stetsons and ball-caps he scanned the
area to find the banner that would lead him toward
the judging area. He finally spotted it toward the
gazebo where someone on the loud speaker called
out the winner of the cake-walk. The huge crowd
gathered in front of the area made him wonder if
he might be late. A quick glance at his watch said
he was right on time. As he started toward the
crowd, the two charmers who'd conned him into
the gig appeared like magician's assistants.

"My, don't you look handsome," Gladys Lewis
said through wrinkly lips smeared with carnation
pink.

"We thought you might have worn your uniform," Arlene Potter commented, giving him a
questionable once-over.

"I apologize, ladies. I'm no longer a member of
the military."

"Good Lord." Gladys gave her cohort a whack
with her lace fan. "You knew that, Arlene."

"I'm sorry."

Not wanting to cause the elderly women to feel
uncomfortable, Aiden flashed them both a smile.

"Too bad, though," Arlene added with a wink.
"Nothing hotter than a man in uniform."

"Good heavens." Gladys rolled her faded blue
eyes. "Come on, young man. Pay no attention to
her. She's just getting old, and her marbles don't
always roll in the same direction."

The women in their floral dresses and straw
hats hooked their arms through his and led him

through the crowd. As they drew closer to the gazebo, the festival attendees turned toward them and began to part like a gaping zipper. The whole scene felt odd and a prickle of alarm crept up the back of his neck. Had it not been for the friendly faces turned his way, he may very well have made a beeline in another direction.

"It's okay, Lieutenant." Gladys gave him a light pat on his arm. He looked down into the reassuring smile on her weathered face. "We're just glad to have you home." She gave a nod toward the gazebo. "Some of us more than others."

When Aiden looked up he saw Paige in a floaty yellow sundress. Her hair had been pulled back in a long braid, tousled by the summer breeze. Her beautiful mouth lifted at the corners. Aiden swore he'd never seen anything prettier in his life. As she held her hand out for him to join her, his heart went warm and fuzzy.

Gladys and Arlene blended back into the crowd, and he took a few steps forward. It was then he realized Paige wasn't reaching out to him. She was letting go of a yellow ribbon that slowly fluttered toward the ground. His gaze followed the ribbon down to the green grass and the large golden dog who sat back on his haunches like the most patient soldier.

Aiden's heart leaped into his throat, and the ever-present ache in his chest disappeared. In a rush of disbelief, he dropped to his knees.

"Rennie!"

The retriever's massive paws dug into the earth, and within a warm flash of sunshine Aiden had his arms around his friend's soft, silky neck. Rennie whined and wiggled and did a doggy happy dance. If dogs could smile, Rennie had a full-on grin. Aiden did, too, as Rennie's long tongue slurped up the side of his face.

"I've missed you, boy."

Aiden thought of all the nights he'd shared his cot with a scared little pup. One who'd grown so big Aiden had considered sleeping on the ground when that cot became too small for the both of them. They'd seen hell together. Shared sorrow. They'd even shared meals. He gave the dog a kiss on the top of his head and laughed at the exultant bark he received in response. With another lick to Aiden's face, Rennie flopped down on his side and rolled over for a shameless belly rub.

Forgiven.

Just like that Rennie forgave him.

Aiden curled his fingers in the dog's thick fur and did his best to hide the tears swimming in his eyes. When he looked up, Paige came toward him with Cricket prancing on a leash by her side.

Paige looked at him with those blue eyes and smiled. "Welcome home, Lieutenant Marshall."

"Welcome home," the rest of his community cheered.

If there had ever been any doubt of where Aiden belonged or who he belonged to or with, it dissipated right then and there.

He stood. "How did you find him?"

"*We* found him," she said. "Eagerly waiting to be brought home to you."

"*We?*"

She gave a nod to those surrounding them. "Sweet. All the people you went off to protect. All the people who've been waiting to welcome you home. They all came together and made this happen . . . because they know how much you love this dog. And because they love you." She tilted her head back and smiled. "Of course, not nearly as much as I do."

A smile burst from his heart as he looked at the faces surrounding him. "I don't know how to thank you. Or how to repay you."

"You owe us nothing in return, Lieutenant Marshall," Bill McBride returned. "You've paid your dues. Just be happy."

Aiden curled his fingers in Rennie's thick fur, wrapped his arm around Paige, and gave the Vietnam vet who'd seen plenty during his own tour-of-duty a nod. "I'll do what I can."

Paige flashed him a smile then turned it toward the crowd. "All right. Y'all have seen enough. Judging starts in thirty minutes."

As the crowd slowly dispersed, Aiden shook his head. "Do they always mind you like that?"

"If they want fresh pickles and crunchy lettuce on their burgers, they do."

He smiled, gazed down into the passion and comfort in her eyes, and brushed a long tendril of

honey-gold hair away from her face. His friends—
better men than he—had not made it back home.
He would not dishonor their memories by taking
life and all it offered for granted. He was grateful
to have an opportunity to love Paige for the rest of
his life. And there was no time like the present to
make that happen. *If* she'd still have him.

"I'm in," he said.

Her soft golden brows pulled together. "In?"

"The partnership. I'm taking you up on your
offer, if it's still on the table."

"Of course it is."

"Good." He tugged her closer. "Then I accept.
On two conditions."

"Which are?"

"I pay my half up front. Equal partners."

"That's one condition." Her hand slid up to his
shoulder. "What's the other?"

"We make it permanent."

She leaned her head back as though he'd offended her. "I would never offer you half the business if I didn't expect it to be long-term."

"Not the business. You and me." He lowered
his mouth to hers—not caring if they had an audience or if the whole world watched—and he
kissed her with everything he felt in his heart.
"We're a good team."

"Yes. We are." Her warm fingers caressed the
side of his face. "You know, you're quite the nego-
tiator. Maybe you should think about running for
mayor in the fall."

"Mayor?"

"Why not?" The music of her laughter danced across his skin. "You've proven to be quite a service-oriented kind of guy. Running the town should be easy after what you've been through."

He nuzzled her sweet-scented neck. "I might be too busy."

"You keep that up and I guarantee you *will* be too busy."

A playful bark interrupted them and they both looked down to where Rennie was busy snuffling Cricket's ear.

"Looks like Rennie's quite at home here." Paige laughed. "He might have even found love."

"He's not the only one." Aiden caught Paige's hand in his and kissed her fingers. *"You're* home to me. And while I may never be the man I was before I left here—"

She pressed a finger to his lips. "That's okay. I'm not the same woman."

No she wasn't. She was more. More than he ever expected. More than he deserved. She was a gift he'd treasure always.

"I love you, Paige. I always have. And I want to be with you for the rest of my life." He gave her hand a squeeze. "Say yes."

"It's always been yes, Aiden." She lifted to her toes, wrapped her arms around his neck, and kissed him. "Always."

Author's Note

The inspiration for *Home Sweet Home* came from an article I read about Nowzad—a charity set up to relieve the suffering of dogs, cats, and even donkeys in Afghanistan. They provide and maintain rescue facilities for the care and treatment of these animals. I read the many rescue/reunion stories they have on their website, and my heart was deeply touched. For more information please check out their website at http://www.nowzad.com and donate if you can.

One Fine Fireman

A Bachelor Firemen Novella

JENNIFER BERNARD

Chapter One

"Here they come! Do we haf enough coffee?" Mrs. Gund called to Maribel from the Lazy Daisy grill, where she was managing twenty breakfast orders with the logistical skill of an air traffic controller.

"I'm on it!" Maribel shot a glance at the gleaming red fire engine that had just pulled up to the curb. She ran to the coffeepot and quickly filled a new filter. She ignored Mrs. Gund's grumbles, which no doubt went along familiar lines. The Bachelor Firemen of San Gabriel often showed up at this time of day, they always wanted lots of coffee, and shouldn't Maribel know all this by now?

"Order is up!"

Maribel left the coffeemaker and hurried to the opening between the grill and the counter.

"Two Lazy Morning Specials for table six." Mrs. Gund, whose tight gray curls were tucked into a hairnet, did a double take. "Maribel, vat is that you are vearing today?"

Maribel looked down at her denim overalls. They were cute, right? In a retro kind of way? "What's wrong with what I'm wearing?"

"We have da most attractive fellows in California about to valk in our door—hero firemen—and you dress like a farmer."

"I'm engaged, Mrs. Gund. It doesn't matter what I wear."

"Do not talk to me about engaged. Vat is this engaged, ven your man never even visits?" Mrs. Gund's stern face grew pink, as it always did when she warmed up to her second favorite topic, after Maribel's occasional lack of focus.

"Duncan visits, Mrs. Gund. You know he does." Maribel took hold of the two plates of Lazy Morning Specials, but her boss seemed reluctant to let them go. "And he wants to talk tonight. About something important. I'm sure it's about setting the date."

Of course, she wasn't entirely sure; she was even less sure about how she felt about that prospect.

"I tell you, he's not the man for you. How long have you vorked here, *elskling*?"

"Please. The eggs are getting cold."

"How long?"

"Six years," Maribel muttered, not liking to admit how long she'd been laboring at what wasn't even close to her dream job.

"Six years I know you. Six years dat man keep you vaiting. Meanwhile, every day these vonder-

ful men come in here and look at you with such
puppy-dog eyes, it makes me want to cry."

"You're such a softy," said Maribel, hiding a
smile. Mrs. Gund, Norwegian to the core, didn't
believe in giving in to her emotions, even though
she had the biggest heart in the world. "I'd better
take these to table six. They keep looking at their
watches."

"Did you hear vat I said about the puppy-dog
eyes?"

"I heard, but really, Mrs. Gund, I've never noticed anything like that. They just come in for
their coffee like all the other customers."

"You don't notice? Of course you don't notice!
That man has stolen your brain! He's—" Maribel
yanked the plates from her grip and fled. Mrs.
Gund was so silly on the topic of Duncan and her
love life. The firemen didn't give her any particular looks. They smiled at everyone. They were
polite and friendly and sexy and gorgeous and . . .

The door opened and three firemen walked in.
Maribel nearly dropped the Lazy Morning Specials in table six's laps. My goodness, they were
like hand grenades of testosterone rolling in the
door, sucking all the air out of the room. They
wore dark blue T-shirts under their yellow firemen's pants, thick suspenders holding up the
trousers. They walked with rolling strides, probably because of their big boots. Individually they
were handsome, but collectively they were devastating.

Maribel knew most of the San Gabriel firemen by name. The brown-haired one with eyes the color of a summer day was Ryan Blake. The big, bulky guy with the intimidating muscles was called Vader. She had no idea what his real name was, but apparently the nickname Vader came from the way he loved to make spooky voices with his breathing apparatus. The third one trailed behind the others, and she couldn't make out his identity. Then Ryan took a step forward, revealing the man behind him. She sucked in a breath.

Kirk was back. For months she'd been wondering where he was and been too shy to ask. She'd worried that he'd transferred to another town or decided to chuck it all and sail around the world. She'd been half-afraid she'd never see him again. But here he was, in the flesh, just as mouthwatering as ever. Her face heated as she darted glance after glance at him, like a starving person just presented with prime rib. It was wrong, so wrong; she was engaged. But she couldn't help it. She had to see if everything about him was as she remembered.

His silvery gray-green eyes, the exact color of the sagebrush that grew in the hills around San Gabriel, hadn't changed, though he looked more tired than she remembered. His blond hair, which he'd cut drastically since she'd last seen him, picked up glints of sunshine through the plate glass wall. His face looked thinner, maybe older, a little pale. But his mouth still had that secret humorous quirk. The rest of his face usually held a serious expression, but his mouth told a different story. It was as if he hid behind a quiet mask, but his mouth had chosen to rebel. Not especially tall, he had a powerful, quiet presence and a spectacular physique under his firefighter gear. She noticed that, unlike the others, he wore a long-sleeved shirt.

His fellow firefighters called him Thor. She could certainly see why. He looked like her idea of a Viking god, though she imagined the God of Thunder would be more of a loudmouth. Kirk was not a big talker. He didn't say much, but when he spoke people seemed to listen.

She certainly did, even though all he'd said to her was, "Black, no sugar," and "How much are those little Christmas ornaments?" referring to the beaded angels she made for sale during the holidays. It was embarrassing how much she relived those little moments.

Tossing friendly smiles to the other customers, the three men strolled to the counter where she took the orders. They gathered around the menu board, though why they bothered, she didn't know. They always ordered the same thing. Firemen seemed to be creatures of habit. Or at least her firemen were.

Scoffing at her own silliness—"her firemen" indeed—she left table six, ignoring their pleas for extra butter, and rounded the counter. Trying to look efficient, she pulled her order pad from the pocket of her apron and plucked her pencil from behind her ear. Nervous, she used a little too much force on the pencil, and it went flying through the air like a lead-tipped missile. Kirk caught it in mid-flight, just before it struck Vader in the temple.

He handed the pencil back to her. Their fingers brushed. Her pulse skittered.

"Something he said?" he asked mildly.

She turned scarlet. Even her eyelids felt hot. "I'm so sorry," she gasped.

"What?" Vader asked, having missed the whole thing.

"Don't worry, Maribel," drawled Ryan. "It could have gone in one ear and out the other and he probably wouldn't notice."

"Notice what?" An ominous frown gathered on Vader's jutting brow.

Maribel had a thing about honesty. "I almost stabbed you with my pencil. Well, not stabbed, because that's more of a deliberate thing, like *Psycho*, you know." She demonstrated with the pencil, jabbing it up and down in the air. It accidentally hit her pad and the tip broke off with a loud crack.

From behind her she heard Mrs. Gund snort. The firemen looked . . . well, she couldn't tell, because she was afraid to look at them.

"That's okay." She shoved the pad and useless pencil into her apron pocket. "I don't need to write your orders down. I know what you want."

"Are you sure?" Ryan said, a wicked twinkle in his eye. His body gave a jerk, as if one of the other firemen had shoved him. Some kind of inside joke, maybe. "I mean, let's hear it. I didn't know we were so predictable."

"Hazelnut quad shot with a Red Bull for Vader, coffee—black for Kirk, espresso with lots of sugar for Ryan—and a dozen muffins of all varieties except bran." She nodded proudly.

"Good job. High five." Ryan reached up a hand and she slapped it. Ryan was the certified dreamboat of the group, but for some reason he didn't make her feel nearly as shy as Kirk did. "How's Pete?"

"He's good. He loves the stickers you guys gave him. He keeps bugging me about getting a ride on your fire engine."

"Open invitation. We'll roll out the red carpet for him."

She smiled delightedly, thinking how thrilled her nine-year-old son would be at the prospect of hanging out with the firemen he idolized.

"Order up," called Mrs. Gund.

"I'll have your drinks ready in a minute," she told the guys. "Be right back."

Kirk spoke, so softly she nearly missed it. "I like the new photographs." He indicated the series of three abstract shots of jacaranda trees Mrs. Gund had allowed her to display.

This time her face went pink from pure pleasure. The photographs were her attempt at art, even though they were nothing compared to Duncan's.

"Thanks." She beamed at Kirk and, as she hurried off to deliver orders, she felt as if she were floating across the scuffed linoleum of the Lazy Daisy. A single compliment on her photography could keep her going through a whole shift. Especially one from the Viking god known as Thor.

As always, the teasing started as soon as they left the Lazy Daisy.

"Eight words. Anyone have eight?" Ryan climbed into the engine and picked up the on-board cell phone. "He said eight words. I had five. Anyone get closer than five?"

The sound of cheering came over the phone.

"All right, Stud, my man. Eight on the nose. Someone owes you a soda. Not me, but someone."

Kirk let the teasing roll off him as he fastened his seat belt. Let the guys joke. After what he'd been through, he couldn't get upset about a little ribbing. Besides, they had a point. Around Maribel Boone, he got tongue-tied. "They were good words," he pointed out. "She liked them."

"They were okay," said Ryan, as Vader steered Engine 1 into the stream of Monday-morning traffic. "Not the words I'd recommend. Nothing resembling, say, 'Would you like to have dinner with me?' "

"Or 'I'd like to bone the sweet bejeezus out of you,' " added Vader.

"Or 'I'm leaving San Gabriel and wanted to declare my undying love before I got on the plane,'" said Ryan.

"Or 'I'd like to lick you like a cherry Popsicle.'"

"Cherry?" Ryan objected. "Why cherry? Where do you even get that?"

"She's got red hair, is all."

Kirk finally spoke up. "It's not red. It's Titian."

Vader, not the station's most dexterous driver, turned the wheel hard as they veered around a corner. All three tilted to the side. "Titian? What's that? Some fancy word for 'tit'? I'm not talking about her boobs."

Ryan let out a hoot of laughter. Kirk shook his head. "Vader, have you ever read a book?"

"What does that have to do with Maribel's rack?"

Ryan was now laughing too hard to explain, and Kirk didn't care enough to. He'd come to blows with Vader in the past over his occasional crudeness, and it never did any good. "It's a shade of red. More like auburn."

"Huh." Since the conversation had veered away from boobs, Vader appeared to lose interest.

From the backseat, Ryan, once he'd gotten over his laughing fit, said in a lowered voice, "I'm serious, Thor. You need to talk to her. Are you going to move away without ever telling her how you feel? You've been crushing on her for years."

"I haven't been crushing."

"Right. More like drooling. I heard you muttering her name in your sleep during our Big Bear campout."

"She's engaged." It hurt like hell to say it, but he'd learned the hard way that you couldn't run from the truth.

"So you're just going to let it go? Disappear into a freakin' glacier? Seize the day, dude. Take the leap. Follow your bliss."

"One more affirmation and I'll shoot you."

"You don't have a gun. And she deserves to know." Ryan sat back with a disgusted air. "For such a tough guy, you sure are a wuss. Strong, silent type, my ass. You're afraid."

"Stay out of it, Hoagie."

Ryan shrugged. It's not like he was saying anything Kirk hadn't told himself a million times, lying awake, sick from chemo, his surgical wounds throbbing. He'd formulated the words many times. "Would you please meet me after work? I have something important to tell you." But as soon as he'd seen her today, with that delicious Titian-red hair in an unruly pile on her head, her dreamy hazel eyes widening with surprise at his compliment, the telltale color coming and going in her apple-round cheeks, he'd gone mute, as he always did.

Maribel left him speechless. Which didn't give him much of a chance to bare his heart to her.

Later, Maribel blamed the shock of Duncan's announcement. An actual wedding date. An actual plan. One of his "friends"—a client who owed him a favor—had offered up his house in the Hamptons for a weekend. It was all too overwhelming and miraculous. She should have broken the news to Pete carefully, gently. Instead she'd burst into his room and said, with openmouthed amazement, "Duncan wants to actually get married. In July! Holy moly, Pete, it's really happening. We're moving to New York!"

Pete was sprawled on his stomach on the floor, surrounded by the drawings and notebooks that comprised his epic fantasy novel. His face had turned red and he'd yelled, "No! I hate him!"

"Pete, you don't mean that."

"I do too! I've told you a million times!"

True, he had said something of the sort, but she didn't believe he really meant it. He'd feel that way about anyone she got involved with. He wanted his mother all to himself. It was understandable.

"I shouldn't have surprised you like that. I'm sorry, Pete."

That helped a bit. The red flooded from his face, leaving behind a sea of freckles. He looked back at the giant sketchbook he'd been writing in. "You don't have to marry him, Mom. We don't need him."

"But honey, I want to marry him. We've been talking about it the last couple of years. Aren't you, you know, used to the idea by now?"

"I don't like him," Pete said sullenly. "He doesn't talk to me."

"Sure he does. When he took us to Disneyland, we talked the whole time. It was so fun, remember?"

Pete scowled at the last sentence he'd written. He had a vague memory of Disneyland, sure, but it wasn't a good one. Duncan was so fake. He'd made Pete go on the baby rides like the stupid spinning teacups. He talked only about boring things—mostly himself. He kept bragging about the famous people he'd photographed and giving Pete nasty looks when he had no idea who they were. Privately, Pete called him Dumb Duncan or, in his angrier moments, Flunkin' Duncan. If only his mother would see the truth about him.

Now his mom was giving him a "be a good boy" sort of look. "Give him a chance, that's all I ask. Can you imagine? Us in New York City! Think of all the opportunities. Museums, concerts, plays, *exhibits*. So many things to photograph, so much to see and do and eat. The best pizza in the world, Pete! We'll still be a family, you and me, with just one extra, that's all . . ."

Pete couldn't stand it another second. He leaped to his feet and ran into the bathroom, slamming the door shut. His mother didn't follow him. One of the best things about his mom was that she knew sometimes he just needed to think. Alone.

When he heard his mother banging around in the kitchen, he skipped back to his room and flung himself on his bed. For a long time he stared at the Harry Potter posters on his wall. If only he could come up with a magic spell for getting rid of an unwanted, nasty fiancé. If only he could point his wand and say *Expelliarmus*! If only Hagrid would show up and give Duncan a pig's tail. That thought made him smile, but it lasted only a second. What was the point of dreaming impossible things? No owl was going to show up with a message luring Duncan off to the Sahara Desert. No giant motorcycle was going to blast through the air and land on top of Duncan.

A rustling sound outside made him jump. Then he went very still. It sounded as if something had landed in the camellia bushes outside his window.

The sound came again. A snuffle. A scuffling sound, like something poking at the shrubs outside.

Quietly, trying not to make a sound, Pete got to his feet. He tiptoed to the window, which was open a few inches, all his mother allowed. Slowly, carefully, he peered out. If it was a magical being, he wanted it to know he was cool with that. Whatever it was, even if it was a troll or an ogre.

It was a dog. Just a dog. A small, white dog with patches of brown and black. Bummed, he let out a long breath.

Then the dog looked up, and Pete knew, without a doubt, that this wasn't "just a dog" at all. His mother was terribly allergic to both dogs and cats, so he'd had very little to do with them in his life. But even so, he knew this dog had to be special. He had such bright, intelligent, curious dark brown eyes, the color of the blackstrap molasses his mom gave him for iron. The dog met Pete's gaze thoughtfully, without blinking, as if any minute he was going to start talking and ask why Pete looked so miserable.

"Hey, boy," said Pete softly. "What's your name?"

The dog cocked his head to one side. He had floppy ears that looked like they'd be soft as his favorite old blankie. Pete noticed he had no collar. Did that mean he was a wild dog? Of course not. This dog couldn't be wild. He looked too nice. But where were his owners?

The dog turned and trotted off, looking over his shoulder as if asking Pete to come play. He seemed to know exactly where he was going. He moved with a tiny hitch in his stride, barely noticeable.

Pete didn't hesitate. He slipped out of his room, ran out the side door into the carport, grabbed his bike, and pedaled after the dog. He needed to call the dog something. Something special and magical. He'd call him . . . Hagrid.

Chapter Two

In his driveway, Kirk revved his Harley, listening to the odd sound he'd noticed the last few times he'd ridden home from the firehouse. Poor bike needed some work. Especially—he gritted his teeth—if he was going to sell it. Which he was. He had to. Not only did he need the money, but it would be insane to cart a Harley all the way up to Alaska so he could ride for the few months a year that had no snow. He'd considered giving the bike to his younger brother in San Diego, but everyone knew Harleys had to be earned, not gifted.

So his beloved bike would have to go. He'd been putting the moment off, but that was silly. It was just a bike. He'd take it to the shop on the edge of town for a tune-up, then post it on Craigslist or something. Unless Gonzalez, the shop owner, knew someone in the market for an older-style, lovingly maintained Harley.

He strapped on his helmet, mounted the bike, and took off down the street. God, he'd miss this feeling, the powerful machine humming between his thighs, the wind lifting his hair, the road rising before him, chasing away every thought other than throttle, downshift, rev, signal.

Well, not *every* thought. Maribel still managed to surface, but he'd gotten used to that constant ache of longing. He didn't understand why he couldn't get her out of his mind. Sure, she was adorable, like a pink-cheeked fairy in an apron. Whenever he walked into the coffee shop, he knew instantly whether or not she was there. He could always pick up her particular scent, a light fragrance like apple blossom filtering through the thick cooking smells of grilled bacon and hazelnut coffee.

She was so creative, with her photographs and her little craftsy ornaments and beaded bracelets and such. She always had things on display at the counter, and he always bought some, whatever they were. He sent them to his family, who'd finally maxed out on the tchotchkes and suggested he share the wealth with the rest of the world. They just didn't appreciate art the way he did.

Maribel was kind too. Most of the time when he tried to buy the ornaments, she'd offer them up for free. He'd come back later and give Mrs. Gund the money. And he'd seen her with her boy, Pete. She'd sit him down at a table in the corner and help him with his homework between customers. She had a gentleness about her, something light and airy and dreamy and joyful; she'd never know how thoughts of her had sustained him during bouts of chemo.

That's why he couldn't tell her his feelings, no matter what Ryan said. He was damaged goods. A cancer survivor. How could he burden such a joyful soul with his crap? Besides, he reminded himself, she was engaged. Although the absence of her fiancé made that hard to keep in mind.

As the cheerful stucco houses of San Gabriel gave way to the grittier businesses of the industrial part of town, he kept an eye out for the cavernous warehouse where Gonzalez had set up shop. Kirk had been doing his own motorcycle maintenance for a while, but now he was under orders to stay out of the sun as much as possible. It was either build his own garage or bring the bike to Gonzalez. Just one more shift in his life.

He almost missed the big, metal-sided shop because it was lacking the huge "Gonzalez Choppers" sign with the flames around the edges. Was the G-Man making a new sign? He pulled into the big parking lot out front and knew something more was up. Usually the place had a steady flow of bikers. But now it was empty. Ominously empty. A breeze whispered through the birch woods behind the warehouse. A "For Lease" sign lay on the browning grass, as if something had knocked it over.

Was Gonzalez Choppers no more?

He knocked on the warehouse door, then realized it was unlocked. He opened it and peered inside. Yup, the place was cleared out. No jumble of Hondas, Harleys, and BMWs. No customers shooting the shit with the huge, tattooed Gonza-lez. The smell was the same. Grease and diesel and leather. And a few tools were still scattered on the counter that used to be chock-full of them. Even the gumball machine that Gonzalez had stocked with mixed nuts still occupied the near corner.

When he took a step forward, his footfalls echoed in the huge, empty space. Cool air settled on his face, a relief from the typically blazing heat of a May day in San Gabriel. The only light came from small windows high on the walls. Oblique and filtered, it did little to illuminate the space. And would pose no threat to his skin.

An idea struck. Why not work on his bike here? No one was using the place, or was likely to, judg-ing by the useless "For Lease" sign. If anyone ob-jected, he could vacate quickly enough. He could probably make do with the tools that had been left behind. If not, he could fill the gap easily enough.

A noise caught his attention, a clanging sound as if someone had knocked something over.

"Who's there?" he called sharply.

The noise stopped with suspicious suddenness.

"Hello?" He spoke into the emptiness. "Gonza-lez? Is that you?"

At his words, the sound came again, followed by a quick clicking of toenails on fast-moving paws. An animal of some kind. Kirk braced him-self. There had been a few wildcat spottings in San Gabriel, not to mention packs of coyotes at night.

But the wild creature that emerged from the

shadows at the back of the shop wasn't too terrifying. In fact, he recognized him right away. A little beagle. Gonzalez's beagle. What was his name again?

"Here pup," called Kirk. "I won't hurt you. What are you doing here, pup? You look like you're half-starved."

The dog's rib cage curved inwards. Poor thing must have gotten left behind. Kirk dug in his pockets for a quarter. Were mixed nuts good for dogs? Dogs ate pretty much anything, didn't they? Except chocolate.

The gumball machine dumped a handful of nuts into his palm, which he then presented to the dog. The beagle sniffed at his hand, gave him an inquiring look, then delicately nibbled at a cashew. Kirk found himself smiling. This dog had better manners than some of the guys at the firehouse. He spilled the rest of the nuts onto the cement floor so the dog could have at them.

"What the heck's your name, pup?" He remembered it had two words, and began with a *B* something. Or maybe it was a *J*. Jelly Bean? Jiffy Lube? He chuckled. "Here, Jiffy Lube."

"His name is Hagrid," said an angry young voice. Kirk jumped up and whirled around. He squinted at the figure silhouetted in the doorway. A boy, wheeling a blue bicycle through the door. Kirk relaxed.

"I don't think so," said Kirk. "I would have remembered that."

The boy came closer. Now Kirk could make out his features. A jolt of recognition shot through him, and his gut tightened. This was Pete. Maribel's kid. He quickly searched the shadows behind Pete but saw no sign of his mother.

"What are you doing out here?" he asked the boy.

"Checking on Hagrid. No one's taking care of him, so I have to."

"The guy who used to own this place must have left him behind."

"That's despicable."

Kirk couldn't argue with that. He looked down at the dog, who was finishing up the nuts. After he'd gobbled down the last one, he trotted over to Pete and sat on his haunches, licking his chops.

Pete swung a small pack off his back and dug inside it. "If you're going to give him all that salty stuff, you should give him water too." He pulled out a water bottle and a bowl. He knelt down and filled the bowl. The dog eagerly lapped at it.

"Good point. Looks like you're taking good care of . . . um, Hagrid."

Pete flashed him a pleased smile. He had his mother's coloring but had missed out on her milky skin. Instead, freckles spangled his face. Kirk ought to warn him to stay out of the sun. Instead, he asked, "Does your mother know you're here?"

Pete gave him a startled glance. "You know my mother?"

"Yeah, from the coffee shop. I'm one of the firemen who come in there."

"Oh. Cool." He seemed to be attempting an unimpressed attitude, but he didn't quite achieve it.

"So, back to my question. Does your mother know you're here?"

Pete looked down at Hagrid—fine, if it made the boy happy—and shook his head. "She doesn't know I come here, but she wouldn't care. She's too busy Skyping her dumbhead fiancé about her stupid wedding."

Ouch. Kirk felt that one like a kick in the gut. "So they're actually doing it, huh?"

"I guess." Pete shrugged.

Kirk felt for him. He recognized that helpless feeling, that knowledge that you had no control over a sudden, huge upheaval in your life. "If it makes her happy, that's a good thing, right?"

"But it—" Pete cut himself off, biting his lip. Damn, Kirk would give a lot to know what he was about to say. But getting inside information on Maribel from her kid seemed kind of low.

He also didn't like the idea of Pete being out here alone. Well, except for the dog, who might be some help if a shady character happened to wander through. Still, he couldn't, in good conscience, leave the boy alone here. Hands in his pockets, he pondered the best way to handle the situation.

"Hey, you want to help me with something?"

"What?"

"I want to see if either of these big doors are working." He indicated the two garage doors installed along one wall. "It might take two of us."

Pete jumped to his feet. "Sure. But what for?"

Kirk didn't answer. He bent to the handle at the lower edge of the door, waited for Pete to grab hold as well, then gave the signal to heave. The door resisted at first, then creaked upward with a rusty shriek. Sunlight poured in.

"It opened! But why? What do you need it open for?" Pete's sullenness had vanished in a blaze of nine-year-old curiosity.

Kirk pointed to his Harley, just visible at the edge of the lot. It glinted cobalt in the late-afternoon sun. "Work on my bike, of course."

Pete's mouth flew open. "That's yours?"

"Yep."

The kid looked from the bike to him, back and forth, over and over. Kirk didn't understand why he should be so amazed. Lots of guys had Harleys. But an expression of wonder passed over the boy's face. He must really love motorcycles. A sudden impulse took hold of Kirk. "Wanna help?"

"Can I?"

"You're here. Bike's here. Why not? As long as you call your mother first and let her know where you are."

He handed over his cell phone. Pete, with a sulky glance, dialed a number and left a grumbling message.

The next couple hours passed in peaceful male harmony. Kirk brought his bike into the warehouse, they closed the door back up, and they turned their attention to the magnificent piece of equipment that somehow brought the warehouse back to life with its presence. Hagrid the Dog dozed nearby, occasionally opening one eye to check on their progress. Kirk didn't do much; he needed more tools. But he walked Pete through the basic mechanics of the Harley. The kid ate it up. He chattered a mile a minute the entire time. He talked about his love for Harry Potter, his strong objections to soccer practice, his passionate arguments for more leniency from his mother.

Kirk wished he'd mention his mother a little more.

One thing became pretty clear. Pete really, really didn't like Duncan, a celebrity photographer who had met Maribel at a gallery opening and been a pest ever since.

Kirk didn't like him either. But he liked Pete, who learned quickly, liked to laugh, and had a firecracker temper.

Neither realized how quickly time was passing until they lifted the door again and discovered night had fallen, or nearly so. The sky held deep sapphire shadows and the first twinkling of evening stars.

Pete looked stricken. "Mom's going to kill me. I'm not supposed to ride my bike after dark. Is this dark? It's not completely dark, right? Still kind of light?"

Kirk squinted at the sky. It looked pretty dark to him. "Do you have any lights on your bike?"

"No. Just a reflector."

"I'll take you home."

"What about my bike?"

"I'll bring it by later in my truck. Your mom will never know."

But Maribel was waiting on the front stoop when they roared up. A shiver of anticipation made Kirk's throat go dry. He'd never seen Maribel outside of the café. It always felt as if he was walking into some magical otherworld when they stopped by. Now here she was, on the front porch of an ordinary, rundown, suburban tract house, with the sort of stunned expression any mother would have at the sight of her son on the back of a motorcycle.

Kirk put his feet on the pavement and waited for Pete to dismount. The kid hesitated, muttering "uh-oh" under his breath.

"It's okay," Kirk called to Maribel, only then realizing he still had his helmet on. He pulled off his riding gloves and struggled with the strap, while Maribel dashed down the porch and strode toward them. Her hair swished around her shoulders, the light from the porch making it gleam like a molten waterfall. Hypnotized, he stood stock-still. He'd never seen her with her hair loose before. Sparks seemed to fly off her.

"How dare you put my son on your motorcycle? Do you know how dangerous that is? And Pete, where have you been? I called all your friends and—"

"I'm sorry, Mom!" Pete looked wretched. "Didn't you get my message at the café?"

"You know I didn't. I never get those messages. That's why you're supposed to use my cell phone."

Kirk shot Pete a sharp glance. *Crap!* He'd let the kid get away with deceiving his mother. Maribel was going to hate him now.

"I forgot. Besides, I didn't mean to stay that long. I didn't see how late it was. I'm really sorry. I didn't want to ride my bike after dark, and he offered me a ride and—"

"You're not supposed to take rides from strangers! It's like candy! Same thing! You know better, Pete."

"But he's not—"

"And you!" She whirled on Kirk again, who took a step back, holding up his hands to show he meant no harm and in the process nearly knocking over his bike. "I ought to call the police. Giving a kid a ride on a motorcycle. What were you thinking? What's next? You're going to buy him a beer? Take him club-hopping?"

"Mom!"

If Kirk could only explain, set her mind at ease, but the strap of his helmet refused to come off. He must look terrifying to her, hiding behind his helmet and black leather jacket.

"Pete, get in the house. Now." She gave Kirk one last, scathing look and turned away. His eyes swept across her pert little rear, encased in a pair of shorts, and her long, deliciously sleek legs. She was barefoot. Her feet were . . . well, kind of big and clunky. For some reason that flaw clutched at his heart. She couldn't leave. Not until he'd explained himself.

He gave the helmet strap one last yank. This time the buckle finally burst open. The helmet bounced to the ground, but he barely noticed, thanks to the pain shooting through his head and the stars dancing in his vision. Had he just punched himself in the face? He had. He felt his jaw, working it to make sure it wasn't broken. He packed a hell of a punch, if he did say so himself.

"Mom! Kirk's hurt."

"Who's Kirk?"

"Kirk! The fireman. The man with the bike."

Maribel froze, then slowly turned. Sure enough, the tough-looking man in the motorcycle helmet was no longer an intimidating stranger, but a wincing silver-eyed Kirk. He seemed to be weaving a little on his feet. "Sorry to scare you," he said. "Pete didn't have any lights on his bike, and it didn't seem safe for him to ride home like that. I'm a very experienced rider. There was never any danger. But I'm real sorry to worry you."

She stared. Was this really the strong, silent Kirk? She'd never heard so many words out of him at once. Maybe that bonk on the head, or whatever had happened, knocked the quiet out of him.

"Are you all right?"

"Oh, yeah. I just . . . had some trouble with my strap." He moved his jaw from side to side.

"You should put some ice on that. Why don't you come in?"

He didn't seem to grasp her meaning, gaping at her blank-faced. Poor guy must have really done a number on himself. She went to him and took his hand, which felt very warm and big. At his touch, a little sunburst seemed to light up her insides. "You'd better come in and sit down. You shouldn't get back on that bike yet. And you definitely need ice. Pete, run ahead and get a pack of frozen corn."

"Peas," Kirk said.

"What?"

Had he said something about having to pee? Unusual thing to mention. He must really be out of it. She paused and looked back at him curiously. But he was looking ahead at Pete—who had just zipped in the doorway—or maybe at her house, or maybe he was just seeing stars. Who knew? At any rate, he didn't notice that she'd stopped walking. He plowed right into her.

As she started to fall backward, he caught her by the shoulders. She clutched at his upper arms, which felt hard as rocks under his black jacket. The smell of pure, manly male—car grease and leather and open road and something else, something she couldn't quite put her finger on—went straight to her head. A liquid thrill shot through the rest of her body.

Oh my! Duncan's presence never made her

lightheaded like this. She inhaled a deep breath, her eyes closing partway so she could savor the scent.

"Sorry," he murmured. But he didn't look sorry. He looked . . . hungry. His head dipped lower, so she got a good, close look at his eyes. They . . . well, they smoldered, there was no other word for it. The intensity in his expression sent another shock of heat blasting through her system. She felt her lips part as she swayed toward him. What would it be like to feel his mouth on hers, taste the essence of Kirk, the power of him? She caught her breath, her lips tingling in anticipation, her body vibrating with one thought, one urge . . . and then . . .

She sneezed. Repeatedly. Helplessly.

Suddenly she realized what that other smell was, the one she couldn't quite identify.

Dog.

Chapter Three

Pete couldn't believe his luck. Good and bad. First there was the good luck of finding Hagrid and the warehouse he called home. Then there was the bad luck that poor Hagrid was starving, so that meant Pete had to keep riding out there and giving him food. Then the good luck of the motorcycle. A motorcycle! If that didn't prove that some magic was working—Hagrid, plus a *motorcycle*—what would? Even better luck, the motorcycle came attached to a really cool guy who let him work on the bike. Even ride it. But that was part of the terrible luck of forgetting to pay attention to the time. That wasn't luck, exactly, but still.

And now, the ultimate bad luck. His mother's sneezing fit meant that Kirk had taken off in a hurry, Pete had been plunged into a long, soapy bath, and he'd now been banned from ever going near Hagrid again.

Right. As if that would fly. Hagrid needed him.

The next day, his mother drove him to school, shooting him stern glances every couple minutes.

Generally speaking, his mom was pretty cool. She was fun and listened to him and didn't get too cuddly at embarrassing moments. If not for Duncan and her dog allergy, she'd be perfect.

"I expect you at the café right after school today."

"Yes, Mom," he said dutifully. No problem. He could leave school early and ride out to feed Hagrid. Besides, his mother had a shaky concept of time. She'd never notice if he was a little late.

"Do you think he likes banana bread better or brownies?"

"Huh?" Pete was used to his mother's random changes of subject, but he couldn't follow this one.

"Kirk. The fireman." He peered up at her, noticing the pink tint of her cheeks. "I feel bad for yelling at him like that. I should apologize."

"Oh, that's okay. Kirk's cool."

"He is?" Her voice sounded odd. He didn't want her to think anything bad about Kirk, so he rushed on.

"He's the coolest guy I ever met. His favorite Harry Potter character is Hagrid too. And he thinks soccer is boring compared to rugby. He played rugby in college and broke his nose three times. And his arm. Next year I'm going to sign up for rugby."

His mother seemed to choke.

"I mean, if that's okay with you," he added hastily, remembering she had some say in the matter as well.

"Do they even have rugby for fifth graders?"

"Huh? I'll ask Kirk. He'd know. He knows a lot."

"That's funny. He's always so quiet."

Pete blinked in amazement. He and Kirk had talked the entire time they'd hung out together. Or at least, he had. He shrugged it off. "Nah, he's cool. Fun to talk to. Not like Dumbo Duncan. You would've seen if only you weren't sneezing so much."

His mom made that choking sound again. "Anyway," she said, "it's not going to come up. No more hanging out at that warehouse. No more dog. And I'll know. The nose never lies."

"Of course, Mom."

Good thing he had a plan.

When Pete didn't show up at the café as commanded, Maribel's already marginal efficiency vanished. She couldn't concentrate on burgers and fries when all her focus was on the street outside. Where was her little boy? And where were the firemen? If Kirk appeared, she could find out where the warehouse was and track down her son. She didn't doubt for a minute that's where he was. She'd recognized that innocent look on his face.

Finally, around five in the evening, Mrs. Gund took mercy on her and told her to leave early and go find Pete. She fled the café, jumping into her car without even bothering to take off her apron. She drove straight to San Gabriel Fire Station 1, the squat brick building in the next neighborhood over. She recognized it from the various TV reports about the Bachelor Firemen of San Gabriel. Just down the street was a busy Starbucks; she wondered vaguely why they came all the way to the Lazy Daisy for their coffee.

She spotted Kirk's Harley in the parking lot, which sent a wave of worry through her. If Pete was at an abandoned warehouse, she'd rather he be accompanied by a strong, capable fireman. By the time she'd found the side door that led into a garage filled with shiny fire engines, hurried down a long corridor lined with cell-like bedrooms, and burst into a living-room area where firefighters were gathered around a long table littered with official-looking pieces of paper, her heart was about to jump out of her chest.

"Excuse me. Hello. I'm looking . . ." Her breath ran out. She panted, desperately surveying the assembled men. And woman.

A lovely green-eyed woman with her hair in a braid down her back rose to her feet. "Are you okay?"

"That's Maribel. Thor's Maribel." Vader goggled at her, as if completely discombobulated by her appearance. "You still have your apron on."

Maribel looked down at her apron, utterly confused. Had he said "Thor's Maribel"?

"Thor!" Ryan called. "Get out here!"

A door opened and Kirk walked out, still fastening his belt. He stopped dead at the sight of her and said, incredulously, "Maribel?" And then, "What's wrong? Is Pete okay?"

Whatever progress she'd made in her attempt to catch her breath disappeared. He was so damn sexy in his uniform, so fit and sturdy. But the best part was the look in his sagebrush eyes. They were wide with concern, exactly mirroring the worry in her heart. Instantly, magically, she felt less alone.

"He didn't come to the café the way he was supposed to, and I don't know where that warehouse is, and I'm sure he went there even though I told him not to, and I kind of hoped you were with him even though then I'd have to kill you both, but you're here and . . ." She stopped, gasping for breath.

Kirk stepped to her side and took her elbow. His touch was firm and infinitely reassuring. "It's okay. It's okay." He turned to a stern-faced man rising at one end of the table. Maribel recognized those remarkable charcoal eyes from the TV reports on the Bachelor Firemen. "Captain Brody, can I run her down to Highway 90?"

"That's okay," Maribel protested. "I don't mean to take you away from your job. Just tell me where it is. I can find it."

Kirk shook his head. "It's a bit out of the way. Not too easy to describe."

Captain Brody came toward them, examining Maribel closely. She nearly took a step back, but felt Kirk's hand squeeze her elbow.

"Captain, I know this isn't a fire, but don't you guys get cats down from trees and that sort of thing? There's a dog out there too, even though he probably isn't in a tree. And who knows what chemicals are at that warehouse? A fire could start . . ." She broke off, swallowing hard. Her attempt to win Brody's consent was backfiring on her, her imagination exploding with all the things that could go wrong.

"Take the plug buggy," said Captain Brody. "Kirk, you can go over the training bulletin later. And keep your phone on."

"Yes, sir."

"Thank you, thank you," said Maribel. As Kirk guided her out of the room, she asked, over her shoulder, "Do you guys like peanut butter fudge? Or I make these really cute puppets from gloves. I call them FingerBabies . . ."

"You can never go wrong with chocolate chip cookies," said Kirk, using his strong grip to navigate her past the fire engines in the garage. "But don't worry. Rescuing damsels in distress is right up our alley. We're supposed to rescue at least one a week."

"Really?" She looked up at him, noticing the curl at the corner of his mouth, the secret smile she'd always known had lurked there. It was just as endearing as she'd imagined. "Oh! You're joking."

"You sound surprised." He opened the door to

a tidy red pickup truck and ushered her into the passenger seat. "Meet the plug buggy. Firehouse truck." Quickly, he jumped into the driver's seat and turned the key in the ignition.

"Well, at the café you don't say a whole lot," said Maribel, returning to the intriguing topic of Kirk's little joke. "It's mostly 'coffee, black,' and honestly, by now I know that's how you like your coffee. You don't even have to say that. But it's fine when you do," she added quickly. "I like it when you do."

He gave her a sidelong, quizzical look. Instantly her face grew warm. She pressed the back of her hand across her cheek, remembering that almost-kiss from last night. At least, she'd seen it as an almost kiss. He probably couldn't get past the sneezing.

It occurred to her, with embarrassing timing, that she had a crush on Kirk. She went even redder.

"I guess I don't generally say a whole lot," Kirk admitted, looking uncomfortable. "But the other guys make up for it. Hard to get a word in edgewise sometimes."

"I guess that explains it. Besides, you probably say more to people who aren't waiting on you." She offered him a cheery smile. "I mean, there's not really much to say to your waitress, I suppose. Other than 'Coffee, black.' Although I do wonder why you don't mention our muffins occasionally. They're really good, you know. But you must have someone making muffins for you. Like, you know, a . . ."

"I don't," he said flatly. "No wife. No girlfriend. If that's what you're asking."

"Really?" If her face were any more red, she'd be a strawberry. Of course she'd been asking him that—in the clumsiest possible way.

They drove over a pothole. She bumped against him as they landed. Her arm tingled even though she hadn't actually touched his skin. "But you're so . . . you must have girls . . . is it the Bachelor Curse?" Rumor had it the San Gabriel firehouse was cursed, so its inordinately handsome crew had a rough time in the romance department.

A smile touched his lips. She wanted to touch them too. Very badly.

"Don't know about that," he said. "It's more of a . . . well . . . it's hard to explain."

"That's fine. You don't have to." Despite herself, disappointment swamped her. She really wanted to know Kirk better. Something lurked behind that silent exterior, something intriguing. But it was hard to pry information out of him. Kind of the opposite of Duncan, who could fill an entire long weekend with anecdotes about photo shoots with Christina Aguilera. "We can stick to 'coffee, black.'" She gazed out the window, trying not to feel hurt. She was being ridiculous anyway. What did a motorcycle-riding fireman and a wannabe-photographer waitress have in common?

Kirk gripped the steering wheel until his knuckles turned white. He'd offended her somehow. Her lovely face had gone closed and stiff. She was no longer chattering about muffins and girlfriends. She propped her elbow on the car door and rested her head on her hand. Her red hair glowed ruby in the twilight, the last rays of the sun turning her skin a vibrant gold. He couldn't believe she was sitting right next to him, like a fantasy come to life, even down to the apron that occasionally turned up in his nighttime yearnings.

What had he said wrong, and how could he fix it? They'd almost reached Highway 90. Shortly they'd arrive at the warehouse and the moment would be gone. Just like the guys said, he should tell her the real reason he went so tongue-tied in her presence. The reason he stuck to "coffee, black" and was damn proud he got that out. If he didn't say anything, she'd continue to think he didn't care to converse with her, or that he saw her only as a food deliverer and nothing more.

"It's not that," he said through gritted teeth. "It's more like . . . a sort of situation." He winced. A situation? What the hell?

She looked confused. "What kind of situation?"

"*Situation's* the wrong word. More of a . . . reaction. A strong reaction. When I . . . well . . ." Damn, this was hard. How could he possibly explain that he'd tried dating other women but kept thinking about her, and that he tended to go mute and awkward in her presence? But that was just part of the story. The rest of it . . . he couldn't tell her that either, she might feel sorry for him or see him as weak. But the expression on her face—wary, trembling on the edge of hurt—reeled him in like a hooked flounder.

"I had skin cancer," he blurted. "Stage Three."

She whirled in his direction. "What?"

Oh lord, now he'd made everything worse. He should have just told her he had a crush on her. No going back now. "I *have* skin cancer," he corrected himself. "I went through treatment. It might be gone. But there's always a chance it could come back."

"Skin cancer," she repeated softly. "Is that why you were gone? You didn't come to the café for a while."

The fact that she'd noticed his absence made him want to crow like a strutting rooster. He tamped down that entirely inappropriate reaction. "Yes. I couldn't work when I was on chemo. I wanted to, but I couldn't. But I'm back now." Not for long, but he didn't want to tell her that. At least not yet.

She put her hand on his forearm. His muscles tensed at her touch. He wanted to look at her, see how she was reacting to his revelation, but instead he stared at the road ahead. Only a few miles to Gonzalez's now. *Way to ruin the mood, asshole*, he lectured himself.

"I'm so glad you're okay now. I wish I'd known. I would have sent you a card or visited you in the hospital." A card. If she had any idea how many times he would have read anything she sent him. She could send her electric bill and he'd pore over it looking for doodles.

"That's okay. I wouldn't want you to worry. Or anyone else. That's why . . ."

"That's why you don't have a girlfriend," she finished for him. "Because you wouldn't want her worrying about you?"

"Right. But more than that. I wouldn't want to make things hard on her. You can't be much of a partner if you're sick all the time."

Maribel was shaking her head back and forth. Every time she did so, another strand of tempting Titian silk strayed from her ponytail. His fingers itched to tuck them back behind her ears. "But that's so wrong."

"I don't want anyone's life complicated because of me. The guys at the firehouse were great. They really came through for me. But the girl I was sort of dating, well, it didn't work out."

"She must not have really loved you."

Hearing the word "love" from her mouth gave him a bittersweet shock. If *she* loved him, he'd be able to lift apartment buildings with one hand, jump to the moon, swim to the stars. But she was engaged. And thought of him as a taciturn occasional customer.

"I'm a firefighter. I watch out for people. Rescue damsels in distress." He tried for a wink, though it came out more as a grimace. "Not the other way around."

"Kirk! You have it all wrong." Her forceful tone gave him a start. "Just look at me."

He took that as an invitation to stare at her, even though she clearly meant it metaphorically. "I'm looking."

"I mean, look at me freaking out about Pete. I'm worried, right?"

"Yes, but you shouldn't be. He's okay, especially if he's with Hagrid. That dog's a lot tougher than he looks. I hung out there working on my motorcycle and no one showed up all day. Just Pete, me, and Hagrid. Believe me, I won't let anything happen to Pete. We'll be there in a couple of minutes and you'll see."

He turned onto the winding road that led to the warehouse.

"That's not the point!" She bounced on the seat in frustration. "I'm worried, but I don't *mind* being worried. I mean, I mind to the extent that I'm going to be pretty darn pissed at that kid and he's going to know it. Consequence city."

"Give him a break. He really cares about that dog."

"Forget the darn dog!" Surprised by her intensity, Kirk screeched to a halt outside the warehouse. Pete's blue Schwinn was right where it always was, and he heard Hagrid bark from inside the building. "It's not the end of the world to worry about someone. I'd rather have someone to worry about than never worry again. If you want to worry about something, worry about why you don't have anyone to worry about you! Except now you do."

"What?"

"Me, you goof. I'm going to worry about you no matter what you say. I don't care if you're a big strong fireman who rescues people with his bare hands. Why should that mean you don't deserve someone to worry about you? Well, you do. And *I do*. So there."

With an emphatic nod of her head, she hopped out of the plug buggy. Kirk rubbed the back of his neck. That conversation was going to take a lot of sorting through. Later, after they'd found Pete. But for now, he kept hearing those two words, "I do," echo through his brain.

God, he was such a hopeless fool.

Chapter Four

The sight of Pete's bike both reassured and infuriated Maribel. So her son had ridden out here in direct defiance of her orders. Maybe Duncan was right and she was too lax, too easy on Pete. Once they got married, would Duncan get more involved in disciplining Pete? They'd never discussed that sort of thing. Pete wouldn't like that much.

Then again, right now she could use a little help in the discipline department. She flung open the door to the warehouse and peered into the dim interior. A sharp flurry of barks greeted her. Something warm kept bumping against her shins, but she couldn't make out anything in the darkness.

"Pete!" she yelled in a panicked voice.

"Down, Hagrid!" came her son's voice. "Down. Be cool." *Hagrid?* Maribel peered at the creature at her feet. As her eyes adjusted, she realized it was a dog. A pretty darn cute dog. Mostly white, but he looked as if someone had spilled black and brown paint on him. He stared up at her with melting brown eyes. She took a step back and collided with Kirk. He put his hands on her upper arms and gently moved her aside so he could step in front of her.

"Come on, boy." The dog, following the firm command in Kirk's voice, trotted after him. "Pete, tie him up. You know your mom's allergic."

Right on cue, Maribel sneezed. Her eyes itched. She blinked madly, blurring the sight of the stubborn scowl on Pete's face. He bent down to snap a rope on the dog's collar. The other end of the rope was tied around a post. He petted the dog, murmuring to it.

Maribel felt like Cruella De Vil. Still, she had to take a stand. "Pete. I told you to stay away from this place. It's not safe. It's an abandoned warehouse, for goodness' sake."

"It's not abandoned. Kirk hangs out here. So does Hagrid. Just because you're allergic doesn't mean I should never get to have a dog. And I don't even *have* Hagrid. I just get to visit him. And now I can't even do that. It's so unfair!"

Oh Lordy. If he'd named the dog Hagrid, the chances of a peaceful resolution to this mess were zero. She cast a helpless glance at Kirk.

"The dog belonged to the guy who used to rent this place," he explained. "He had a motorcycle shop here. Looks like he left his dog behind."

"That's terrible."

Pete's face brightened. Maribel tried to steel her heart against all sympathy for the dog.

"Pete found him, and he's been taking good care of him. Pete says he's actually put on a little weight."

"When I got here, he was sleeping and I thought he might be sick. I didn't want to leave him all alone. Look, I taught him a trick."

He gave Hagrid an elaborate, spiraling hand signal. Hagrid, with what looked distinctly like a sigh, rolled over quickly, then popped back to his feet again.

Kirk laughed, which made Maribel glance at him in surprise. She'd never seen him look carefree before. He always seemed so serious, even when ordering coffee. "Hagrid's a smart dog. He used to ride with Gonzalez sometimes. The shop owner. He sat in front, even had a helmet. Cutest thing you ever saw."

Maribel shook her head in despair, then sneezed again. "Pete, what do you want me to do? We can't bring the dog home. You know we can't."

"Because we're moving to New York?"

Maribel felt Kirk glance sharply in her direction. Her face went warm. Should she have told Kirk they were leaving? But they didn't know each other that well yet. "That's not why and you know it."

Pete bent to cuddle the dog again. As he scratched between Hagrid's floppy ears, the dog's tail thumped the floor. "Then why can't I just keep doing this for now? Take care of him out here? He likes this place. So do I. It's fun."

"Because . . ." Maribel put a hand to her forehead. Was she in the wrong here? Where was the section in the nonexistent motherhood manual that covered this situation? What would Pete's father say? Then again, his father, having left town and changed his cell number the instant two lines appeared on the pregnancy test, probably wouldn't be the best guide. "Because it's an abandoned building. If I let you play here unsupervised, they'd take away my Mom card."

"There's no such thing as a Mom card."

"I'm sorry, Pete. It's just not safe." She took a deep breath. "I think we should take Hagrid to the animal shelter so they can find him a good home."

"*What?* They kill dogs there. You know they do!"

Maribel winced. Wrong move. "We won't let that happen. We'll keep checking in. If no one adopts him, we'll find someone ourselves."

"But we don't know who's going to adopt him! It could be someone horrible who never takes him for walks and feeds him crappy food and doesn't care about him!"

"Pete, be reasonable."

Pete screamed at the top of his lungs, "*You're not being reasonable! You're being horrible! You should . . . they should . . . take away your Mom card!*"

Maribel felt the warehouse shift around her. She thought Pete had outgrown his terrible tantrum phase. His outbursts could be horrible. Nothing made her feel worse or more incompetent as a mother. And Kirk was about to witness the whole thing, see how inept a parent she was, how little control she had over her son, how . . .

She felt a hand drop to her shoulder, a strong, warm hand. Kirk's calm voice carried through the charged atmosphere like headlights through fog.

"Your mom's right, Pete. I'd never have been able to play alone out here when I was a kid. I'd have been grounded about ten times over by now."

Pete gave a surprised hiccup. Had Kirk managed to stop the hurricane before it truly got going?

"But I do have an idea. Pete, can you give us a minute? I'll run it by your mom first and see what she says." Not giving Pete a chance to answer, he took Maribel by the elbow and led her outside into the bright air.

"I'm sorry about that," she mumbled, mortified. "He can be pretty fierce sometimes."

Kirk shrugged, as if it was no big deal. "I was wondering how you would feel about Pete coming to feed Hagrid if I'm with him."

"You mean . . ." She frowned. "You'd bring him out here? Every day?"

"Not every day. Can't when I'm on shift. But most days I could. I'm working on my bike here anyway. It's no trouble."

"No trouble?" She looked at him skeptically. "You're basically offering to babysit my kid and his stray dog. Don't you have other things you'd rather do?"

A funny look crossed his face. He opened his mouth, then shut it again quickly.

"Anyway," she continued, "it's not a long-term solution. He'll just get more attached to the dog and . . . I don't know anything about that dog. What if he has rabies or fleas or mad cow disease or . . ."

Kirk seemed to bite back a laugh. "I can vouch for Hagrid. Gonzalez always took good care of him. But I'll take him to a vet and get him checked out."

"But . . . we're going to be moving and . . ." She swallowed. Strange how hollow that last statement made her feel.

Kirk didn't seem to like the sound of it any better than she did, judging by the way his body stilled. "Pete and I will work on finding a home for Hagrid. Someone Pete likes. I'd take him, but . . ." He snapped his mouth shut, as if he'd nearly said too much.

"You mean, you'd help him with the transition to a new owner."

"Yeah, I guess."

"Transitions are hard on kids," she explained. "That's what all the parenting books say."

His silvery eyes looked down on her with such sympathy, she found herself spilling out more confidences. "I read a lot of parenting books. My parents weren't . . . well, they travel a lot. All over the world. Everywhere except here. The air's bad here." Yes, that sounded just as lame is it had when her mother explained it to her.

After a moment, Kirk asked, quietly, "What about Pete's father?"

Her eyes flicked away from his and focused on the chest muscles under his dark blue SGFD shirt.

"Pete's never met him. I know it must be hard. That's why I want some stability for him. A male figure in his life. Duncan thinks Pete needs a stronger hand. He's probably right. Pete used to have these tantrums . . ."

Even though she was still concentrating on his broad chest, she caught a glimpse of his jaw tightening. A muscle flexed in his neck. It was fascinating, watching these little signs of his inner thoughts.

"I don't know about that," he finally said, as though he were restraining himself from saying something much different.

"Know about what?"

"Pete's a good kid. You see a lot of kids in my line of work. There's nothing wrong with your son."

As much as Maribel wanted to believe that, she couldn't help giving him a skeptical frown. "But you aren't a father, are you?"

"No. Is Duncan?"

Good lord, was that jealousy in his voice? And what was that hard look in his gray-green eyes, as though the next celebrity photographer he spotted would go flying across the room in a bloody blur?

Something inside her thrilled to the restrained force etched in every line of his body. What would it be like to feel that strength against her . . . inside her? She shivered.

"Mom? Kirk?" Pete called from inside the warehouse. "What are you doing?"

What *were* they doing? Kirk stared down at her with a look that screamed possessiveness. And she . . . she was gazing back, lips parted, breath coming quickly . . . Were they suddenly standing closer to each other than they had been two minutes ago? She didn't recall stepping forward, or seeing him do so. And yet, her skin was tingling at his nearness, the little hairs on her arms were standing on end, as were her nipples . . .

Good Lord almighty, this had to stop! She took a wild step backward, only to feel Kirk's hand catch her before she tripped over a chunk of concrete.

"See?" she said triumphantly, waving a finger at him. "Pete could stub his toe on something like that. He could fall on his face, start bleeding, get a concussion, not be able to find his way home . . ."

The confusion in his silver-lit eyes brought her back to earth.

"Ugh, there I go, catastrophizing again. Bad habit."

He just kept looking at her as if she were the most fascinating being on the planet. "What's that?"

"Think of the worst possible thing. All possible worst possible things. I do it a lot, ever since I became a parent."

"It's good to prepare for the worst. We do it when we fight fires too."

"Yeah, but I think I might go overboard sometimes. It's hard to say. It's not like they have a catastrophe chart in any of the parenting books."

Amusement lit his quiet face, transforming it from handsome to dazzling. A dimple appeared in his cheek, erasing his tired, drawn look. "I think you're doing great, Maribel. You don't need to worry so much."

Pleasure flooded her, chasing away the thought that Duncan said pretty much the opposite.

"Mom!"

"Fine," she said quickly, knowing from the impatient tone in Pete's voice exactly how much time they had left. "You can bring Pete out here to take care of Hagrid. But you have to be with him the whole time. And if he has schoolwork or soccer practice, that comes first."

"That's fair."

"And you promise you'll help him find Hagrid a good home?"

"Promise."

At his solemn tone, that of someone taking a sacred vow, she felt an unstoppable urge to thank him. Before she knew it, she was teetering forward, rising on tiptoe, and touching her lips to his jaw. The slight roughness of his past–five o'clock stubble tickled her mouth. The sunny, open-road scent of his warm skin went right to her head. His head started to move, his mouth coming toward hers, she could feel his hot, intoxicating breath against her cheek, she swayed toward him, wanting him, wanting all of him, but for now this would do, just the feel of his mouth against hers . . .

A brief, scalding contact sent fire racing through her veins. *Holy crap*, she thought wildly, before feeling his body pull away from hers, his lips lift away from her mouth. The door was flung open and Pete stared at them like an indignant, red-headed avenging angel.

"I've been yelling and yelling in there. Are you both deaf?"

"We've been working something out for you, Pete," said Kirk calmly, though his eyes had darkened and his chest rose and fell more quickly than normal. "I'll be your Hagrid-feeding escort. Every other day or so, we'll come out here and bring him some more food, play with him and so forth."

"Every *other* day?"

"I gotta work. You know, putting out fires, saving lives." A smile ghosted across his lips. The lips that had just been touching hers, that had kissed her with a kind of intensity she'd never imagined from quiet Kirk. She put a hand to her mouth.

"I guess that's okay," said Pete.

Maribel made a mighty effort to get a grip on her unruly reaction to the sexy fireman. "Pete, Kirk will be in charge. He's doing a really nice thing for you, and I want you to appreciate it."

"I do. I do. Thank you." Pete bobbed his head fervently.

"And your schoolwork comes first."

"Sure."

"No schoolwork, no Hagrid," she repeated, just to drive home the point.

"Mom, I get it."

"And you're grounded for two days because you disobeyed the rules and came out here today."

He groaned. "Fine."

She dared a glance at Kirk, almost afraid she'd burst into flames of lust if she looked directly at him.

He was nodding gravely. "Very fair."

"Grrrr." Pete whirled around and disappeared back inside the warehouse, leaving Maribel and Kirk staring at each other awkwardly.

"I . . . I'm sorry," he muttered. "I know you're engaged, and I shouldn't have done that."

Her jaw dropped. Horror-struck, she stared at him. *Engaged.* Good lord, she'd forgotten all about Duncan. Not just during the kiss, but after, all the way until he'd brought it up. If he hadn't, when *would* she have remembered? Sometime before the wedding, she hoped.

She stammered something and spun around to go after Pete. This wasn't good. Not good at all.

As soon as she'd put Pete to bed, she called Duncan. Good thing he kept rock-and-roll hours to match those of his clients. "Duncan, you have to come visit. Really."

"Why, baby? This is a busy month, you know. I have three shoots in the next two weeks."

"But Pete needs to get to know you better." She landed on the first mentionable reason she could think of. "He's freaking out about us getting married. I was thinking some time alone with him would be good."

If it worked for Kirk, why not Duncan? Logically it made a certain amount of sense, even though she had a sneaking suspicion it wouldn't be the same at all.

"Time alone? If I'm coming all the way out there, I want time alone with my babycakes."

"Well, of course, that too." That was the main point, wasn't it? To get Kirk out of her brain and Duncan back into it? "I miss you."

"I miss you too, Mari. But just think, before long we'll be together all the time. Can't wait, baby!"

"Me neither. So you'll come?"

"Let me check my schedule . . ." He put her on speaker so he could pull up his calendar. "Yes, let's do it. Maybe I can set up some meetings while I'm out there. You wouldn't mind a road trip to LA, would you? I could take you to Bar Marmont. Bet Pete would like that. Maybe I can wrangle a run-in with Daniel Radcliffe."

Now that, Maribel had to admit, would actually impress Pete, though he normally scoffed at all of Duncan's celebrity references. When she hung up, she felt a little better. Duncan loved her, surely he did. He could have any number of high-profile girlfriends. And he had, before he'd met her. He'd even dated a Victoria's Secret model and one of Madonna's dancers. But he claimed Maribel was perfect for him, his haven from the fame-hungry world in which he lived.

Yes, Duncan loved her . . . and respected her, right? Sure, he laughed a little at her reverence for the "art" of photography. Not that she claimed to be an artist, of course, but she had an awestruck admiration for those who were. Duncan found it adorable in the same way he found her photographs adorable. But that was good, right? She didn't need him to think she was a genius. As long as he respected her, which he did, didn't he?

Anyway, he'd finally picked a date, they were getting married, and that was that. Pete would grow to appreciate Duncan's good qualities, as well as the amazing Manhattan lifestyle they were about to adopt—think of the schools, the museums, the culture—and he'd forget all about a goofy dog named Hagrid and the kind, pulse-poundingly handsome fireman he'd befriended.

Uninvited, thoughts of Kirk came flooding back. Not just the kiss, but everything he'd told her in the plug buggy. His bout with cancer. His refusal to be a burden on a girlfriend. Maybe he thought that was heroic, but it made her angry all over again. Damn it, someone like Kirk, someone strong and thoughtful, someone who spent his life watching out for other people, running into fires, helping out little boys, taking care of abandoned dogs . . . someone like Kirk ought to have a woman standing by him. Babying him. Loving him. Making love to him . . .

She groaned and went to take a shower. Duncan better get here soon.

Chapter Five

Kirk's only question about what had happened at the warehouse was: How badly had he screwed up? Maribel had snagged Pete and run out of there so fast, he'd barely had a chance to scribble his number on a piece of paper and hand it to the kid. But maybe the deal was off now anyway; no phone call so far, and it had been two days.

Worried about Hagrid, he'd gone out to the warehouse alone with a can of Science Diet, tossed a stick for the pup until they both got bored, then scratched his ears and said goodbye.

But not before he'd shared a few secrets with the dog, who made a comfortable, floppy-eared confidant. "She liked that kiss as much as I did, you know. And she kissed me first. Sure, it was a little peck on the jaw, but when she put her lips on me, I couldn't think straight anymore. Can you blame me? Well, *she* might blame me. Then again, I think she was mad at herself more than me. She's not the type of woman who would cheat on her fiancé. She's probably beating herself up. Catastrophizing." He smiled at Hagrid, who cocked his head, apparently following the one-sided conversation perfectly well. Or else wondering when Kirk would break out the next snack.

"I'm just not sure what to do next. Ryan would probably say, 'Ask her to dinner.' But that would make it worse, wouldn't it? Then she might think that I thought she was the type of woman who would two-time her fiancé. You know what I mean?"

Hagrid laid his head on his paws. Kirk stroked his soft ears until his tail thumped happily.

"It's tricky. And it makes it worse that it's her. Because I don't want to make a wrong move. Freak her out. Even more than she already is, I mean. Damn. Maybe I'll see what the guys think."

Even Hagrid seemed to think that was a terrible idea, judging by the snuffling noise he made as Kirk scratched the notch between his shoulder blades.

"I know. Bad idea. Not happening anyway."

What could he do, besides hope that Pete would give him a call soon? He surged to his feet, so frustrated he tossed the empty tin of dog food in the garbage can with enough force to make it ring like a bell of doom. God, how pathetic could a man get, waiting for a call from a nine-year-old boy? Why had he made that offer anyway? All it guaranteed was time with Pete, not Maribel. He felt like a man wandering the streets, pressing his face against the window of a cozy home for a glimpse of the happiness inside.

Pete was going to be someone else's stepson. Maribel was going to be someone else's wife. He was going to move to freaking Alaska. And Hagrid? He'd make a few calls, see what he could drum up.

In the meantime it would probably be best for them all if his number got irretrievably lost in the chaotic jumble that lived inside Pete's pockets.

But it didn't. The next day, Maribel called. Actually, the next evening. Kirk was playing pool when his cell phone rang and ruined his bank shot into the corner pocket.

"Yeah," he answered abruptly, not bothering to check the number.

"Is this Kirk?" The sound of her soft voice made him straighten up, knocking the chalk off the side of the table.

"Yes. Sorry." He swung around so the guys couldn't hear him. "Maribel?"

"Wow! Good guess."

Right. As if he wouldn't know her voice anywhere.

"I . . . uh . . . have kind of a strange favor to ask. My babysitter canceled and I've been calling around everywhere, but no luck. Pete came up with the idea of hanging out with you tonight. I told him you were probably already busy, or else working, but I promised him I'd check. So this is me, checking. Please don't be offended that I even asked; it was Pete's idea and he gave me your number, and . . ."

"Sure."

"Really?" The delight in her voice sent blood rushing to his head. "You're free?"

"Well, I'll be home soon. Say, ten minutes?"

"Oh my God, you're a lifesaver. I can . . . maybe I can bring you some cookies or something? Fudge brownies?"

"Don't worry about that. You can set me up with some more ornaments next Christmas, how's that?" Kirk winced. His family would stage a revolt if any more ornaments came their way. He'd have to find a worthy charity.

"Done! For the next five Christmases, if you like. I always have a lot left over."

Kirk gave her his address, then handed off his pool cue to Vader. Of course nothing was that easy; as soon as he explained, the teasing followed him right out the door.

"Thor, you wuss. Who are you, Mary Poppins?" Ryan winked. "Bet you're after that spoonful of sugar."

"Adventures in babysitting, dude. Adventures in babysitting," said Vader cryptically.

"My sister watched that movie about a hundred times," said Fred the Stud with deep nostalgia.

"I saw that one," said Ryan. "Elizabeth Shue was cute in it. Damn, I just remembered . . . the bratty kid in that movie liked Thor. Wore a helmet and everything."

"Thor the Babysitter. Never thought I'd see the day." Vader shook his head.

Kirk managed to escape without bloodying anyone's nose, which he considered a personal triumph. He cruised home on his bike, barely making it ahead of the battered old Volvo containing Maribel and Pete.

The thrill of Maribel at his front door, of his porch light striking copper starbursts in her glorious hair, of her apple-blossom fragrance drifting inside his living room, gave him a high that ended only when Pete explained, gloomily, that Duncan was in town and Maribel wanted some time alone with him.

At that point, Kirk figured he deserved every scrap of ribbing the guys could dish out—and then some.

Maribel rushed home, where Duncan was still finishing up a phone call. He didn't even look up when she burst into the house. "Ready!"

"Who'd you find?" Duncan asked vaguely, though Maribel knew he didn't really care and wouldn't remember the answer if she told him. Maybe the news that a handsome fireman was looking after Pete would make him sit up and take notice, but probably not. If Duncan was jealous of other men, he'd never shown it during six years of a long-distance relationship.

"Just a friend." A friend who'd kissed the sense out of her, but no need to go there.

Their dinner date was not what Maribel had hoped for. Duncan's phone call had put him in a bad mood. Maribel knew the signs. Prolonged silences, preoccupied glances, sudden bursts of animated ranting. Moments of great charm directed at the waitresses alternating with sullen monologues about why the West Coast scene was entirely inferior to New York's. There was no point in debate; Maribel knew her role. Listen sympathetically, offer unquestioning support, be the haven he saw her as.

The thing was, she didn't feel like a "haven." She had things on her mind. Pete, for one. When Duncan's flow of complaints seemed to be easing, she grabbed the opportunity. "Have you thought about what you want to do with Pete while you're here?"

"Huh?" He looked at her blankly, almost as if he'd forgotten she knew how to speak.

"You know, some Pete-and-Duncan alone time. To give you two a chance to bond."

"Oh." He waved his fork, on which perched a chunk of baked Brie. "I don't think that's going to happen this trip, baby. Next time."

"What? Why not?"

"Haven't you been listening? The Chicksie Dicks are freaking out. They want a reshoot."

The Chicksie Dicks? That didn't sound right. She really had been zoning out while Duncan vented. She wanted to ask if the Chicksie Dicks were a real group or if he was making fun of the Dixie Chicks, but now she didn't dare. He'd never forgive her if he knew she didn't hang on his every word.

"But Duncan, you keep talking about being Pete's stepfather. You want us to be a family."

"Of course I do."

"Shouldn't you get to know him better?"

"What's to know? He's a nine-year-old boy. I was nine once. I know what it was like. It sucked. If someone had come along and offered me backstage passes to the Beastie Boys, I'd have been his slave for life."

"But Pete's not that into music. He likes to read. He's got a great imagination. You should hear some of the things he makes up. He's convinced an owl will show up when he's eleven with an invitation to Hogwarts. He's even written his own novel—well, started it. But he's two chapters in and it's fantastic . . ."

But Duncan's phone had buzzed; a text had come in. He immediately began scrolling through the message and cursing. Maribel wanted to scream with frustration. His distraction had never bothered her until now. It hadn't really mattered because their lives were so separate. But if they really were going to become a family, it did matter. She couldn't let this slide. She waited until he finished his reply text, watching the top of his sandy brown head as he hunched over his phone. Duncan was good-looking in a bland, prep-school sort of way. He'd grown up in the suburbs of New Jersey with the sole dream of breaking into the Manhattan hip crowd. He'd done it too, and wore the black jeans and horn-rimmed glasses to prove it.

She'd assumed the fact that he'd chosen her, someone with no social connections or any kind of status in his world, meant he wasn't really the snob he appeared to be. But was that really true? Why did he want her?

"Duncan," she said, when he'd finished his text. "Why do you think we should get married? I mean, things are good the way they are, right? We do okay, for a long-distance relationship. We're both busy with our careers. I've got Pete, you don't really want more kids." This gave her a secret pang. Pete would love a sibling. She forged ahead. "Why mess with a good thing?"

Duncan dragged his gaze from his phone. "What?"

"Did you hear any of that? Do I need to repeat the whole thing?"

"Sorry, baby. You know how it is." God, his phone seemed to have a gravitational pull stronger than Jupiter's. It was winning again; she was losing his attention.

She kept it short and sweet this time. "Why do you want to get married?"

"What?" He frowned behind his horn-rims. "I told you. Because you're my haven."

"Okay, but . . . do you think you could elaborate just a little? How am I a haven?" And how was that not like being compared to a retirement home? *Ooooh.* She drew in a breath. Was that it? Did Duncan see being with her as the equivalent of an emotional retirement from the Manhattan dating scene?

"It means"—he shot an angry glance at his phone, where apparently things were not going well—"you're not needy and demanding. You let me do my thing without wanting to take over my life. And usually you don't irritate me. But right now . . . Jesus, Mari, do you think you could back off?"

She flinched back in her chair in shock. In six years, Duncan had never spoken to her like this. They'd always had a romantic, swoony kind of relationship, full of endearments and sappy little e-mails and kissy-faces over Skype. He'd swept her off her feet with expensive dinners at the Ivy and weekend getaways to Santa Barbara. He found her amusing and adorable, and never got impatient with her occasional dreamy fogginess—her creative mode—which drove most people crazy. But he understood, because he was an artist too, right?

"Duncan, I'm not trying to annoy you. I'm just concerned about my son. I want to make sure we're on the same page."

"I highly doubt that," he said brusquely. "Fortunately for him. But seriously, Mari, your timing

sucks. I can't deal with this crap now. I've got a su-
perstar rock group imploding on me, and you're
bugging me about . . . what, again? I don't even
know. Can we just finish dinner so I can get back
and take care of this mess?"

Fury such as she had never known swept Maribel to her feet. "Consider it finished." She threw
her car keys on the table. "I'll grab a cab."

"Mari, chill out. For God's sake."

She ignored him and made for the exit, afraid
she'd throw his Portuguese bouillabaisse in his
face if she stuck around any longer. She could put
up with a lot—she did put up with a lot, probably
too much, but that was another story—but she absolutely would not put up with someone dismiss-
ing Pete in such a callous way. It wasn't in her; she
couldn't do it. Even for Duncan, who she . . .

But *did* she love him?

Luckily, a cab was just dropping someone off in
front of the restaurant. She snagged it and gave the
driver Kirk's address. She spent the drive fuming
over Duncan's attitude. How could she marry
him? How could she marry a man who thought
Pete was just like any other little boy, that they
were all the same, not worth the trouble of getting
to know individually? The need to be with her
son, her precious, one of a kind son, beat through
her veins like a bongo drum.

Kirk opened the door with a finger to his lips.
Barefoot, he wore drawstring workout pants and
nothing else. His chest was a muscular blur in the

dimmed light of his living room. "He fell asleep during *Hannah Montana*," he mouthed.

"*Hannah Montana?!*"

"I knew he'd think it was boring and I figured he needed some sleep."

"How'd you know?"

"What?"

"How'd you know he wouldn't like it?" She edged past him to check on Pete, who was sprawled on Kirk's blue-plaid sofa, his mouth open, eyes shut tight. With one part of her mind, she took note of Kirk's bachelor décor. With another, she realized Pete must really trust Kirk to fall asleep so deeply on his couch. But most of her mind was taken up with one all-consuming question. "Is it because all nine-year-old boys are the same?"

"What?" Kirk looked nervous. He ran his hand over the back of his neck, a gesture she'd seen him make before. "Of course not."

"Prove it."

"Excuse me?"

"What, am I being too demanding? Prove it!"

"Huh?" Poor Kirk seemed truly bewildered, and she couldn't blame him. She was bewildered herself. None of this had anything to do with Kirk. But for some reason she found it a lot easier to yell at him than at Duncan.

"Tell me why my son, Pete Boone, wouldn't enjoy an episode of *Hannah Montana*."

"Well," said Kirk slowly, as though drawing

out each word in the hopes she'd calm down. "As you know, I'm sure, Pete's not really into music or TV or singing, which is what *Hannah Montana* is about. He's more into fantasy and magic-type stuff. He wanted to work on his book but he'd left it behind. He told me the plot. At length. Pretty cool, what I can remember."

She felt tears well in her eyes. In all the times Pete had told her the plot of his book, she rarely remembered the details either. They seemed to change too. It was a work in progress, as was her occasionally temperamental, sometimes fierce, always wonderful son.

"I'm done with Duncan," she said, almost choking on the words. "He doesn't deserve to be in Pete's life. And he can't have me without Pete, can he?"

Kirk went very still. Now that her eyes had adjusted to the light, she couldn't help staring at his bare chest. It was spectacular, though it looked as though a shark had taken three bites out of his torso. The wounds had scarred over, but they didn't affect his magnificence anyway. It was as if Michelangelo had returned to chisel a flesh-and-blood work of art. Ripped muscles ran in a syncopated pattern from the waistband of his pants to his taut shoulders. In the center of his chest, a light covering of blond fur begged to be petted.

"Sorry," Kirk said, pulling on a T-shirt. "When he fell asleep, I decided to work out for a bit. I'm still trying to get my strength back."

"That's okay," she said in a strangled voice. "It's fine with me."

"So you were saying, about Duncan."

Who? she almost asked. Then the temporary daze created by his bare chest wore off, and the memory came flooding back. "He thinks all nine-year-olds are alike. And he thinks I'm a haven. Translation: I'm supposed to shut up and not bother him."

"Are you sure about that?" Kirk gestured for her to follow him into the kitchen so they wouldn't wake Pete up.

She waited until they'd reached the cozy kitchen and he was pouring her a glass of water from the faucet. "You weren't there, watching him with his Brie and his bouillabaisse and his stupid phone."

"It's just that . . . never mind."

"What? Are you taking his side? What is it with you men? Maybe *you're* all alike!" She put down the glass of water with a click, the liquid sloshing onto the table.

"The word 'haven' doesn't sound like an insult, that's all."

"Forget it." She turned away, intent on collecting Pete and getting the hell out. Of course he didn't understand. Why should he? Just because he was nice to Pete and cared about dogs didn't mean he knew anything about her. Or cared, for that matter. "I'd better go."

"The hell with that," she heard him mutter

through her blur of frustrated tears. Then strong arms came around her. Her feet were lifted off the ground. She was being held tight against a hot male chest.

Chapter Six

It was the wrong move. Of course it was. He was supposed to be showing her how much he respected her, not mauling her the second she dumped her fiancé. But she felt so good in his arms, a bundle of warm, sexy, tender woman. And the fact that she hadn't even blinked at the sight of his scars made him want her even more.

"Kirk!" She gaped at him, but she didn't look like she minded.

He stared down at her hazel eyes, noticing the way the gold-flecked irises had nearly disappeared as her pupils went wide and dark. "You're so beautiful," he said in a whisper.

Oddly, that statement seemed to confuse her. "You think I'm beautiful?"

"Why do you think I can never put two words together when I'm around you?"

Her mouth fell open, and that was that. He couldn't resist a second longer. Lowering his head, he brushed his lips against hers, savoring the incredible softness of her mouth. It wasn't a kiss so much as a question, tender and tentative. Her lips tasted so sweet—was that coconut? What had she been eating at dinner with Duncan? The reminder of Duncan made him draw back. This was stupid. Asking for trouble. What if they'd just had an ordinary fight and would be back to normal by tomorrow?

Then she wrapped her arms around his neck and all regrets were obliterated. She grabbed him with passionate enthusiasm and suddenly her mouth was on his, hot and eager. This one wasn't a kiss so much as a statement. *I want you. I will have you.* He kissed her deeply, completely, irrevocably. Unable to get enough of her, he explored her mouth with his tongue: the slippery hardness of teeth, the pointed tip of her tongue, the delicious slickness of the roof of her mouth. She slipped out of his arms and pressed her entire body against him. He gripped her head in both his hands, tilting it to dive deep, to take her into him like air into lungs.

Then the rest of her body called to him, and he slid his hands down her sides, brushing the slight swell of her breasts crushed against him. He felt her shudder and nearly came in his workout pants. Speaking of which, she must be feeling every bit of his fierce erection pressed against her pelvis. All of a sudden he felt too exposed. All this time he'd hidden his longing for her. But you couldn't hide a boner the size of a tire iron behind a thin layer of cotton.

Not that she seemed to mind. She pushed her hips closer to him—*oh God!*—and made a moaning sound.

He got even harder and fought not to embarrass himself by coming all over her like a teenager under the bleachers. "Maribel," he forced himself to say, "I don't know about this."

"Why not?" Her breath was coming in quick, jagged gasps, and her glorious hair tumbled around her head like a halo of sunset. She looked like a fallen angel. "If you're worried about Pete, forget it. It practically takes a fire alarm to wake him up. You want me. I can tell."

He snorted, then groaned as the motion pushed his cock against the soft gap between her legs. "You think?"

Her eyes closed halfway, as if desire was dragging her eyelids down. "I want you too," she said, like a siren crooning to her next victim. "You can probably tell."

She put his hand on her breast and he wanted to weep, she felt so tempting. He caressed her soft, round apple of a breast, her aroused nipple nudging through her clothes. She was wearing a silky-looking dress with one of those peasant-type necklines, like a country wench in a tavern. It was held up by a ribbon tied in a bow right at the front, and lord help him, there was no possible way he could resist a gift-wrapped Maribel. His hand shaking slightly, he pulled the end of the bow and drew down her top so her breasts peeked out from a satiny, creamy nest of a bra. Her skin was one shade darker, more pink, than the bra, and a thousand times silkier. He drew his finger reverently across the rise of her breasts and into the dip between.

She gasped and leaned her upper half toward him. Color came and went in her cheeks. The knowledge that he was turning her on went to his head like a shot of vodka. He moved his hand to cup her breast, pulling down the edge of her bra with his thumb. Her nipple seemed to leap into his hand as if it belonged there, as if that velvety morsel was created to be touched by him. It swelled deliciously hard, begging for more attention.

He bent down, put his hands on her curvy ass, and picked her up, depositing her on the kitchen table.

"Oh!" she said, her mouth open in a shocked oval of surprise.

"You have no idea what you do to me," he muttered as he bent to her breasts, which were somehow, miraculously, both exposed now. Had he done that? Maybe he possessed magical powers of undressing women he wanted, women he . . . well, *loved*. No getting around it.

He gorged himself on her breasts as if they were snow cones on a hot day. Helped himself to her nipples as if they were chocolate-covered cherries. She threw her head back and let his hands roam at will, welcomed his ravaging tongue, writhed under the long sucklings of his mouth.

"That . . . feels . . . so incredible . . ." she panted. "Is there somewhere . . . else . . . ?"

He knew what she was trying to ask. They could go only so far on the kitchen table. Pete might be a sound sleeper, but then again, what if a fire alarm did go off? Catching his mother and his friendly neighborhood fireman screwing on the kitchen table might cause all kinds of nightmares.

His bedroom was just down the hall. It had a door. They could put something under the knob so no one could open it, so that if Pete woke up and wandered around looking for them, they'd have enough time to get decent before explaining that Kirk had been showing off his collection of . . .

A cold wave of sanity hit him. He couldn't let her inside his bedroom. Kirk closed his eyes, battling the drumbeat of lust and the throbbing of his cock. He'd started this, in a moment of sheer, panicked refusal to see her walk out of his kitchen. But if they didn't stop now, they'd end up in bed, and as much as he wanted that, she'd probably regret it quicker than a cat in a bathtub. He called upon all his higher angels, every speck of moral fiber, every ounce of the endurance he'd honed during chemotherapy.

And he firmly put her aside.

"Maribel." He gritted his teeth. "We can't do this. What about . . ." He cast around for something to throw cold water on the moment. "Duncan?"

"Duncan's a dick." She looked shocked at her

words and clapped a hand over her mouth. "I didn't mean to say that." But his mention of her fiancé had done its intended job.

"Dick or not, he's probably waiting for you. Maybe he wants to apologize."

"He's probably sulking because I ditched him." She wrenched herself off the table and stalked around the kitchen, wringing her hands. "He sulks. He doesn't appreciate my son. He assumes I'm going to move to New York and stay home and be his haven."

Kirk prayed for the right words. The name Duncan, fortunately, had worked like magic on his erection. Time to start thinking with his head. The real one. "You don't want to move to New York?"

"No, I do. I think. I mean, I did. Oh fudge! What am I doing?" She squeezed her hands together in apparent agony.

"It's my fault. Don't blame yourself."

She cast him a skeptical glance. "Don't you dare let me off the hook here. I would have had sex with you on the kitchen floor."

Arousal pulsed again through his cock. *Focus, man, focus. Even if it hurts like a motherfucker.* He braced himself. "Do you love Duncan?"

Her face went flaming red. "I'm the wrong person to ask."

He let out a surprised snort of laughter. "Who else would know?"

"What I mean is, I'm not a big fan of love. I

thought I loved Pete's father because his hair flopped over his forehead when he played the drums. It's important to know your flaws and shortcomings, right? I make bad decisions about men. I realize that. So I have to make decisions based on what's best for Pete."

He supposed that made sense, in an odd sort of way. And a tiny tendril of hope awoke in his heart. *She hadn't said that she loved Duncan.* "Okay, I can buy that. You're a single mother; you have to watch out for your son. So what is best for Pete?"

"Well, moving to New York, of course." She frowned, giving him the impression she was trying to convince herself. "It's the greatest city in the world, after all. All the writers live there, and he loves to write. Publishers too. He'd get a much better education, especially because Duncan wants to send him to private school. Probably so he can make connections with famous people's kids, but even so. It's a great opportunity for Pete . . ." She trailed off.

"And what about you?" He made himself ask the question. "Are you excited about the move?"

"Sure!"

Maybe it was his imagination, but her cheerfulness seemed forced. And were her knuckles turning white as she gripped the edge of the kitchen counter behind her back? He felt bad, pushing her like this, interrogating her, but something told him she hadn't asked herself the tough questions. He waited patiently for her to continue.

"I'm ready for new horizons. San Gabriel's been wonderful, but I can't work at the Lazy Daisy forever, and it's not as if my photography career is taking off. I think I've sufficiently documented the jacarandas around here. Maybe it's time for subway tunnels and neon billboards." She looked forlornly around his kitchen, like a kitten caught in a storm. Suddenly she went still. Kirk followed her gaze. *Oops.*

Maribel stared at the abstract study of a yucca plant in bloom. The spiky red flowers looked like ominous red-painted claws. The long rays of the late-afternoon sun made every bulbous thorn stand out in horror-movie relief. It wasn't the most warm and fuzzy photo she'd ever taken. She'd been in a funk at the time. But here it was, framed and hung in Kirk's kitchen, right over a wall-mounted magnetic strip that held his kitchen knives.

Her eyes drifted to the hallway outside the kitchen. She could just make out the edge of a frame. Tilting her body to the left, she took in the sight of one of her pretentious black-and-white portraits of Mrs. Gund in her hairnet. Her boss stared sternly at the camera from the Lazy Daisy grill. Mrs. G. had actually paid her to take the photographs. They both knew it to be a mercy commission: Maribel had been facing some daunting medical bills after Pete had fallen off the roof during an unauthorized attempt to see if he could play Quidditch with the kitchen broom. Mrs. Gund had loved the photos and proudly displayed them in the coffee shop, but Maribel thought they were embarrassingly clichéd. Then, one by one, they'd been purchased.

Now here was one of them . . . no, two, she realized as she paced toward the hallway door. Three. Four. Five. All five. Except for the one Mrs. Gund had kept for herself. Five portraits of Mrs. Gund's impassive Norwegian face framed against various coffee-shop backdrops. The menu board. The coffee maker. The long counter. And so forth. The entire series—perhaps the low point of her creative learning curve—paraded down Kirk's hallway.

"You were the one who bought my Mrs. Gund photos," Maribel said numbly.

"Yes."

"Why? You can't possibly like them."

"Why not?"

"No one could. Except Mrs. Gund. Which I never understood, by the way."

She dared a look at Kirk. He was rubbing the back of his neck in what she now knew was a signal of discomfort. His intent, lustful look was gone, replaced by an awkward shifting of his eyes.

"I like them. Why else would I buy them? I like all your work."

Suddenly struck by a thought, Maribel dashed out of the kitchen.

"Wait," called Kirk, but she ignored him. She ran down the hall toward the open doorway at the end. Maybe it was rude to barge through someone's house like this. But she had to know.

Sure enough, there in his tidy blue-plaid bedroom, near the punching bag that swung from the ceiling, hung another of her photographs. At least she was proud of this one. A flash flood had crashed through the desert outside San Gabriel one rainy January, and she'd gotten an amazing shot of a drenched sparrow taking refuge on a cactus, clinging to the thorns with frantic little feet.

It wasn't the only work of art gracing Kirk's bedroom, but it was the most prominent. He also had a dreamy Irish landscape with two horses and a poster advertising the Rugby World Cup. Really, his décor was sad. From the bedside table came the low murmur of a police scanner.

"How come you never told me you were a fan of my photography?" she asked without turning, knowing he was right behind her.

"I did."

"When, right between 'coffee' and 'black'?"

"I always buy your Christmas ornaments."

"That's different. Those are goofy little craft items I make for extra cash. This is my *art*." Duncan always laughed at her when she referred to her passion as art, but what the hell, Duncan wasn't here right now.

Kirk was looking slightly panicked. "Should we go check on Pete?"

"Forget about Pete. He's fine." Maybe she

sounded like a heartless mother, but she knew her son. He'd probably sleep through a collision with an asteroid, then be really bummed that he'd missed it. "Wait! I know! You're just storing these here because Mrs. Gund ran out of room. It's not like you actually bought them all."

But Kirk raised reluctant, silver-smoked eyes to meet hers. "No. I bought them."

"But that's . . ." She tallied up the photographs she'd seen so far, added in the cost of framing, and flinched. "A lot of money."

"Over the years, maybe. It's not like I liquidated my savings or anything."

"Did you do it to help me out? Did I seem that desperate? The clichéd struggling single mom trying to make ends meet on a wing and a prayer?"

"That's not fair." He looked so hurt she instantly felt bad.

"You can't possibly like all those pieces. The sparrow, I'll give you that one. It's one of my better efforts. But you can't convince me you always dreamed of having five portraits of an expressionless Norwegian coffee-shop owner filling your hallway."

His eyes darted around the room, as if looking desperately for escape. It occurred to her that she wouldn't get far in her career if she was this hard on everyone who bought one of her pieces. But . . . one, she could understand. Seven?

"Do you have others?"

"No. This is it."

She took a step back and folded her arms across her chest. "Do you think these will be worth something someday? I hate to break it to you, but the chances of that are very, very minuscule."

"They're worth something now." He flushed in a rather endearing way. "To me, anyway."

"Why?"

"Because . . . because they're . . . you. You made them. That's worth something."

She shook her head with disbelief. "You felt sorry for me. You knew I needed money. They were mercy purchases."

"No! *Damn!*"

He turned away and slammed a fist against the punching bag that hung in the corner. It spun away in a blur of red leather. When it swung back toward him, he sent it whirling again with another roundhouse punch. After a minute of this, a minute during which she berated herself for upsetting her one and only collector, he deliberately stopped the bag and turned to face her.

"Okay, I knew it would help you out, but that's not the only reason. I like looking at your photographs. I like the way you see things. I'm a fan. That's all."

"That's all?" It felt like something was missing, but the hell if she knew what. She frowned, oddly disappointed, and shrugged. "Okay, I guess. I'm flattered. To the best of my knowledge, you're my only fan. So, thanks."

He gave her a frazzled glance, like a drowning man watching the last lifeboat disappear. She took a step toward the door, more than ready to end this awkward scene.

"Wait! That's *not* all." There went his hand to the back of his neck again. "For God's sake, Maribel, don't you get it? I love your art. I love everything about you. I love *you*."

Chapter Seven

"*What?*"

Now that Kirk's silent-type shell had cracked, he kept talking, as if he couldn't stop himself.

"I've loved you forever, it feels like. Since I don't know when. Early on. Why do you think we always come to the Lazy Daisy? But I couldn't have you. You were with someone. At first I figured it was a crush and it would go away. But it hasn't. I still feel it, more than ever."

She shook her head, trying to clear it, unable to grasp what he was saying. "That's why you bought my photographs?"

"I like them. I wanted to support your career because . . . I think you're really good. That's just my opinion, and I know I'm not an expert."

He looked so wretched, she couldn't stand it. "It's okay. I'm glad. I mean . . . I'm glad they're here." She gave one last wild glance around the bedroom. She thought about Duncan waiting at home, and what she'd almost done here, with Kirk. Who said he loved her.

But she couldn't think about that now. Couldn't take it in. "I have to go." In the living room, she scooped Pete up, barely managed a stammered goodbye, and fled. Thankfully, her son slept through the short wait for the cab, insertion into the cab, and the drive home, which gave her lots of time to lose herself in her windmilling thoughts.

For the last six years, she hadn't spent time with any man other than Duncan. Being with Kirk wasn't anything like being with Duncan. Kirk made her feel more—how to pin it down?— *interesting*. Duncan claimed to find her adorable and enchanting, not to mention his haven, but he tended to glaze over when she talked. This had never bothered her. He was a celebrity photographer, after all, and she was a teenage mom turned waitress turned amateur shutterbug. But now that they were really, as opposed to hypothetically, getting married, big alarm bells were going off right and left.

Duncan didn't inspire any sort of urge to have sex on a kitchen table. Duncan hadn't ever spent one dime on any of her photographs. Duncan didn't look at her as if he never wanted to stop. He didn't listen to her much at all. He'd certainly been in no hurry to get married; in fact, she still didn't know why he'd suddenly decided the time had come. Surely a free weekend in the Hamptons wasn't enough of a reason.

As the driver waited at a stoplight, she watched

his digital clock change to midnight. She never stayed up this late, yet she was wide awake, as if she'd stuck her hand in a socket and every nerve had been jolted awake. And she knew it was because of Kirk. His kisses, his touch, his strength . . . his shocking declaration.

Don't think about that. It was too much to grasp. All this time, Kirk had been in love with her? How could she not have known? *Since I don't know when,* he'd said. A secret warmth filtered through her as she thought of all the times Kirk had come into the coffee shop. She'd always looked for him, been extra aware of him, felt a special zing when their hands brushed over a to-go cup and some change. She'd admitted to herself that she found him attractive, that she had a crush. But she'd never allowed herself to follow up on the idea. She was *engaged*. To a man who could have anyone but who wanted her. Her awe at Duncan's presence in her life had blinded her to everything else.

When the cab reached her house, she paid the driver and roused Pete enough so he could make it inside on his own two feet. He made a good zombie; she could probably make him brush his teeth, change into pajamas, and maybe even do some homework without him remembering a thing the next day. But her car was in the driveway and her bedroom lights were on, so she told Pete to go crawl into bed.

Confrontation with Duncan was at hand.

She heaved a sigh as she guided Pete toward his room. Oddly, she didn't feel guilty about anything that had happened with Kirk. She probably ought to, and she gave it a good effort, but it went nowhere. Kirk was . . . he was . . . he was magic. He made her feel like Wonder Woman and Greta Garbo combined. He made her feel alive and desired and appreciated. Was that selfish? Maybe it was.

Maybe it was time to get a little selfish.

Duncan was waiting in her bed, working on his laptop. His silk striped pajama top was open at the neck, showing off the sunburn he always got when he came to San Gabriel. His mouth had a sullen cast to it, but as soon as he looked at her over the rims of his glasses, he shifted. He must have seen something unfamiliar in her expression, because he set aside the laptop and patted her side of the bed.

"I'm sorry I upset you," he said. "Can we give our little convo another chance, now that I'm not so distracted?"

"Our little convo?" She stayed in the doorway, unwilling to get any closer to him.

"You wanted to know why I thought we should get married."

"Right." Truthfully, other concerns had taken over by now, but that one still loomed.

"The thing is, I feel different when I'm with you, Mari. I don't have to prove anything. It's comfortable. Homey."

"Homey?"

Duncan shoved his glasses back up his face, looking uncharacteristically awkward. "That sounded all wrong. What I mean to say is, I want to come home to you. I've been giving all my attention to my career and only a tiny bit to you. Look at the way I was at dinner. I barely heard what you were saying; you were like an irritating buzz in my ear. I'm not proud of that, Maribel. If we get married, it won't be like that anymore. Don't you want to save me from being a hopeless workaholic?"

His usually charming smile fell flat. "So that's why you need me? To keep buzzing in your ear until you stop working?"

"Maribel. Don't be harsh. That's not you. You're always so lovely and soft; that's what I love about you."

"Duncan." Her abruptness took both of them by surprise; she even jumped a bit. "What do you think of my work?"

He blinked behind his horn-rims, like a blond, bland owl. "Your work?"

"Not my waitressing skills. My photography. What do you think, really? Your honest opinion."

"Not bad, if you like that sort of thing," he answered promptly. "Pretty good, in fact. Not my cup of tea, but I'm not ashamed to be marrying the creator." He offered a conspiratorial smile.

Not ashamed . . . hadn't she read about this in a psychology book? If he came up with the word "ashamed," then he was ashamed, no matter what he said. Or had been. Maybe he'd convinced himself he wasn't.

"Define 'that sort of thing.' "

"Excuse me?"

"That sort of thing. The sort you don't like but maybe other people do. What sort of thing? Come on, Dunc, it's not difficult."

"What's gotten into you, baby? You're not usually like this. And where did you go when you stormed out of the restaurant like that? I've been waiting for hours."

"Diversion tactic."

"What?"

Never had she been so grateful for her obsession with parenting books. Not that she'd ever imagined she'd be using her knowledge on Duncan.

"I'm not falling for your diversionary tactics. What sort of thing is it that I create?"

"Sweetie, it's not such a big deal. I like photographing people. You like nature. I find nature clichéd. But did you ever think it might be a good thing we're not in the same field? We're not competing against each other." He laughed, as if the entire idea of the two of them competing was, well, laughable.

She turned away, mostly to avoid throwing something at his smug face. Instantly he was out of the bed and striding to her side. He put his hands on her shoulders just the way Kirk had, but the shivers Duncan inspired felt more like spiders skittering up and down her arms. Time was, he'd been like a meteor streaking through her life at unpredictable moments. Where was all that dazzled, starstruck awe he used to inspire?

"Come on, baby, let's table this for tonight. I love you. I want to marry you. Still do, even though you walked out on a fabulous raspberry terrine."

"You stayed for dessert?"

"Ran into an old Exeter friend of mine. We hung out for a while and caught up on old times. What was I supposed to do? Crawl home and hide under the blankets? Watch Lifetime and gorge myself on Haagen-Dazs?"

She pushed his hands away. The very sight of him, sandy-haired and self-satisfied, his mouth quirked to produce his supposedly witty quip, made her gag. "I'm going to check on Pete."

"Honey, we can get through this. After six years together, we can get through anything. Right?"

But as she gazed at the sleeping lump of her son, she wondered if they'd ever really been "together." He was never around when she really needed someone, and she'd never asked him to be. He'd been more of a glamorous god occasionally descending into her life. Never a partner or a helpmate.

Was that a basis for a marriage?

But the next morning, after a restless night sleeping next to Duncan, who kept trying to throw his leg over her thigh, she knew she wasn't ready to take any drastic steps. She needed to think things through before she made any irrevocable decisions.

Around nine, while she was making banana pancake batter, her phone rang. Electric thrills ran through her at the sight of Kirk's number. Duncan, still in his silk pajamas, was immersed in a new series of text messages and barely noticed when she answered, breathlessly, "Hello?"

"Maribel, it's Kirk." His voice, deep and resonant, brought to mind a quiet wind rustling pines in the forest. Her heart felt as if it would burst out of her throat, it was pounding so hard.

"How are you?"

"Embarrassed. Apologetic."

"No need. Really." She shot Duncan a surreptitious look, but he was muttering furiously at his iPhone. "I'm the one who should be."

"I . . . uh . . ." He cleared his throat. "I wanted to let Pete know that I've located Gonzalez, Hagrid's former owner. He's in Colorado. I sent him an e-mail letting him know we found Hagrid, though I remembered his name used to be Z-boy. Short for Zeus."

"Zeus? Like the god Zeus?"

Duncan looked up, raising an eyebrow in curiosity.

"Yep. No idea why. Not sure why I forgot either, because the guys at the firehouse call me Thor, and Gonzalez always got a kick out of that. At any rate, I'll let Pete know as soon as I hear anything. For all we know, Gonzalez lost track of the dog and wants him back."

"Oh, that would be wonderful! I mean, if he

could be reunited with his real owner. Even Pete would be okay with that." Pete was in his room, staging his usual late appearance at breakfast when Duncan was visiting.

"It seemed like a good solution all around."

"Thank you so much. I really appreciate it. Pete's gotten so attached to him in such a short amount of time." She bit her lip. Hagrid wasn't the only one Pete had gotten attached to.

"Maribel . . . wait, don't hang up. I've been beating myself up all night over the things I said."

"This isn't . . ." Feeling her face heat, she glanced at Duncan, who, mercifully, seemed oblivious to her embarrassment. "Wait, you're saying you didn't mean those things?"

"Oh, I meant them. Every word. And then some. But I didn't mean to dump all that on you. You have enough to worry about."

"Oh."

He was doing it again, trying to spare other people the trouble of . . . what? Worrying about him? Caring about him? But she couldn't say all that, not with Duncan sitting right there in his tan-and-white—sorry, fawn-and-mint—striped silk.

"So don't feel awkward next time I come into the coffee shop, okay?"

"I won't. But . . ." She trailed off, hating the fact that she couldn't speak freely. Words choked in her throat like debris piling up at a dam.

"And don't feel funny about the photos. I think they're a good investment."

She murmured, "If you like that sort of thing." Duncan looked up sharply.

"So we okay?"

"Of course." She hung up numbly. Even the phone felt funny in her hands, as if the sensation of it was muffled. Duncan's voice seemed to come from some other planet.

"Who was that?"

"Oh, just a friend."

With a sidelong glance, she noticed the suspicious furrow between his eyebrows.

"Of Pete's."

"A friend of Pete's?"

"Well, of both of us. There's this dog, and Pete's really worried about him, and this fireman is helping find the owner, and . . ." But Duncan had apparently heard enough to realize he wasn't really that interested. He waved a hand and went back to his texting.

"I'm going to let Pete know the pancakes will be ready soon."

"Mmmhh."

She knocked on Pete's door, then went inside. Pete was, as usual, sprawled facedown on the floor, chewing on the end of his pen, his notebook under his chin.

"Pete, I . . . uh . . . Kirk called about Hagrid."

Pete looked up eagerly. "Yeah?"

"He might have found his original owner." When Pete scowled, she added, "That's good, right?"

"No."

"Why not?"

"His owner *abandoned* him, that's why not! He doesn't deserve to have him back."

Maribel walked all the way in and sat on his bed. "We don't know that. Maybe he just lost him."

"Same thing. If I had a great dog like Hagrid, I wouldn't *lose* him. That's just stupid. I bet Hagrid ran away from him. He's probably a big jerk."

"Pete. Let's give him a chance, huh?"

"You always say that. Give him a chance, give him a chance! I'm sick of giving people a chance. What difference does it make anyway? Nothing changes!"

Maribel knew what he was talking about. Duncan. How many times over the years had she urged Pete to give Duncan a chance?

"Sweetie, I know you don't really like Duncan. But he's been there for us, right? He's never walked away. That counts for something, doesn't it?" She didn't say out loud the other part of that thought—he'd never walked away, unlike Pete's father.

"No, it doesn't. He's never here to begin with. And when he is, he doesn't *do* anything. I mean, not anything fun."

"Like play wizards, for instance? Or Dungeons and Dragons?"

"Like *anything*," Pete said fiercely. "You can marry him if you want, but I don't have to talk to him. And I'm going to name the giant slug who lives in the Cave of Torment after him. You can't stop me."

"I guess not. Artistic license."

"And I'm naming the fire dragon Kirk."

"Because he's a fireman? That makes sense, I guess."

"No, not because he's a fireman. Don't you ever listen to my story? I have to tell the whole plot all over again! The fire dragon's really a noble-man, see? He was cursed by a witch who turned him into a dragon who gets burned by the sun. That's why he's a fire dragon—he catches on fire. It's really painful but he never cries. And no one understands what's happening to him, so they're scared of him, but he's really noble and kind and rescues people in the middle of the night when the sun can't burn him."

Maribel opened her mouth but couldn't speak a word. Kirk the Fire Dragon. Noble and kind. Burned from the sun.

Did Pete know about Kirk's cancer? Or had his imagination concocted a good reason for Kirk to work on his motorcycle in a place sheltered from the sun?

"Does he . . . um . . . what happens to Kirk the Dragon?"

"Mom, I don't know! I'm only on chapter three of Book One. And there's going to be at least seven books. But I know what happens to Duncan the Giant Slug. He's going to get squished. A big boul-der is going to—"

"Okay, okay, I get it. Anyway, pancakes are just about ready, honey. And please don't squish Duncan until after breakfast, okay?"

"Fine."

After she left Pete's room, unable to face Duncan yet, she took shelter in the bathroom. The scent of rose-petal potpourri greeted her, along with the sight of her pale face in the mirror.

The image of Kirk as a fire dragon pounded through her brain. It was eerily perfect. There was something else Pete had said, that it didn't matter that Duncan had never walked away, because he'd never really been around to begin with.

Abandonment wasn't the problem here. It had already happened. This time they'd been pre-abandoned by a distracted, self-absorbed workaholic.

But whose fault was that?

Maybe she'd never wanted Duncan around that much. Maybe that's why they'd lasted six years. They'd never had to confront anything difficult until now.

Maybe her son was right. Maybe she should have listened to him a little more. Maybe she needed to tear off her rose-colored glasses and get real.

Chapter Eight

Kirk handed the keys of his Harley to Bruce, who'd answered his Craigslist ad.

"Take it easy. Speed limit's thirty-five around here. And I know all the cops."

"No worries, dude." Bruce, a young snowboarder from Tahoe, kick-started the Harley and grinned. "Suh-weet. Be right back."

He roared off. Kirk leaned against his truck, which was already heating up from the morning sun. He ought to go inside, but the hell with it. Before long he'd be far away from the intense desert rays. Besides, he needed to conserve energy for the important stuff: packing and thinking about Maribel.

Two weeks had passed without a single encounter with her. Two crucial weeks during which Kirk felt something die inside him. He'd taken his shot. Bared his heart. Spilled his guts. He'd never done anything so tough in his life. Firefighter exam, chemotherapy, the decision to leave San Gabriel—

it all paled next to the leap off a cliff he'd taken under Maribel's incredulous hazel gaze.

Bruce zoomed back into sight and veered into the driveway, stopping on a dime before he hit the truck. The kid could ride, no doubt about that. "You got all the maintenance records?"

"Yup. Not much there; it's been a good bike. Couple tune-ups, that's about it."

"Harleys, man. They don't need much." Bruce passed his hand reverently across the still-purring body. "Why you selling her again?"

"I have to leave town. Moving to Alaska."

"*Alaska?* You a snowboarder too?"

"No, no. I . . . uh . . ." Kirk eyed the guy's sunburned face. Wouldn't hurt to warn him. "I got skin cancer. It could come back. I decided I'd be better off somewhere where the angle of the sun isn't so direct. Alaska's so far north, the UV index is a lot lower." Bruce was goggling at him. "You wear sunscreen?"

"No."

"Tell you what. I'll give you two hundred dollars off the price of the Harley if you spend it all on sunscreen."

"Rad. Thanks, dude."

"So you want the bike?"

"Hellz yeah."

A couple thousand dollars richer, Kirk watched his bike ride off into the midday sun with Bruce the Snowboarder. It ought to make him sad, but it just added to the growing hole in his heart. One more snip of the ties binding him to San Gabriel and his old life.

His big regret was that he hadn't been able to give Pete one more ride on the bike before he sold it. He hadn't seen the kid since the night he babysat him. Every time he checked on Hagrid, he saw that someone had brought food for him. Maybe Maribel was bringing Pete to the warehouse. Or maybe Duncan was.

But he'd finally gotten an e-mail from Gonzalez and needed to share it with Pete, so he'd left a message for Maribel and any day . . . hour . . . minute . . . he'd hear back from one of them. And that would be the final loose end. One last beer with the guys, one last viewing of the desert sunset from the tailgate of his truck, and he'd be gone.

Pete waited to call Kirk back until his mother had shut herself in her bedroom with her laptop. Ever since Duncan's last visit, things had been different. The wedding was off, along with the move to New York, even though she still talked to Duncan on the phone. And she'd been nice about driving out to see Hagrid—but mean about Kirk, saying she needed some time to sort everything out.

He had no idea what that meant, but if it meant less Duncan, he was all for it.

When he heard the sound of his mother's voice, Skyping from her bedroom, he dialed Kirk's number.

"Hi. It's Pete."

"Hey, buddy. I've got good news for you about Z-boy. Hagrid."

Pete's stomach dropped. Even though Kirk was cool, he was still a grown-up, and their ideas about good news always differed from his. "What is it?"

"Gonzalez e-mailed me. He didn't leave Z-boy behind on purpose. He said the dog jumped out of the truck when they left the shop. Ran away and wouldn't come back, no matter what they did. They stuck around for another day trying to lure him back with fried liver and bacon, all his favorites, but he didn't bite. They never saw him again. He was really happy to know we've been taking care of him."

Pete did a silent air-punch of glee. Hagrid had run away. That mean he wasn't Gonzalez's dog anymore. "Cool."

"There's more. He's willing to pay to ship Hagrid to Colorado if we can get him into a carrier. He's got a friend flying out of San Gabriel tomorrow; he can take him."

"What?"

"He misses Z-boy. Says he's a special dog. He told me his whole history. He was trained as a rescue dog for San Gabriel County Search and Rescue. Then he got injured in an earthquake rescue. Said he still has a limp, but I never noticed it."

Pete mumbled an answer. He'd noticed the limp right away, but that was because he cared about Hagrid so much.

"Anyway, they retired him with honors, and that's when Gonzalez adopted him. He has a plaque floating around somewhere. So I guess we have to convince Hagrid—Z-boy—to let us put him in a carrier. What do you say we go out and do it together?"

"No!" Pete burst out. "He doesn't want to go to Colorado. Why do you think he ran away?"

"Aw, Pete. Don't you think he probably misses Gonzalez?"

"No." If Hagrid had been so crazy about Gonzalez, he wouldn't have jumped out of the truck. Seemed obvious to Pete.

"Maybe you should talk to your mom about this. Maybe she has some good ideas."

"Nah." A lump of sheer resentment nearly choked him. "She's too busy all the time." He felt bad as soon as he said it. It's not that he was mad at his mother exactly. It wasn't her fault she was allergic to dogs. It wasn't her fault Duncan was such a douche bag.

"Wedding plans keeping her busy?" Kirk's voice sounded a little funny.

"No. They're not getting married. That's one good thing. He keeps calling though."

"Really? The wedding's off?"

"Don't tell her I told you. It's supposed to be a secret."

"Oh." A short silence followed. "So, about Hagrid. I told Gonzalez I'd try to deliver him to his friend tomorrow night. You want to go out to the warehouse tomorrow afternoon?"

"Um . . . I have to ask my mom."

"Sure. Let me know."

Pete hung up. Gonzalez didn't deserve to have Hagrid back. What would Harry Potter do in this situation? Or better yet, his own hero, Robin Dareheart, who had just discovered a magic stalagmite in the Cave of Torment that gave him the ability to change into any living being at any given moment? He'd never just sit back while disaster struck.

Tomorrow afternoon Kirk would be heading out to the warehouse. That gave him plenty of time.

Life as the former fiancée of Duncan Geller felt very odd, as if Maribel had just shed an outer layer of skin. On the one hand, she felt raw and vulnerable. Her relationship with Duncan had been a shockingly huge part of how she saw herself. She hadn't been just a waitress; she'd been the chosen one of the great celebrity photographer. It was as if her childhood blankie had been yanked away from her.

On the other hand, she knew she'd done the right thing. She felt lighter and more awake, as if her mind was filled with clear, sparkling water. She and Duncan were all wrong for each other. They had a certain amount of chemistry but nothing earthshaking. He patronized her, while she had spent countless hours listening to him, never admitting to herself how much he bored her. The only reason they hadn't figured it out earlier was that convenient three thousand miles between them.

"So stupid," she muttered as she refilled the cute little milk jugs of creamer that graced each table.

"What?" asked Mrs. Gund.

"Nothing."

She hadn't yet told Mrs. Gund she'd broken up with Duncan. That might unleash an onslaught of setup attempts with one or all of the Bachelor Firemen. Everything in her longed to run to Kirk, jump into his arms, tell him she was free and that the memory of his kisses hummed under her skin every moment of every day.

But she'd checked out a few books on breakups and knew the dangers of a rebound relationship. Better to give it some time, right? Let things settle down, let Duncan get all his over-analyzing out of his system, maybe do that therapy session by conference call he kept proposing. She felt awful hurting Duncan. She owed him a respectful breakup process, even if he did keep mentioning the shoot he had coming up with Lindsay Lohan as if that was supposed to make her jealous.

The door jingled open. Her heart jumped into her throat at the familiar sight of the dark blue T-shirts and suspenders of the Bachelor Firemen, even though she saw in an instant that neither one

of them was Kirk. Ryan and the boyish-looking
one they called Stud, but whose name was actually Fred, were walking toward the cash register.
Her hands shaking, she put away the half-and-
half and went out to take their order.

"Mornin', gorgeous," said Ryan with a wink.

"Back at you." She smiled widely at him. Ryan
sure was a sight for sore eyes even for someone
like her, who couldn't stop thinking about his
quiet coworker.

"I'll have an espresso with lots of sugar. But you
already knew that, didn't you?" He offered up his
knee-weakening smile.

"Yup. And a cappuccino with cinnamon for
you, Fred, right?"

Fred turned as red as the fire engine parked at
the curb. "Right. Thanks."

She turned to the espresso machine. Not that
she was counting the days or anything, but she
hadn't seen Kirk in . . . well, since *that night*. She
hoped he wasn't avoiding the Lazy Daisy so he
didn't have to see her. He'd told her not to feel
awkward, but what if he felt uncomfortable?

"Should I . . . um . . . throw in a black coffee for
Kirk? I mean, Thor? Or is he off-shift today?"

"He's off-shift all right. His last day was Friday.
Weird to see his locker emptied out." Ryan shook
his head. "It's hard to see him go. He's like a
brother. But at least he's . . ." He trailed off, as if
he'd gone too far.

"Alive," said Fred helpfully. "Close thing too."

"Stud!" hissed Ryan.

Fred turned even redder. Maribel's thoughts were wheeling like a flock of surprised swallows. Kirk had left the firehouse? He'd never mentioned anything about leaving the station.

"Did he quit or something? Transfer somewhere else?"

Ryan and Fred exchanged glances. "He's leaving California," Ryan finally answered. "Going to Alaska. For the climate. It's a long story, but if you want to hear it, you'd better ask him."

Maribel dropped the espresso cup onto the floor, where it bounced on the non-skid rubber mat. Black liquid spilled onto her sneakers. "He never told me. Why didn't he tell me?" Was he really going to leave town and never say a word? "I'm going to strangle him."

"Hey." Ryan reached out a hand to her forearm. "Go easy on him, okay? He's been through a lot."

She shook him off and dashed from behind the counter, nearly tripping over the dropped espresso cup. "Be back later, Mrs. Gund."

"What?" Mrs. Gund squawked.

"Don't worry, we got you covered, Mrs. G.," said Ryan. "Cap wants us back in half an hour, but until then, we're all yours."

"Herregud!" Mrs. Gund clapped her hand over her mouth, though she was the only one in the room who had any idea what that meant.

Maribel flew out of the Lazy Daisy and into her car. She ripped off her apron and tossed it in the backseat—not making that mistake again. Too bad she couldn't commandeer the fire engine. If this was a romantic comedy movie, the guys would drive her to Kirk's, where she would tell him . . . something clever and touching, and they would hug and kiss and . . . dissolve to the next scene. Truth was, she didn't know what to say. All she knew was she had to see him. The thought of him leaving the state was unbearable. Plain freaking unbearable.

She banged on his door, ignoring the unacceptable sight of the moving van parked in the driveway.

It felt like forever until the door opened and the sight of Kirk filled her vision. He looked harassed and tired, his hair mussed, his eyes shadowed. He wore a threadbare, long sleeved, faded blue shirt with a smudge of dust across the sleeve. His feet were bare. He was the sexiest thing she'd ever laid eyes on.

"How could you?" Her hurt spilled into the question, making an accusation out of it. She flung her arms in the air, but he caught her wrist before she could accidentally make contact. "Let go."

But he didn't. He held onto her arm, his eyes burning. "How could I what?"

"Leave! Without telling me!"

But he didn't look apologetic. If anything, he looked even angrier. "And you're the honest one here? How could you break up with Duncan without telling me?"

"What?" Her mouth fell open. "How did you know . . . ? That's different!"

Kirk pulled her inside and shut the door. He crossed his arms over his chest. "Different how?"

"It's . . . it's personal." She wasn't ready to explain about Duncan and her all-over-the-place feelings.

It was as if a wall of ice came down over his face. "So I'm not entitled to know things about your personal life. Fine. We're even. Thanks for stopping by." He put his hand on her shoulder and spun her around toward the door. She ducked under his arm and spun herself right back.

"That's not what I meant."

One of his eyebrows rose in a question. "Let me have it then. What did you mean?"

"I meant . . ." Oh God. Why was it so hard to say the important things? But for six years she'd avoided saying the important things to Duncan, and look where that had gotten her. "I meant . . ." He was leaving. A moving van stood in his driveway. Hurt lurked in his silvery eyes.

She loved him.

"I meant," she continued in barely a whisper, "that I want to be with you. You're like this pool of beautiful sunshine in my heart, and every time I think of you I get happy, and believe me, that's a lot, I think about you all the time, but I didn't want you to be a rebound guy, not that you would be, but I wanted to make sure. So I was sort of . . . waiting . . . but then Ryan said you were moving to Alaska . . . *Alaska*, do you know how far away that is?"

"Maribel," said Kirk, his voice rough, his eyes gone deepest gray. "I took a job in a small town up there that needs someone to train their volunteers. If figure I'll be inside more and it'll be easier to avoid the sun that far north. The UV level is lower. It's still a risk. I'll always have to be careful. The doctors say the cancer could come back."

Tears clogged the back of her throat, tears at the thought of no more Kirk, at the thought that he'd nearly died, that he could still die. "I understand all that. But you would just leave without saying goodbye?"

"No." He reached in his back pocket and pulled out a sheaf of paper covered with tiny writing. "Here's my goodbye."

"A *letter*?"

"You know me. I'm not so good when it comes to talking. But it explains everything."

His wobbly smile was too much for her, the icing on the cake of his irresistibility. She threw herself into his arms. Well, technically, against his chest, but he quickly wrapped his strong arms around her. His heart beat fast against her chest, a rapid patter that told her he was just as rattled as she was. Being back in Kirk's arms felt wonderful, better than wonderful, like a miracle.

"I don't want your letter, Kirk," she murmured into his warm neck.

"You don't?"

"I want you. Right now. And later on too."

"You sure?" He leaned his head back to peer into her face. "What about the rebound thing?"

"Forget that. You're not a rebound guy. You're the guy I've had a crush on for years but never let myself admit it. The guy I want to make love to for the next twenty-four hours straight. The guy who's kind to children and animals and women and total strangers whose houses happened to catch fire. The guy who makes my heart want to dance right out of my body every time you touch me. The guy who . . ."

He silenced her with a deep, spine-tingling kiss. "All right. Not that I don't love listening to you, but is there any action to go with that talk?"

"See?" She rained kisses on his dear, tired, handsome face. "You love listening to me. I love that. That's important, right? I've had enough of not speaking up for myself. No more of that, no way. If you want to be with me, you have to care what I think. And want."

"Oh I care, all right." He lifted her legs, one by one, so they wrapped around his waist. "Especially if you happen to be wanting me."

"I am." Her voice came in a rough whisper. "Oh Kirk, I am. So much. I'm sorry I didn't come right away, as soon as I knew that I . . ."

"That you what?" He sounded distracted, maybe because he was trying to kiss her neck as he made his way past packing cartons down the hall to his bedroom.

"Well, as soon as I thought I might love you."

"Might?" He kicked open the door to his bedroom, which, thank the lord, still held a bed. "Let's see if we can't do better than that."

Chapter Nine

Now that Kirk had Maribel where he wanted her, where he'd dreamed of having her for so long, no way was he going to drop the ball. He whisked her into the bedroom as if she weighed less than a pillow and flung her onto his bed. Her glorious auburn hair tumbled around her ears as she looked up at him, eyes wide with delight, mouth gaping adorably.

He stood over her, feeling like Tarzan and a Viking marauder rolled into one. He was practically beating his chest. "Mind if I rip your clothes off now?" he said with rough-edged courtesy, so as to distinguish himself from his pillaging Scandinavian ancestors.

"Feel free," she laughed.

So he did. Off went the pale green T-shirt with the retro Cadillac printed on it. The bra underneath, which was some blurred shade of white that he'd never be able to identify again, seemed to melt under the intensity of his lust. Her lovely breasts—there they were, just as he'd remembered during his restless nighttime fantasies—the size of perfect new apples, just as juicy and perky as a man could want. His mouth watered at the sight of her hard little nipples, already erect before he'd even touched them. Her skin was so delectable, so smooth and faintly freckled here and there. After he lifted her legs to pull off her jeans and underwear—a vague shade of pink—he parted her legs in awe to find a fluffy patch of ginger curls simply begging for his tongue.

He obliged, of course, but not until he'd done a thorough taste test of the rest of her body. She was full of sensual puzzles. How could the skin over her bottom rib taste like vanilla, whereas the curve to her waist tasted like green apples? Why did she quiver when he swirled his tongue around her belly button, but flat-out moan when he explored the dip between her hipbones? He could swear that one nipple was slightly plumper than the other, but he had to keep switching from one to the other to make sure. That brought on a whole cascade of sounds from Maribel, every one of which acted like a shot of adrenaline to his rearing cock.

He was so hard he could hang a fireman's coat on his boner. And as he knelt over her, licking and savoring, it kept bumping against her satin skin, each little brush a fresh torment of temptation. He wanted to bury himself inside her, make her his in the primal, ancient way of men, feel her heat from the inside, hear her cries as she surrendered her body and heart to him.

But first he wanted her to know how much he felt for her. His mouth had never been his best tool, word-wise, but now he put it to use loving every last inch of her. With hands, body, tongue, lips, he told her how much he loved her, how much she inspired him, how he'd lay down his life for her, how everything he had was hers. And when he finally allowed his tongue to brush against the delicate tissues hiding behind that soft puff of hair, her desperate writhing—and the death grip she had on his head—told him he didn't have to wait another second.

He reared up and placed his cock at her entrance. So close, so close . . . then a moment of sanity surfaced and he flung himself off her as if he'd been electrocuted.

"What? What?" She sat up, wild-eyed. "What happened? Why'd you stop?"

"Condom," he gasped. "Protect. You. Safe." Yes, words had definitely deserted him; he was apparently doing his own version of "Me Tarzan, you Jane."

"Well, *hurry*!"

He hurried. He scrambled to his bedside table, where he usually kept a few condoms, then realized he'd packed everything up. Wallet. Where'd he put his wallet?

Maribel moaned. He dropped to his knees, cock bobbing in front of him, and scrabbled through his pockets to find his wallet. There, between his

Visa card and his video-store punch card, sat one lone condom.

Maribel was kneeling on the bed, watching him anxiously, when he arose, now fully sheathed. She looked so beautiful, her sunset hair a crazy tangle, her hazel eyes foggy with desire, that he wished he had an ounce of artistic talent so he could attempt to capture a tiny portion of her glory.

"I love you, Maribel," he said with sudden soberness. "I'm not doing this casually, just so you know. This means everything to me."

"I know," she whispered. "I understand." She reached for him and drew him against her soft body as if welcoming him home after a long, dangerous journey.

They moved against each other with none of the usual first-time awkwardness. When she slid her legs apart, still kneeling on the bed, he put both hands on her ass and pulled her hard against his hips. With a gasp from her and a groan from him, they joined in a burst of star-spangled joy. When he thrust into her body, the warmth rushed through him like hot brandy on a cold winter's night.

Long, luscious moments passed as he immersed himself in the wonder of Maribel. He felt suspended in a world with no time, where all that existed was the feel of her body, the quick beat of her heart against his chest, her hot, panting breath in his ear, the scent of aroused woman, then the frantic, triumphant cries as she tilted over the edge into release. The butterfly tremors of her inner channel around his cock pulled him along with her and he surrendered, helplessly, to the shocking joy of exploding inside her body.

He muttered her name as he came, he who never said much during sex. Now he couldn't stop babbling things like, "So good . . . Maribel . . . sweetheart . . . oh God . . ." and probably other goofy nonsense stuff. She didn't seem to mind, holding him tight and laughing breathlessly as he poured himself, heart and soul, into her sweet body.

Maribel drifted happily on a magic carpet through a sunshine landscape of golden sunflowers and capering clouds. It seemed absurd that such bliss could exist without her having known about it. She'd had sex before—obviously. But she hadn't had *this* before. This . . . insanely beautiful, heart-to-heart, soul-to-soul experience. It felt as if she and Kirk had somehow exchanged parts of themselves as they'd made love. Essential parts, parts that meant they now belonged to each other in some basic kind of way.

She sighed happily. She was a fool for love, that's what she was. Six years of trying to be smart, to be careful and make good choices, gone in a burst of gloriously orgasmic impulsiveness. But to hell with it. This was right. She knew it with every singing cell of her satisfied body.

Next to her, Kirk lay equally stunned, or perhaps asleep. She blew on his ear. "Kirk."

"Shh." He lifted a hand abruptly. She drew back, confused. That wasn't a very romantic afterglow kind of response. Then she saw he was listening closely to the low murmur of his police scanner.

"Sounds like there's some sort of fire out on Highway 90."

"Highway 90?" She sat up. "Where that warehouse is?"

"Yeah. A lot of other buildings too. Hang on." He got up and walked to the scanner, which sat balanced on the windowsill in the absence of a bedside table. With absolutely no apparent concern for his naked, scarred state, he leaned over and turned up the volume. Maribel experienced a wave of sheer awe at his physical condition, at the body that had withstood an assault of cancer and chemicals. The hollows of his pelvic bones probably dipped deeper than they used to. He probably moved with less energy. She hated the fact that she hadn't been there for his bout with chemo. As soon as she could, she was going to learn every detail of what he'd gone through.

The voice of the dispatcher intruded. The woman spoke fast, in a kind of code Maribel didn't understand. She caught the words "structure fire" and "three alarm," "incident report" and "uninhabited."

"Uninhabited. That's good, right?"

But Kirk didn't answer, waiting tensely until the address came through again. "Three thousand Highway 90." Then he wheeled on her. "It's the warehouse. Pete isn't out there, is he?"

"No, of course not. He's in school. Besides, he knows he's not supposed to go out there alone."

"You sure he's at school? I told him I was going to pick up Hagrid this afternoon and put him on a plane to Colorado."

Maribel got a sick feeling in her stomach. She scrambled to her feet and looked around for her purse. Kirk located it and tossed it at her. *Cell phone.* It was off. When had she turned it off? *Doesn't matter. Turn it on.* One unheard message. From Pete's school.

Kirk was already pulling on his clothes. Maribel's hands were shaking so hard she could barely play the message. Kirk plucked the phone out of her hands and clicked on the speaker.

"Ms. Boone, this is Janet from San Gabriel Elementary. Your son Pete hasn't been seen here at school since this morning. Please give us a call as soon as you can and let us know if you took him home."

"Come on," said Kirk roughly. "Get dressed, we're going out there." He picked up his own phone and clicked a speed-dial key. "Captain Brody, it's Thor. That warehouse fire out on 90, there might be a kid inside. Nine-year-old boy going after a dog. Ten-four. I'm on my way."

He stuffed the cell phone in his pocket and helped Maribel finish dressing. "Do you want to stay here, honey? Captain Brody and the guys are on it, and they're the best. I want to be there because Pete knows me. But if it's too much for you—"

"I'm going," she said tensely.

"Okay." He didn't argue, as she was afraid he would. They ran through the house to the driveway, where her car was parked behind his older-model brown truck, blocking him in. "We can take your car, it'll be faster. Mind if I drive?"

She dug in her purse and threw him her keys. If she drove in this state of mind, every telephone pole between here and the warehouse would be in danger. She dashed for the passenger seat and fastened her seat belt.

Good thing too, because her little Volvo had never been driven like a race car in the Indy 500 before. In Kirk's hands, her car suddenly acquired powerful acceleration, precision turns, speed limit-obliterating velocity. They screamed down the highway. She wouldn't have been at all surprised to find a platoon of state troopers behind them by the time they'd reached the city limits. But luck was with them, and before long they spotted giant billows of black smoke belching above the horizon.

"Oh my God," she started chanting, a thick dread clutching at her throat. Her boy, all that black smoke . . . But he couldn't be there. It must be a mistake. She should call Janet back and make sure. She punched redial on her phone. When a woman answered, she babbled, "Pete Boone, I'm calling about Pete. Is he there?"

"Ms. Boone? We've been trying to reach you. We called your workplace number too. No, no one's seen Pete since lunch. Are you saying he's not with you?"

Maribel dropped the phone, all her focus now on the looming black cloud a half mile away . . . a quarter mile . . . down the next road . . . at the end of the—Oh good Lord!

A hellish sight waited at the end of the road. The warehouse was completely engulfed in a thick, toxic-looking mass of roiling smoke, lit by a red, eerie glow. Orange flames darted here and there, like flickering snakes' tongues. Several fire engines were parked at different angles around the building, and helmeted, tank-bearing firemen were dragging hoses and setting up ladders.

"This could be a hazmat situation," muttered Kirk, peering into the mess. "Who knows what chemicals are in there? See how they're staying upwind to be safe? You'd better stay here."

"But Pete—"

"I don't see his bike. He usually drops it right by the front door. See?" He pointed to the front door, which, amazingly, was still intact. The fire was concentrated toward the back of the building. The front step was empty; no little blue Schwinn. Maribel went faint from relief. Maybe Pete had gone to the Lazy Daisy, or home to work on his book. He'd get a consequence—scolding, no computer games, something big—but at least he wasn't caught in a toxic inferno.

"Do you have a scarf or something?" Kirk was asking.

"What? Why?"

"I don't have any gear with me."

"Gear? Kirk, you can't go in there." She clutched at him, absolutely appalled.

"I'm just going to check it out. I'm not going inside, don't worry. How about that apron?"

She reached into the backseat and tossed it to him. He folded it, wrapped it around the lower half of his face, then tied the strings at the back. Above the rough cotton, his gray-green eyes stared at her intently. He looked like a pirate or a spy. Then he waggled his eyebrows, completely ruining the effect and making her burst into hysterical giggles.

"Be right back," he said, muffled in cotton. "Keep the windows closed." And he was gone, dashing toward the horrible gushing smoke. She watched him until he disappeared behind a fire engine. Even through the glass windows, she heard the hollow roar of the fire, like a blowtorch multiplied to a monstrous size, and the occasional yells of the firemen. The stench drifted in—through the vents, maybe? She put her hand over her mouth, gagging a bit.

She found her cell phone and called the house. *Pick up, Pete. Come on, sweelie.* But the only answer was her own voice on the outgoing message. Next, the Lazy Daisy.

"Haf not seen him, Maribel. And I'm on my own, cannot talk."

"Sorry. Call me if he comes in, would you? I'm getting frantic."

"I vill."

She hung up and looked back at the fire, a fresh wave of panic sending flutters to her heart. Where was Pete? With a sudden chill of dread, she knew he'd come here. Maybe he'd left his bike somewhere else for once. Maybe it was even now being incinerated in a chemical bonfire . . .

She had to get to Pete. Get him out. She jumped out of the car. The sickening smell of the fire nearly knocked her off her feet. "Pete!" she yelled, running toward the warehouse. Her voice sounded weird, nearly inaudible over the vast roar of the fire. But she kept at it anyway, yelling "Pete, Pete," until someone slammed into her and swooped her off the ground.

"What the hell are you doing?" Kirk yelled in a hoarse voice. "I told you to stay in the car!" He held her against his chest while she struggled against him.

"Pete . . . not at home . . . can't find him," Maribel panted. "Have to find him."

"The guys are on it. They haven't seen a bike. No sign of anyone. You're just going to get killed if you go in there."

"But Kirk . . ." Tears were flowing down her cheeks. "I know he's here. I just know it. Please. You have to listen to me."

He stilled, scrutinizing her face. Would he listen? Would someone, for once, hear her?

"Okay," he said, putting her back on her feet but keeping a tight grip on her arm. "But you can't run into a burning building. That's what firefighters are for. We'll circle around the edges. And you don't make a move without me. Here."

He pulled a red bandanna from his pocket and tied it around her mouth and nose. The soft cotton, with a pleasant tang of laundry detergent, was a balm after the nasty, harsh stench of the smoke. "I had this stashed in Engine 1. Now come on."

But before they'd taken more than a few steps, he squeezed her arm so tightly she yelped.

"Shh!"

He waited, stock-still, until Maribel heard it too. The sharp bark of a dog. "I think that's Hagrid. That's the bark a rescue dog makes when they've found something. Let's go."

He ran toward the sound, which didn't come from the building but from the birch woods behind it. She ran after him, keeping her hand over her mouth so the bandanna didn't slide off. Even though they gave the burning warehouse a wide berth, it was absolutely terrifying, like a grotesque smoke monster bellowing and thrashing. In quick, fascinated glimpses, she saw yellow-suited firefighters brave the smoke, aiming streams of water into its depths. The flow of water looked puny compared to the crazed beast of fire, but the firemen seemed undaunted. They worked together seamlessly, at least to her eye. It occurred to her that Kirk would have been right there with them if he hadn't quit the department.

Awe at his courage—at their courage—battled with sheer relief that he wasn't risking his life at the moment.

At the edge of the woods, a small white blur raced toward them. Pete's little dog.

"Hagrid! Z-boy!" Kirk rushed toward him. Man and dog met halfway, the dog nipping eagerly at his leg. Maribel caught a glimpse of his dark brown eyes, bright with urgency. Then the little guy wheeled around and raced back into the woods.

Chapter Ten

Something wet was sliming Pete's cheek. He opened his eyes, then squinted them shut right away. A bright shaft of light from above had nearly blinded him. And what was that black slippery stuff all around him? He tried to struggle to his feet, but he kept sliding around in the mud.

The mud.

Memory flooded back. He'd been running through the woods, away from the sneaky-looking men who'd shown up at the warehouse, when the ground had disappeared from under him and everything had gone black. He must have fallen into some kind of hole, like a trap.

His heart raced. Where was he? Where were those men?

He lifted his head and listened. Should he try to climb out of the hole? Was it safe? What would Robin Dareheart do if he saw a bunch of creepy men with red plastic containers that smelled like gasoline?

Robin Dareheart probably wouldn't have run.

At least he'd grabbed Hagrid, although he'd had to leave his bike behind. Maybe it was a good thing Hagrid hadn't wanted to get in the saddlebag he'd brought.

"Hagrid," he whispered. "Are you here?"

Then he remembered. Halfway between the warehouse and the woods, he'd heard a shout, then a sharp *pop*.

Hagrid had wormed out of his arms and raced back toward the warehouse, barking like a maniac. Terrified, Pete had kept running until he reached the woods, then kept on, going in wild zigzags, until blackness had swallowed him up.

He gave a sob. *Hagrid*. Hagrid must have gone back to attack those men, scare them away. He'd probably gotten shot. That *pop* must have been a gunshot, right? He was probably lying dead outside the warehouse while those horrible men set it on fire. The building was probably burned to a crisp by now and Hagrid, poor brave Hagrid . . .

A sharp bark made him jerk. That sounded like . . . Was Hagrid still alive?

"Hagrid, shh!" He spoke in a loud whisper that hopefully wouldn't carry too far in case the men were still out there.

Quick little scrabbling sounds came from overhead, followed by the thump of running footsteps. Oh no, the men were after Hagrid. He had to get out of here, had to help . . . He made his hands into claws and dug them into the muddy sides of the hole. The light wasn't too far above him, just a few feet. If he could grab onto a tree root or something . . . He craned his neck at the opening overhead. Something was blocking the light. He squinted.

A furry white head peered down at him and gave a soft bark. The footsteps were still coming after him.

"Hagrid! What are you doing, boy? Run and hide. Hide!"

Then another figure appeared next to the dog. "Pete, is that you?"

Kirk. Dizzy with relief, Pete slid back down to the bottom of the hole. "I'm down here. Are those men still here?"

"The firemen? Yep, they're here, but they're a little busy."

"No," said Pete, but it didn't seem worth explaining right now. "I'm kind of stuck down here."

"So I see. Hang tight, I'll get a rope. You okay for a few more minutes?"

"Oh sure. Take your time." Now that Kirk and Hagrid were here, all fear left him. Kirk disappeared, but then his mother knelt next to Hagrid, the sunlight making a red halo out of her hair.

"Pete! Are you hurt?" She'd obviously been crying; he could tell from her voice. And he felt horrible all of a sudden. He'd snuck out of school, broken the rules, been shot at, nearly gotten Hagrid killed.

"No," he said in a thin voice. He hadn't felt

like crying until this very moment. But now . . .
"I'm not hurt. And I'm really sorry, Mom. You can
ground me. I don't mind."

"Oh sweetie. You look pretty grounded already." She went for a laugh, which partly worked.

She'd made a joke. His mom, who must have
been freaking out, had tried to make him laugh.
Tears sprang out of his eyes. He wiped them away,
getting mud all over his face.

His mother sneezed.

"Mom, you'd better get away from Hagrid. He's
making you sneeze."

"Not yet. We're fine for now, me and Hagrid."
He saw a movement up above that looked like a
pat on the dog's head.

"You're going to have to take a bath when we
get home," he said.

"I have a feeling I'm not the only one. Just how
muddy are you?"

"About as muddy as the giant slug in the Cave
of Torment."

"Wow! But sorry, I don't think we have a bathtub big enough for the giant slug."

Another joke! Everything was going to be okay.
And then Kirk was back, and he knew for sure
that everything would be fine.

"Okay, buddy. Time to show off your climbing skills." A rope, knotted at the end so he could
easily grip it, slowly made its way down the hole.
"You can tie it around your waist or just hold on."

"My hands are really muddy."

"Then tie it around your chest, under your arms. No hurry, Pete. Take your time, tie a good knot. That's right. Good job."

Kirk's calm voice made all the difference. Pete wasn't nervous at all as he tied the knot. He felt a little goofy dangling from the rope as Kirk hauled him up. He used his feet to hold himself off the sides of the hole. As his head cleared the opening, the first thing he felt was Hagrid's enthusiastic, joyful licking of every inch of his face. Next came his mother's arms, scooping him up tight, never mind the mud all over him. And then the unfamiliar, reassuring weight of a strong male hand clapping him on the back.

Maribel could barely stand to hear the details of Pete's adventure. A rescue ambulance came and paramedics checked him out and wrapped him in a blanket. Even though it was eighty degrees outside, her son kept shivering. Shock, they said. Luckily, they didn't feel a trip to Good Samaritan hospital was necessary. She stayed with Pete, sitting close to him on the tailgate of the rescue ambulance, and listened to the details of his story. He'd planned to stash Hagrid in the garden shed behind their house. Since she never did anything resembling yard work, it might have worked, if Hagrid had never barked or ventured outside during daylight hours.

"Honey, I wish we could keep Hagrid. I really do. But—"

"I know. It was stupid. I don't care anymore. I mean, I care, but I'm just glad he's alive."

They both glanced over at poor Hagrid, whose ear was being swathed in ointment by Fred, who'd spread out a blanket on the grass to tend to the dog. The fire was now a smoldering shadow of its former terrifying self, and the firefighters were putting away their equipment. A few of the fire engines had already left, but the San Gabriel crew was still there.

"He's a great dog," said Maribel softly. "You were right, Pete. He's special."

Pete nodded wearily. She wanted to throw up at the thought of everything he'd gone through—gunshots, arson-witnessing, getting knocked unconscious. She put her arm around him, wondering how she was ever going to let him out of her sight again.

Captain Brody walked over to them and surveyed Pete with sober charcoal-gray eyes. "Pete, the arson investigators are going to want to talk to you. Are you okay with that?"

"Why?" Maribel asked in alarm. "He's just a kid."

"But he's a smart kid. If he saw something that might help locate the arsonists, we might be able to lock them up so they don't do anything like this again. We might not even know it was arson if Pete hadn't seen as much as he did. These are dangerous people, professionals probably hired by the owners when they couldn't find a new renter It's not only arson, but attempted murder."

The blood drained from Maribel's face. She hadn't thought of it in those terms. "And Pete's the witness? But he didn't see anything. And they didn't see him, did they, Pete? Just from the back while you were running into the woods?"

Pete's eyes were wide with fright. "I don't think they saw my face."

"Don't worry, they'll never know his name. He'll be protected."

"Yes, he will be," said Kirk, stepping to Brody's side. His face looked grim and angry, his eyes like chips of quartz in a wall of granite. "I'll make sure of that."

Maribel was so glad to see him, she forgot that no one else knew they were—well, in love—and clutched his hand to her heart. "Kirk, where've you been?"

"Trying to figure out what happened. I'm guessing Hagrid went after the bastard—excuse me—who shot at Pete. Some gasoline spilled on his ear and a spark must have landed on it. That's one lucky dog."

"Brave too," said Captain Brody. He knelt on the blanket next to Fred and looked Hagrid in the eye. Hagrid gazed back with soulful brown eyes.

"Good dog," said Brody finally, reaching out to scratch Hagrid's uninjured ear. "You did good. But you know that. I hear you were a helluva rescue dog."

Hagrid gave a soft yip and licked at Brody's hand.

"His ear isn't too bad," said Fred. "As long as it doesn't get infected, he should heal pretty quick. It's going to scar up though."

"Hear that, pup?" said Brody. "A battle scar. All the girls will love you."

Hagrid's intelligent gaze traveled from face to face, but always went back to Brody. He must have recognized the top dog in this pack of firefighters.

Brody scratched the dog under the chin, making his eyes close in bliss. "We'll have to make sure you're well taken care of, won't we?"

Pete piped up. "He doesn't want to go to Colorado. He's a California dog."

"Is that right?" The captain didn't seem to think it strange that Pete would speak for Hagrid. "Then again, maybe his work here is done." Another long moment of communion with Hagrid followed, while Maribel fought back tears. If Hagrid had been killed in the fire, or by the arsonists, would they have found Pete in that old sinkhole?

She held tightly to the lifeline of Kirk's hand. The warmth of his body, standing so close to her, felt more than reassuring; it felt essential.

Pete, apparently jealous of Hagrid's newfound dog-crush on Captain Brody, hopped down from the ambulance and knelt next to Hagrid. He kept the blanket wrapped around himself, but Maribel could tell he felt better. She snuggled closer to Kirk and rubbed her cheek on his arm.

"What did you mean when you said you'll make sure Pete's protected?" Maribel murmured.

"I'm going to make sure. Personally. I'm going to stay and watch over him."

"What?"

"Listen to me." She let him pull her away from the ambulance, out of Pete's earshot. "The police will probably offer some protection, depending on what the arson squad determines. But it's not enough. I'll sleep on your couch. I'll drive him to school. I'll check with the school officials about security there. I'll be his personal bodyguard until the danger's passed."

"Kirk! That's crazy. You're supposed to be moving to Alaska."

A stubborn look came over his face, a very Thor-like expression that really ought to be accompanied by a thunderbolt. "Pete might be the only witness to arson and attempted murder. What's to stop them from trying to finish the job?"

Maribel shuddered. "But they didn't see him!"

"We don't know that. What if they had someone on lookout in the woods? We can't take a chance."

"But the police—"

"Are perfectly competent. But I'm not going to leave it up to them."

"Kirk . . ." She wrung her hands together. "You're scaring me. Of course. That's it: you're catastrophizing!"

"Maribel. Look at me." She did, and the dead-serious look in his eyes sent a chill straight through her. "I'm not catastrophizing. I'm being smart and careful. In fact, it would be even better if . . ."

"If what?"

But they were interrupted by Pete running toward them. "Hagrid might get a special award! Captain Brody says he's earned it."

"That's great, honey. Of course he's earned it."

Pete looked from one to the other of them. "What's wrong?"

"Sweetie, would you mind if Kirk stayed at our house for a little while?"

An exuberant hug around Kirk's waist, blanket sliding to the ground, was answer enough for Maribel.

"Fine," she told Kirk. "But we need to talk more about this."

That stubborn thunderbolt look came back, but he nodded. "What about Hagrid?" He turned to the captain. "Maribel's allergic. Any ideas who could take care of him for now?"

Brody stroked his stubbled chin thoughtfully. "I'll take him to the station, see if any of the crew wants to take him home. I'm sure we'll get some takers. Maybe even a bidding war. When everyone hears his story, they'll be fighting over who gets to adopt him."

"What about you, Cap? He really likes you." Hagrid had torn himself away from Fred's ministrations and was plastered to Brody's leg, gazing up at him adoringly.

"Not a good time," he said vaguely. "Rebecca, you know, well . . . not a good time." He strode toward Engine 1, Hagrid trotting eagerly at his feet. They watched the dog hop into the fire engine as if he'd been doing it for years. Maybe he had been, in his former career. Hagrid had many secrets, Maribel realized.

"Well." She took in a deep breath and smiled at her son and her . . . Kirk. "Shall we go home?"

Kirk passed an uncomfortable night on Maribel's royal-purple overstuffed couch. After she'd put Pete to bed, she'd cuddled with him and things had gotten interesting, but neither had felt comfortable going any further with Pete liable to wake up any minute from a nightmare. Which he'd done, later on. Kirk heard Maribel slip into his room, heard the murmur of her voice soothing him, the soft lullaby she sang him. His heart hurt from the beauty of it. Everything he wanted was in that room. Maribel, a family, a bright boy, love, warmth, life. Nothing was going to hurt anyone in that room, he vowed; he'd give his own life to make sure.

The next day, Pete stayed home from school. Kirk had to go back to his house to move the last few boxes out. He called the movers and put everything on hold for a week. He'd have to talk to the police about their take on the situation. How would he know when it was safe to relax? Would he ever feel comfortable about Pete's safety, especially when he was thousands of miles away? He doubted that would ever happen. He'd have to consider canceling the move to Alaska.

When he got back to Maribel's house, she met him with a tender smile and a happy-to-see-you hug. "Pete's asleep in my room," she whispered. "Out like a light. We've got hours until he wakes up." She tugged him toward the living-room couch. He sank into its soft cushions with a sigh that seemed to come straight from his core. She knelt next to him, nudging him to twist a bit to the side. Then cool, gentle hands were playing across the back of his neck, stroking his tight muscles, rubbing out the knots of tension. His eyes drifted halfway shut at the pleasure of her caresses, the sweetness of being taken care of.

When he thought he'd reached a state of unmatchable bliss, it got better. Those sweet little hands reached around his front and tugged his shirt up. He raised his hands like a child, although the lower half of his body was all adult. The X-rated kind of adult. In no time flat.

She seemed happy about that sudden bulge in his jeans, if her next actions were any indication. Slipping off the couch, she came around in front of him and straddled his lap. Her cottony pink skirt flowed over his legs. It was like having a summer flower sit on him.

"Lie back, you stud. It's my turn." Her voice was huskier than usual, and he noticed an extra wash of pink on her round cheeks. Since resistance seemed pointless, he lay back and let her run her hands over his chest, her expression rapt as a kid at Christmas. Her light touch made his senses swim;

it was as if she were a blind person reading him with her fingers. He closed his eyes. Instantly, his whole world shrank to the tracking of her every move, anticipation of her next exploration.

Her fingers discovered everything: the two chunks of missing flesh, the biopsy scar, the swirls of hair around his nipples, the skipping of the pulse in his neck, the way his very heartbeat danced to her touch. Her hands did more than discover; love flowed from her fingers through his ravaged skin into his heart, which seemed to expand into an unbearably bright sun, an inside sun that could never hurt him.

"You, my dear," she murmured as she trailed her hands to the top button of his jeans, "are one fine fireman."

"Is that right?" His voice was hoarse.

"Oh yes."

Her voice now came from the region of his crotch. He jerked his eyes open to find her kneeling between his legs, unzipping his jeans. "What are you doing?"

"I'm sure you've heard of it." She smiled up at him, her pink lips already parted.

"Yes, but . . . you don't have to."

"Look, buster." She narrowed her eyes at him. "I love every piece of you, and I want to show you just how much. I don't want to hold back or tiptoe around you or hide what I want. If you have a problem with any of that, you'd better tell me right now."

"No. No. I . . . uh . . . no problem."

"Then zip it. Not this"—she reached inside his fly—"but that." She gave his mouth a scolding look, then wrapped her precious lips around his cock.

Oh sweet lord. *Give it up, Kirk. This woman owns you.* Scraps of thoughts flew through his brain as she moved her warm mouth up and down his shaft. Anything . . . forever . . . I'm yours . . . so good . . . Oh God . . . Maribel . . . inside . . . need . . . now . . .

When she paused for breath, he swooped in and whirled her onto the couch. "I've got to be inside you."

Maribel gave a little gasp, staring dizzily up at the man who'd been at her mercy one second ago. Now he braced himself over her, every ripped muscle vibrating with tension, his voice gritty from lust. She could just about faint from the desire written in every line of his usually serious face. It looked as though the restraint had been scorched out of him by raw, white-hot need.

"I want you, Maribel."

"Oh, me too." She brought his hand under her skirt, between her legs. She knew he'd find her wet and ready. Loving him with her mouth, feeling his instant response, the swell and surge of him, was an incredible turn-on. He practically ripped her panties down her legs. That sudden show of strength made her gasp again. Then his hands were on her, those work-roughened, all-knowing hands. She nearly moaned from the happiness of having him touch her again. When was that first time . . . yesterday? It felt like eons had passed.

But it didn't matter; they were together again, hands on flesh, skin against damp skin, lips on mouth, heart against heart, him inside her, her around him.

She wrapped her legs around his hips, reveling in their power as he thrust into her body. Each flex of his hips set off a sparkling fountain of pleasure, each one deeper and sweeter and more piercing. "I love you, Kirk," she chanted in a whisper. "I love you, I love you."

She had no choice; her body, soul, and heart pushed the words out of her.

His answer seemed torn from the deepest part of himself. "Oh sweetheart. God, how I love you, Maribel."

And then great waves of pleasure lifted them up and away, spun them around, and launched them into endless, exquisite wonder.

Afterwards, they went into her sunny kitchen, where she put him in the chair farthest from the window and brought him coffee. "Coffee, black?" she asked, her voice still adorably sex-husky.

"Like old times." He smiled at her over the mug, blinking like a lovesick puppy.

She sat across from him, her pink skirt floating around her. He'd never forget that skirt.

"Pete and I are supposed to meet with the arson investigator tomorrow. Do you think you could come?"

The request made his heart glow. "Of course. Pete's not going anywhere without me for a while. I told you."

With a nervous, sidelong look, she plucked at the fabric of her skirt. "Kirk, while you were gone, Pete and I talked. We don't like what you're doing. It's not right."

Now that was a punch in the gut. He put the coffee mug down on the rickety side table by the couch. "Don't start, Maribel. You're not going to change my mind."

"But Kirk, have you forgotten you're *moving*? You're supposed to stay out of the sun, and it's nothing but sun here. It's bad for your health. We can't accept that."

Agitated, Kirk jumped to his feet. Maribel stood as well, arms folded, her hair a rumpled tangle around her head.

"It's my choice. I'm at risk either way, whether I move or don't. It won't kill me to stay a little longer."

"But you said the UV level is higher here."

"I'll take the chance, Maribel. I stay covered up, I use sunscreen. But I'm not taking chances with Pete's life. I won't. Don't ask me to, sweetheart." He took her by the shoulders, willing her to understand. "Last night I lay on your couch and promised myself I wouldn't let anything happen to you or Pete, if I can do anything to stop it. Nothing matters to me more than the two of you."

Tears swam in her wide hazel eyes, hung on her eyelashes. Fiercely, she dashed them away and glared up at him. "Don't you get it, Kirk? We don't want anything to happen to you either! We want to come with you to Alaska." Her face went pink as a peach. "I mean, if you want us."

"Wh . . . what?" He clutched her tighter, not sure he'd heard right. "Come to Alaska?"

"Ye . . . es." Her gaze dropped away, as if she was embarrassed. "I asked Pete how he'd feel about going with you. I said, 'I'm sorry you can't have a dog, but what about a fireman instead?' Kind of joking, you know. I explained that I loved you, and that you'd said you loved me too, and asked what he'd think of us all being together as a family and moving to Alaska and—are you okay?"

Sure, he was okay, as long as breathing wasn't absolutely essential. He managed to choke out some words. "What did he say?"

"He loves the idea," she said simply. "He thinks you're the best thing on two feet. Hagrid's the best on four, of course. Oof!"

He didn't remember how it happened, exactly, but he was suddenly squeezing the breath out of her, making her laugh and hug him back in a blaze of bright, shining joy that threatened to lift the little house off its foundations and float all the way to Alaska.

Fairness compelled him to double-check, though. "Are you sure? All the way to Alaska? I never thought . . ."

"It'll be an adventure," she said firmly. "I'll expand my artistic horizons and Pete can work some other climate zones into his epic novel. And we'll be safe from . . . you know. They're not going to hunt him down in Alaska. And, most important, we'll be with you."

True.

Of course, they'd have to discuss a wedding, or at least an engagement, but for now it was enough to hold her tight and feel happiness seep like a healing balm through every cell of his body.

Kirk brought Pete to the firehouse with him to say goodbye. Maribel was training her replacement at the Lazy Daisy but sent along a few dozen farewell muffins, everything but bran. All the Bachelor Firemen and the newest female member of the crew, the pretty, turquoise-eyed Sabina Jones, gathered around to shake his hand, clap his shoulder, and offer hugs. After the milling and chattering had died down, Captain Brody cleared his throat for attention. Hagrid was at his feet; his ear already looked nearly healed. Pete dropped down to pet him and scratch his neck until his tail threatened to pound a groove into the floor.

"The crew has voted. We all feel— unanimously—that the fairest thing to do with a dog as brave and fearless around fire as this one is to turn him into a firehouse dog. We checked with Gonzalez in Colorado and he's fine with it. So if it's okay with you, Pete, we'd like to adopt Hagrid here at San Gabriel Station 1."

"Really?" Pete looked up from his mutual adoration-fest with Hagrid.

"Yes. But I have to tell you, there's a catch."

"What?"

Kirk started to smile. He knew exactly what was coming.

"According to tradition, every firehouse dog here at Station 1 has been named Constancia. After Constancia B. Sidwell."

"Ill-fated bride of Virgil Rush, who left him in the lurch and inspired our bachelor curse," explained Ryan with a wink. "Which some of us call a blessing in disguise."

"Constancia? That's a horrible name!" Pete cried, appalled. "He's a boy, first of all."

"Good point. Besides, he just doesn't look like a Constancia to me. It's a bit old-fashioned. What do you say to the name Stan?"

"Stan," muttered Pete, stroking the dog's floppy ear. "Good boy, Stan, good boy." Hagrid/7-boy/ Stan cocked his head in answer. "That's fine. He's okay with Stan."

"Stan it is."

A cheer went up from the firefighters. Captain Brody smiled broadly. As Pete got to his feet, the captain clapped him on the shoulder. "You can visit him any time."

Ryan elbowed his way through the crowd. "You'll probably hear about him on the news way before that."

"Why?" Pete asked. "Because he's such a hero?"

"No, not that. We're going to spread it around that two dogs were at the scene and Stan slept through the fire. Throw off the arsonists. Nope, Stan's going to be known as the official Bachelor Fire Dog of San Gabriel. Now he'll never find a Mrs. Stan."

Sabina snorted and rolled her eyes. "You guys don't really believe in that curse, do you?"

Quiet descended.

"Anyone else notice how Kirk didn't hook up with Maribel until after he quit the department?" Vader said in a spooked voice.

"Hey," Kirk protested, with a quick glance at Pete. "We didn't 'hook up.' We're getting married."

The firemen let loose another round of cheers and hoots, before quieting again. "Weird, though," said Vader, as though telling a ghost story. "Six years without saying ten words at a time to her—"

"Record was seventeen," Fred pointed out. "Last Christmas. Sixteen on July 13."

Vader ignored him. "And suddenly, they're getting married. Makes you wonder."

"No, it doesn't," said Brody firmly. "Back to work, everyone. Pete, Kirk . . . good luck in Alaska. Keep in touch."

"Will do, Cap."

One last bear hug from the best captain he'd ever known, a last wave of goodbyes, one more lingering cuddle with Stan the Bachelor Fire Dog, and Kirk and Pete headed home, where Maribel, the moving van, and life itself awaited.

Keep reading for excerpts from
the authors' latest books

RUN TO YOU
Rachel Gibson
Available Fall 2013

ANYTHING BUT SWEET
Candis Terry
Available July 2013

SEX AND THE SINGLE FIREMAN
Jennifer Bernard
Available Now

Run to You

RACHEL GIBSON

Chapter One

Back Door Betty Night at Ricky's Rock 'N' Roll Saloon was always the third Wednesday of the month. Back Door Betty Night was all about freedom of expression. A pageant of diversity that lured drag queens in from Key West to Biloxi. Lady Gay Guy and Him Kardashian competed for the Back Door crown with the likes of Devine Boxx and Anita Mann. The Back Door crown was one of the more prestigious crowns on the pageant circuit and the competition was always *fierce.*

Back Door Betty Night also meant the bartenders and cocktail waitresses had to dress accordingly and show more skin than usual. In Miami, where short and tight ruled the night, that meant practically naked

"Lemon!" Stella Leon hollered over Kelly Clarkson's "Stronger" yowling from the bar's speakers. On stage, Kreme Delight did her best impersonation of a shimmering, leather-clad dominatrix. That was the thing about drag queens. They loved sparkles and glitter and girl-power songs. They were more girl than most girls, and loved girl drinks like appletinis and White Russians, but at the same time, they were men. Men didn't tend to order blender drinks. Stella, like most bartenders, hated making blender drinks. They took time, and time was money.

"Lemon," a male bartender dressed in tiny white shorts and shimmer hollered back.

The Amy Winehouse bouffant pinned on the top of Stella's head stayed securely anchored as she raised a hand and caught the yellow fruit hurled at her. Around the base of the bouffant fastened to her head, she'd tied a red scarf to cover the many bobby pins holding it in place. On a normal night, her long hair was pulled up off her neck, but tonight she'd left it down and was hot as hell.

She sliced and squeezed and shook cocktail shakers two at a time. Her breasts jiggled inside her leopard-print bustier, but she wasn't worried about a wardrobe malfunction. The bustier was tight and she wasn't a very busty girl. If anything, she feared the bottom curves of her butt might show beneath her black leather booty shorts and invite comment. Or worse, a slap. Not that that was a huge fear tonight. Tonight the males in the bar weren't interested in *her* ass cheeks. The only person she had to worry about touching her butt was the owner himself. Everyone said Ricky was just "friendly." Yeah, a friendly pervert with fast hands. They also said he had mafia connections. She didn't know if that was true, but he did have "associates" with names like Lefty Lou, Fat Fabian, and Cockeyed Phil. She definitely remained on high alert when Ricky was around. Lucky for her, he didn't usually show up until a few hours before closing, and Stella was usually long gone by three A.M. She wasn't the kind of person to hang out after her shift ended. She wasn't a big drinker, and if she had to be around drunks, she wanted to get paid.

"Stella!"

Stella glanced up from the martinis she'd set on a tray and smiled. "Anna!" Anna Conda was six feet of statuesque queen all wrapped up in reptilian pleather. Over the past few years, Stella had gotten to know several of the queens fairly well. As with everything in life, some of them she liked. Others, not so much. She genuinely liked Anna, but Anna was moody as hell. Her moods usually depended on her latest boyfriend. "What can I get you?"

"Snake Nuts, of course." The tips of her shiny green lips lilted upward. If it wasn't for Anna's deep voice and big Adam's apple, she might have been pretty enough to pass for a woman. "Put an umbrella in it, honey." Applause broke out as Kreme exited the stage, and Anna turned toward the crowd. "Have you seen Jimmy?"

Jimmy was Anna's leather daddy, although neither was exclusive. Stella grabbed a bottle of vodka, amaretto, and triple sec. "Not yet." She scooped ice into a shaker and added the alcohol and an ounce of lime juice. "He'll probably wander in." Stella glanced at the clock. It was after midnight. One more hour of competition before this month's Back Door Betty was crowned. While the stage was set for the next contestant, a mixed murmur of male voices filled the void left by the music. Besides the employees, few true females filled the bar. Although Back Door Betty Night tended to get loud, it never rose to the same level as a bar packed with real women.

Anna turned back toward Stella. "Your Amy eyeliner looks good."

Stella shook the cocktail, then poured it into a lowball glass. "Thanks. Ivana Cox did it for me." Stella was fairly competent when it came to makeup, but Amy Winehouse eyeliner was beyond her capabilities.

"Ivana's here? I hate that bitch," Anna said without rancor.

Last month she'd loved Ivana. Of course, that had been after more than a few Snake Nuts. "She did my eyebrows, too. With a thread." Stella grabbed a straw and a little pink umbrella and stuck them into the drink.

"Hallelujah. Thank God someone finally got rid of that unibrow." Anna pointed one green fingernail between Stella's eyes.

"It was painful."

Anna's hand fell to the bar and she said in her

deep baritone voice, "Honey, until you tuck your banana in your ass crack, don't talk to me about pain."

Stella grimaced and handed Anna her drink. She didn't have a banana, but she did have an ass crack and she was positive she'd never purposely tuck anything in it. She did wear thong underwear, but the string of a thong was nowhere near the size of a banana. "Do you have an open tab?"

"Yeah."

Stella added the drink to Anna's already impressive bill. "Are you performing tonight?"

"Later. Are you?"

Stella shook her head, then looked at the next drink order. House wine and a bottle of Bud. Easy. Sometimes, on a slow night, she took the stage and belted out a few songs. She used to sing in an all-girl band, Random Muse, but the band broke up when the drummer slept with the bass guitarist's boyfriend and the two girls duked it out onstage at the Kandy Kane Lounge in Orlando. She grabbed a bottle of white wine and poured it into a glass. Stella had never understood why women fought over a man. Or hit each other at all. High on her list of things never to do, right above tucking anything the size of a banana in her ass crack, was getting punched in the head. Call her a baby, but she didn't like pain.

"Break me off a piece of that."

Without looking up and with little interest, Stella asked, "Of what?"

"Of that guy who just came in. Standing next to the Elvis jumpsuit."

Stella glanced through the dimly lit bar to the white suit behind Plexiglas bolted to the wall across from her. Ricky claimed the suit had once belonged to Elvis, but Stella wouldn't be surprised to discover it was as big a fake as the signed Stevie Ray Vaughn Stratocaster above the bar. "The guy in the baseball cap?"

"Yeah. He reminds me of that G.I. Joe guy."

Stella reached into the refrigerator beneath the bar and grabbed a bottle of Bud Light. "What G.I. Joe guy?"

Anna turned back to Stella, and the light above the bar caught in the green glitter in her lashes. "The one in the movie. What's his name . . . ?" Anna raised a hand and snapped her fingers, careful not to snap off her green snakeskin nails. "Tatum . . . something."

"O'Neal?"

"That's a female." She sighed as if Stella was hopeless. "He was also in my all-time favorite movie, *Dear John*."

Stella frowned and grabbed a chilled glass. Of course. Anna loved Nicholas Sparks.

"I wanna bite him. He's yummy."

Stella glanced at the orders on the screen in front of her. She liked Anna, but the queen was a distraction. Distraction slowed her down. The bar was hopping, and slowing down cost money. "Nicholas Sparks?"

"The guy next to the Elvis suit." A frown tugged at the corners of Anna's shiny green lips. "Military. I can tell just by the way he's leaning against the wall."

Stella removed the bottle cap and set it and the glass next to the wine on a tray. A waitress dressed as a zombie Hello Kitty whisked the tray away. Out of all the men in the bar, Stella wondered how Anna noticed the guy standing across the bar. He was dressed in black and blended into the shadows.

"He's straight. A real hard-ass," Anna answered as if she'd read Stella's mind. "And so on edge he's about to explode."

"You can tell all that from here?" Stella could hardly make out his outline as he leaned one shoulder into the lighter wood of the wall. She wouldn't have noticed him at all if Anna hadn't pointed him out. Just one more unsuspecting tourist who'd wandered in off the street. They didn't usually stay long once they figured out they were surrounded by queens and every other flavor of the rainbow.

Anna raised a hand and made a circle with her big palm. "It's in his aura. Straight. Hard-ass. Hot sexual repression." Her lips pursed around the straw and she took a sip of her drink. "Mmm."

Stella didn't believe in auras or any of the woo-woo psychic stuff. Her mother believed enough for both of them, and her grandmother was a staunch woo-woo follower. Abuela was into miracles and Marian apparitions and claimed to have once seen the Virgin Mary on a taco chip. Unfortunately, Tio Jorge ate it before she could put it in a shrine.

"I think I'll go say hey. You'd be surprised how many straight men troll for queens."

Actually, she wouldn't. She'd worked at Ricky's too long to be surprised by much. Although that didn't mean she understood men. Gay or straight or anywhere in between. "Could be he is a tourist and just wandered in."

"Maybe, but if there's one bitch to turn a straight man, it's Anna Conda." Anna lowered her drink. "G.I. Joe needs to be thanked for his service, and I'm suddenly feeling patriotic."

Stella rolled her eyes and took an order from a heavyset man with a thick red beard. She poured the Guinness with a perfect head and was rewarded with a five-dollar tip. "Thank you," she said through a smile and stuffed the bill into the small leather pouch tied around her hips. She had a tip jar, too, but she liked to empty it regularly. There had been too many times when drunks had helped themselves.

She glanced up as Anna headed across the bar, blue and green lights blinking in her size thirteen acrylic heels with each step she took.

Roy Orbison's iconic "Pretty Woman" rocked the bar's speakers as Penny Ho strutted the short stage in thigh-high boots and blue-and-white hooker dress, looking remarkably like Julia Roberts. Apparently, "Pretty Woman" was popular among drag queens and tiara tots.

Over the next hour, Stella poured shots, pulled drafts, and gave the martini shakers a workout. By one-thirty, she'd changed out of her four-inch pumps and into her Doc Martens. Even with the thick cushion of the floor matting, her feet had not been able to hold out for more than six hours. Her old Doc boots were scuffed, but they were worn in, comfortable, and supported her feet.

After Penny Ho, Edith Moorehead took the stage and shimmied in a meat gown to Lady Gaga's "Born This Way." It just went without saying that the dress was an unfortunate choice for a big girl like Edith. Unfortunate and dangerous for the people who got hit with a flying flank steak.

Stella fanned her face with a cardboard coaster as she poured a glass of merlot. She was off in half an hour and wanted to get her side work done before the next bartender took her place. In the entertainment district of Miami, bars were open 24/7. Ricky chose to close his between five and ten A.M. because business slowed during those hours, and due to operating costs, he lost money by staying open. And more than groping an unsuspecting female employee, Ricky loved money.

Stella lifted her long hair from the back of her neck and gazed across the bar. Her attention stopped on a couple in fairy wings going at it a few feet from the white Elvis suit. They'd better take it down a notch or one of the bouncers would bounce them. Ricky didn't tolerate excessive PDA or sex in his bar. Not because the man had even a passing acquaintance with anything resembling a moral compass, but because, gay or straight, it was bad for business.

Wedged between the fairy couple and the Elvis suit, Anna's G.I. Joe sat back farther in the shadows. A slash of light cut across his shoulder, wide neck, and chin. The strobe at the end of the stage flashed on his face, cheeks, and the brim of his hat. By the set of his jaw, he didn't appear happy. A smile twisted a corner of Stella's lips and she shook her head. If the man didn't like queens and in-betweens, he could always leave. The fact that he still sat there, soaking in all the homosexual testosterone surrounding him, likely meant he had a case of "closet gay." Anger was a classic sign, at least that's what she'd heard from homosexual men who were free to be themselves.

After Edith, Anna hit the stage to Robyn's "Do You Know." Her lip-synching was spot-on. Her stage presence was good, but in the end, Kreme Delight won the night and the Back Door Betty crown. Anna stormed off the stage and out the front door. Stella glanced across the room toward the white Elvis suit. G.I. Joe was gone, too. Coincidence?

At one forty-five, she was caught up on most of her side work. She sliced fruit and restocked olives and cherries. She washed down the bar and unloaded the industrial-size dishwasher. At two, she closed out, transferred tabs, and stayed around long enough to get tipped out. She untied her leather tip purse from around her hips and stuffed it into a backpack along with her heels and hairbrush. Out of habit, she took out her Russian Red lipstick. Without a mirror, she applied a perfect swipe across her mouth. Some women liked mascara. Others rouge. Stella was a lipstick girl. Always red, and she never went anywhere without ruby-colored lips.

She fished the keys to her maroon PT Cruiser from the backpack. The car had over one hundred thousand miles on it and needed new shocks and struts. Riding in it jarred the fillings from your teeth, but the air conditioning worked and that was all Stella cared about.

She said good-bye to the other employees and headed out the back door. June, warm and slushy, pressed into her skin despite the early morning hour. Stella had been born and raised in Las Cruces and was used to some humidity, but summers in Miami were like living in a steam bath, and she'd never quite gotten used to how it lay on her skin and weighted her lungs. Occasionally she thought about returning home. Then she'd remember why she left, and she remembered that she could never go home again.

"Little Stella Bella."

She glanced up as she shut the door behind her. Crap. Ricky. "Mr. De Luca."

"Are you leaving so soon?"

"My shift was over half an hour ago."

Ricardo De Luca was a good seven inches taller than Stella and easily outweighed her by a hundred pounds. He always wore traditional guayabera shirts. Sometimes zipped, sometimes buttoned, but always pastel. Tonight it looked like tangerine. "You don't have to leave so soon." His lifestyle had aged him beyond his fifty-three years. He might have been handsome, but too much booze made him pink and bloated. He had thick black hair and a black soul patch that he wore under the delusion that it made him look younger. It made him look sad.

"Good night," she said, and stepped around him.

"Some of my friends are meeting me here." He grabbed her wrist, and his booze-soaked-breath smacked her across the face. "Party with us."

She took a step back but he didn't release her. Her Mace was in her backpack, and she couldn't get to it one-handed. "I can't." Anxiety crept up her spine and sped up her heart. *Relax. Breathe,* she told herself before her anxiety turned into panic. She hadn't had a full-blown attack in several years. Not since she'd learned how to talk herself out of one. *This is Ricky. He wouldn't hurt you.* But if he tried, she knew how to hurt *him.* She really didn't want to shove the heel of her hand in his nose or her knee in his junk. She wanted to keep her job. "I'm meeting someone," she lied.

"Who? A man? I bet I have more to offer."

She needed her job. She made good money and was good at it. "Let go of my wrist, please."

"Why are you always running away?" The lights from the back of the bar shone across the thin layer of sweat above his top lip. "What's your problem?"

"I don't have a problem, Mr. De Luca." And she pointed out rather reasonably, or so she thought, "I'm your employee. You're my boss. It's just not a good idea for us to party together." Then she topped it off with a little flattery. "I'm positive there are a lot of other women who would just love to party with you." She tried to pull away but his grasp tightened on her wrist. Her keys fell to the ground and an old familiar fear turned her muscles tight. *Ricky wouldn't hurt me*, she told herself again as she looked into his drunken gaze. He wouldn't hold her against her will.

"If you're nice to me, I'll be nice to you."

"Please let go." Instead, he gave her wrist a hard jerk. She planted her free hand on his chest to keep from falling into him.

"Not yet."

A deep rasp of a voice spoke from behind Ricky, "That's twice." The voice was so chilly it almost cooled the air, and Stella tried in vain to look over Ricky's left shoulder. "Now let her go."

"Fuck off," Ricky said, and turned toward the voice. "This is none of your business. Get out of my fucking lot."

"It's hot and I don't want to work up a sweat. I'll give you three seconds."

"I said fuc—" A solid thud snapped Ricky's head back. His grasp on her relaxed and he slid to the ground. Her mouth fell open and she sucked in a startled breath. Her Amy pouf tilted forward as she stared down at the tangerine lump at her feet. She blinked at him several times. What had just happened? Ricky looked like he was out cold. She pushed at his arm with the toe of her boot. Definitely out cold. "I don't think that was three seconds."

"I get impatient sometimes."

Stella glanced up from Ricky's tangerine shirt to the big chest covered in a black T-shirt in front of her. Black pants. Black T-shirt, baseball cap, he was almost swallowed up in the black night like some hulking ninja. She couldn't see his eyes, but she felt his gaze on her face. As cool as his voice and just as direct. There was something familiar about him.

"He should have listened." He tilted his head to one side and glanced down at Ricky. "This is your boss?"

"Yeah." She looked down at Ricky. He *was* her boss. *Not now.* She couldn't work for him now, which was moot because she was pretty sure she was fired. And that made her mad. She had rent and utilities and a car payment. "Is he going to be okay?"

"Do you care?"

Ricky snored once, twice, and she glanced back up into the shadows beneath the brim of the stranger's hat. Square chin and jaw. Thick neck. Big shoulders. Anna's G.I. Joe. Did she care? Probably not as much as she should. "I don't want him to die."

"He's not going to die."

"How do you know?" She'd heard of people dying from one blow to the head.

"Because if I wanted him dead, he'd be dead. He wouldn't be snoring right now."

"Oh." She didn't know anything about the man standing in front of her, but she believed him. "Is Anna out here with you?" She looked behind him at the empty parking lot.

"Who?"

Stella knelt down and quickly grabbed her keys by Ricky's shoulder. She didn't want to touch him, but she paused just long enough to wave her hand in front of his eyes to make sure he was good and truly out. "Ricky?" She peered closer, looking for blood. "Mr. De Luca?"

"Who's Anna?"

"Anna Conda." She didn't see blood. Which was probably a good sign.

"I don't know any Anna Conda."

Ricky snored and blew his gross breath on her. She cringed and stood. "The drag queen in the snake gown. You're not out here with her?"

He folded his arms across his big chest and rocked back on his heels. The shadow from the brim of his hat brushed the bow of his scowling top lip. "Negative. There isn't anyone else out here." He pointed to her and then to the ground. "Except you and Numb Nuts."

Sometimes tourists wandered into the lot or parked in it illegally. What did a girl say to a guy who'd knocked out another guy on her behalf? No one had ever come to her defense like that before. "Thank you," she guessed.

"You're welcome."

Why had he? A stranger? G.I. Joe was big. A lot bigger than Ricky, and it didn't look like an ounce of fat would have the audacity to cling to any part of his body. She'd have to jump up to deliver a stunning nose jab or eye poke, and she suddenly felt small. "This is employee parking. What are you doing out here?" She took a step back and slid her pack off her shoulder. Without taking her eyes from his, she slid her finger to the zipper. She didn't want to Mace the guy. That seemed kind of rude, but she would. Mace him, then run like hell. She was pretty fast for a short girl. "You could get towed."

"I'm not going to hurt you, Stella."

That stopped her fingers and brought her up short. "Do I know you?"

"No. I'm here on behalf of a second party."

"Hold on." She held up a hand. "You've been out here waiting for me?"

"Yeah. It took you a while."

"Are you from a collection agency?" She glanced

toward the front of the lot, and her PT Cruiser was still in its slot. She didn't have any other outstanding debts.

"No."

If he were going to serve her with a subpoena, he would have when he'd first walked in the bar. "Who is the 'second party' and what do they want?"

"I'll buy you coffee at the café around the corner and we'll talk about it."

"No thanks." She carefully stepped over her boss but kept her eyes on him just in case he woke and grabbed her leg. "Just tell me and let's get this over with." Although she could probably guess.

"A member of your family."

That's what she thought. She was so relieved not to feel Ricky's pervy hand on her leg, she relaxed a fraction. "Tell them I'm not interested."

"Ten minutes in the café." He dropped his hands to his sides and took several steps back. "That's it. And we should get moving before Numb Nuts comes around. I don't like to put a guy down twice in one night. Could cause brain damage."

What a humanitarian. Although she'd really rather not be around when Ricky woke up, either. Or when one of his sleazy "associates" rolled in. Or have G.I. Joe "put him down" again and cause brain damage. Or in Ricky's case, *more* brain damage.

"And it will save us both the trouble of me knocking on your door tomorrow," he added.

He was as relentless as he looked, and she didn't doubt him. "Ten minutes." She'd rather hear what he had to say in a busy café than at her front door. "I'll give you ten minutes and then I want you to tell my family to leave me alone." Behind her, Ricky snorted and snored, and she looked back at him one last time as she moved toward the street.

"That's all it will take."

She walked beside him from the dark lot into the bright, crazy nightlife of Miami. Tubes of pink and purple neon lit up clubs and Art Deco hotels. Shiny cars with custom rims, booming systems that thumped the pavement. Even at three in the morning, the party was still going strong.

"Maybe we should call an ambulance for Ricky," she said as they passed a drunk tourist puking on a neon-blue palm tree.

"He's not that hurt." He moved closest to the street as he dug into a side pocket of his pants.

"He's unconscious," she pointed out.

"Maybe he's a little hurt." He pulled out a cell and punched a few numbers on his phone. "I'm on a traceable. I need you to call Ricky's Rock 'N' Roll Saloon in Miami and tell them there's someone passed out on their back doorstep." He laughed as he took Stella's elbow and turned the corner. The commanding touch was so brief, it was over before she had time to pull away. So brief yet left a hot imprint even after he dropped his hand. "Yeah. I'm sure he's drunk." He laughed again. They moved to the curb and he stuck out his arm like a security gate as he looked up and down the street. "I'm headed there in about an hour. It should go down easy." Then he pointed at the café across the street as if he was in command. In charge. The boss.

No one was in charge of Stella. No one commanded her anymore. She was the boss. Not that it mattered. She'd give this guy ten minutes of her time and then it was sayonara, G.I. Joe.

Anything But Sweet

A Sweet, TX Novel

CANDIS TERRY

Chapter One

Trouble rolled into downtown Sweet on the spinning wheels of a yellow Hummer. Inside the gas guzzler, the crew for cable TV's makeover show *My New Town* waved their arms out the windows to the legions of enthusiasts extending a big Texas welcome.

On an ordinary day, there wasn't much to attract outsiders to a town that progress had ignored. No interstate to bring in the tourists—just a poorly paved road with too many ruts to be comfortable even in the most luxurious limousine. With the exception of Goody Gum Drops—the candy store painted like a peppermint stick—most of the town's cedar-sided shops were faded with age. Their metal overhangs more rust than steel. Their signs in various stages of chip and peel.

A few years back, Mayor Gary Gleason had promised to put a little zing into the ancient buildings that lined Main Street. Talk was he never got any further than the side-street boutique rumored to have a back room that sold naughty lingerie and large quantities of AA batteries.

Frustrated with the mayor's lack of gumption, the over-seventy crowd who met on a daily basis at Bud's Nothing Finer Diner for coffee, pie, and gossip, put their gray-haired heads together. They conjured up the outrageous idea to contact a reality makeover show to come in and give the town a face-lift.

The harebrained proposition churned up gossip for weeks and kept the town abuzz, like the hive wreaking havoc below the marquee at the Yellow Rose Cinema.

So on this steamy summer day, with wildflowers dotting the meadows and a curtain of brilliant blue draped across the sky, Tinsel Town came calling.

Everyone was excited about the change.

Everyone except Reno Wilder, who stood in the shade of the warped overhang above Wilder and Sons Hardware & Feed watching the parade of trucks and trailers thunder down Main Street.

Dust and gravel kicked up in the wake of the intruders as the community jumped up and down like they were at a Rangers doubleheader.

Arms folded across his chest, Reno leaned a shoulder against a rough-hewn post and crossed one booted ankle over the other. The muscles in his neck tightened as he shook his head.

He wanted no part of this insanity.

There wasn't a damn thing wrong with his hometown.

Sure, it was a little weathered at the wings. Tarnished at the joints. But that's what gave it character and charm. Yeah, maybe the place had been established in the mid 1800s, and all the downtown buildings were original. What was wrong with that? He liked historic. Traditional. If folks wanted new and trendy, they could go to Austin. He liked his little town just the way it was—like his favorite pair of boots. A little worn at the heels but real comfortable.

"They've all lost their minds." The statement came out a grumble.

"Come on." Former Army Ranger Aiden Marshall chuckled as he dumped the bag of dog food he'd just purchased into the bed of his truck. He reached through the open window and gave the golden retriever and border collie waiting in the cab a rub between their ears. "This is the most excitement we've had since I came home from Afghanistan."

Reno raised a brow. Within weeks of Aiden's return, he'd reconnected with Paige Walker, the love of his life. Word had it a wedding was in the works. An invasion from Hollywood hardly seemed a fair comparison.

"Yeah, well, that would be the *Army* part of your brain working in the wrong direction."

Aiden laughed out loud. "Then I guess that

means the former *Marine* part of your brain is working overtime."

"Semper Fi, my man."

The good-humored ribbing they tossed back and forth wasn't unusual or meant to be unkind. Didn't matter what branch of the military a man served, they were all brothers in arms. The joking helped bury the memories they'd rather forget. Eased the pain that still lingered.

After the darkest day in America, any man able to pass the scrutiny enlisted. That list included Reno and his brothers. Aiden and his best friends. Some came home. Some didn't. Reno knew that grief too well.

"Think they brought any good-lookin' women with 'em?"

In unison, Reno and Aiden glanced down at the bald pate of the old codger standing between them. At eighty years old, Chester Banks was every bit the skirt chaser he'd been all his life. Reno didn't know if Chester had been a handsome man in his youth; today he was all nose and sunken eyeballs.

"Doubt it," Reno said. "Looks like you'll have to stick with Gertie Finnegan. I hear she's taking fox-trot lessons over at the senior center just for you."

"Pfft." Chester waved an arthritic hand. "That woman ain't got no sense. She should be learnin' that cha-cha like they do on *Dancing with the Stars*. 'Course, Gertie ain't built like those hot little dancers."

"Don't expect she is." Reno squinted against the

glare bouncing off another truck bearing the TV show logo. "Hard to maintain a killer bod when you're pushing ninety."

Chester's hopeful smile slid into the abyss. "Ain't that a fact."

"Paige mentioned something about the designer host's name being Charli," Aiden said.

"Probably light in the loafers." Chester gave an all-knowing nod.

"That's an awfully big assumption," Reno said.

The old man looked up at him. "I don't see you pitchin' a hissy over polka-dot chintz or chandeliers with them dangly little crystals."

"I'm not much into fabrics or lighting," Reno agreed. "Unless my sheets need washing or my Maglite needs new batteries."

"Exactly." Chester said this in the same way one would holler, "Eureka!"

"Why are y'all standing over here?" All three men looked up as Paige Walker honey blond ponytail swinging—jogged toward them. "The party's across the street." She came to a stop in front of Aiden, grabbed hold of his T-shirt with both hands and pulled him in for a kiss. Paige had always been a take-what-she-wanted kind of girl. Not that Aiden seemed to mind.

"We can see fine from here," Reno answered. Not that she was really listening. Reno's heart cramped as he watched his buddy's arms go around the woman he loved.

He'd had that once. That crazy, can't-get-enough-of-her fire in his blood. Like everything else, he'd lost it. Tragically. Horribly. Unforgettably.

Never one to take no for an answer, Paige lifted her head, wrinkled her nose, and zeroed in on the weak link of the bunch. "Chester? Don't you want a better look?"

"Ah." He waved a shoofly hand. "I ain't interested in no girly men."

Paige laughed. *"Girly* men?"

"You know," Chester said, doing a little dance on bowed legs. "The tiptoe-through-the-tulips type. Like that Charli fella."

"You mean Charlotte Brooks? The designer?"

Chester's rheumy hazel eyes widened. "Charli's a *girl?"*

"Was the last time I saw her on TV." Knowing she'd won at least one of them over, Paige gave a victorious grin. "She's kind of a knockout too."

"Now you've done it," Reno said, as Chester found a sudden giddyap to his get-a-long.

"Y'all come on." Halfway across the street, Chester waved the three of them over. "In case I have me a heart attack."

"I'm good right here," Reno mumbled. He had no intention of setting foot anywhere near those who planned to seek and destroy his quiet, humble little town.

"No, you're not." Paige grabbed both him and Aiden by the arm. "And if y'all are having any ideas of taking off for the hills, think again," she added, "I've got on my running shoes."

Didn't matter that the front door to his hardware store stood wide open, Reno knew better than to mess with any female who had Texas running deep in her veins. They built them strong in the South. And when a Southern woman used *that* tone, they meant business. A lesson he'd learned years ago and would not soon forget.

Paige hauled them across the street and pushed them toward the front of the crowd, where the big yellow Hummer and parade of trucks had rolled to a stop at the curb of what the folks liked to call Town Square. In reality, it was only a patch of grass with a few trees, picnic tables, and a gazebo with half the roof gone from a random windstorm last spring. Yet more weddings and birthday parties took place there than anywhere else within a ten-mile radius.

With the mayor directing the Hollywood interlopers, the Hummer cleared the curb and drove up onto the lawn, mashing the grass Ernie McGreavy had spent hours the day before meticulously mowing. Like a swarm of killer bees, the crowd of locals surrounded the yellow monstrosity and let out a cheer when the doors popped open. Cameras were already rolling when four passengers stepped out—a tiny blonde with a studious look and a clipboard hugged to her chest and a ragtag trio of men who looked as though they'd pounded a few nails—or heads—in their day.

The last to emerge was the driver—a brunette in a snug skirt that hit her midcalf and a blouse that molded like a second skin over high, firm breasts, and a narrow waist. A tall, *curvy* brunette, whose ankles wobbled when she stepped down from the vehicle. A tall, curvy, *smiling* brunette, whose skyscraper heels sank deep into Ernie McGreavy's perfectly clipped grass.

Reno covered a laugh with a cough.

Looked like *Charli* was going to find out fast that her big city ways—and shoes—wouldn't fly in this small Texas town.

"Whoops!" She giggled as the mayor reached out to steady her. Then she looked up with wide eyes, and asked the crowd, "Do you mind if I dispense with propriety?"

The crowd responded with a cheer.

Reno watched in surprise as she reached down, pulled off her shoes, and instantly shrunk several inches. She wiggled her painted pink toes in Ernie's grass with a long "Ahhhhhh." Then she flashed another smile through full lips tinted a soft coral.

Paige had been right.

The woman was a knockout.

Appearances could be deceiving. Anyone knew that. While Reno had to admit that *Charli* made a pretty package, it wouldn't take long for the rest of the town to realize what he already knew. They'd made a huge mistake. Faster than roaches out the kitchen door of Mabel's Grits and Grog, they'd send her and her cohorts packing.

"This is going to be so much fun." Beside him,

Paige practically vibrated in her white sneakers. She grabbed hold of Aiden's arm and grinned. "Maybe we can even pick up some design pointers for our B&B."

For what seemed like the millionth time that day, Reno shook his head. If Paige took so much as a hammer to Honey Hill, her Aunt Bertie— the elderly relative from whom she'd bought the place—would pitch a hissy all the way from the Texas Rose Assisted Care facility.

A loud screech of feedback ripped Reno's attention back to the mayor and the TV star. After brief introductions, she took the microphone like she'd been born to hold one in her hand. Reno imagined that manicured hand had probably never seen a day of hard work. Most likely she used it for pointing and ordering others around.

As she addressed the crowd, Reno watched her perfectly bowed lips break into another smile, which flashed her straight white teeth. You could tell a lot about a person from their smile—though these days it was hard to tell with all the collagen, Botox, and veneers going around. He ran his tongue along the slight chip in his front tooth—a gift he'd received during a tussle with his brother about fifteen years back. Not everyone came perfectly put together. Some folks were a little rougher around the edges.

All the better in his mind.

The makeover star made eye contact with several eagerly nodding folks in the pack of humans squished together, vying to be in a camera shot. In Reno's book, direct eye contact spoke volumes about a person. If a man—or a woman—wouldn't look you square in the eye, you'd best figure out how to defend yourself. He'd learned that the hard way. Had the scars to prove it. There were other wounds inside him too. The ones in his heart might be invisible to the eye, but that didn't mean they weren't just as devastating.

After several syrupy comments from Ms. Brooks about how happy she was to be there and how those on the show planned to give Sweet a shot in the arm and help turn it into a wonderful tourist destination, Reno had had enough. He started to back out of the crowd, only to be stopped by the woman who'd raised him.

"Where y'all going, son?" Jana Wilder stood barely tall enough to reach the bottom of his chin, but she wielded a mighty sword that he and his brothers yielded to—if they valued their hides. And they did. On most days.

By the flash in her bright blue eyes and the tilt of her big blond hairdo, he knew he was about to be on the receiving end of a lecture. "Left the door open on the store," he said. "Need to get back."

"This is Sweet, sugarplum." She reached up and patted the stubble shadowing his jaw. "Who's going to pay attention?"

He angled his head toward the makeover crew. "Strangers in town."

"Oh pooh. Don't be silly. These nice folks came here fixin' to help. Not rob us."

"That's a matter of opinion."

His mother smiled. "Don't be such a fuddy-duddy."

"Yeah." Paige gave him an elbow nudge. "Lighten up a little."

Reno looked for a little masculine support from Aiden and Chester. Knowing they'd be wasting their breath, they both shrugged. Tempted to go the battle alone, Reno put on his best glare. "Y'all might want to reconsider your enthusiasm before this town you love so much disappears. You let something like this in, next thing you know you'll have a McDonald's and Walmart on every corner."

His mother chuckled. "Didn't your daddy ever tell you that life was just one big ol' adventure, and you'd best snatch it up with both hands?"

"Yes." *The day before he died, in fact.* Reno fought back the huge sense of loss that remained as powerful today as the day two years ago, when they'd buried the man who'd saved his life.

"Then turn around and grab it," his mother dared with a big smile.

As Reno turned back to the circus, he found *Fancy Pants* leaning into that big gas guzzler. Her efforts hiked up her skirt and gave him, and anyone else who cared to look, a splendid view of the backs of her firm thighs.

Chester let out a wolf whistle. Paige gave the

old skirt chaser a poke in the ribs. Reno had to admit that as much as he did not want change in his little town, he was a man. One who recognized a gorgeous woman even as everything inside him tried to ignore the warning bells and whistles.

The gathered crowd waited with hushed whispers until the TV host backed out of the Hummer with something in her arms. That *something* happened to be a tiny, apricot-colored poodle sporting a sparkling rhinestone collar.

Charlotte Brooks took a step forward, coming close enough for him to catch a whiff of her sweet perfume. Her brown eyes traveled down the length of his body and slowly climbed back up to his face. She flashed him a grin that seemed to say she approved.

"Hold Pumpkin for me, won't you, handsome?" Her voice was the kind of sexy low and husky a man wanted to hear in the bedroom. Whispering his name. As she begged him to take her again and again.

The sensual spell she cast crashed down as she thrust her prissy pooch in his arms, then sauntered away to continue wowing the crowd.

Pumpkin?

Reno glanced down at the pathetic excuse of a dog shivering in his arms. For Christ's sake, it had glitter-painted toenails on its raccoonlike feet. Who the hell would do that?

Chester elbowed him, leering and nodding like a bobblehead figurine. "She likes you."

Reno could barely think beyond the irritation burning through his veins. That was when something warm and wet spread across the front of his shirt.

Shocked, he stared down into bugged-out brown eyes that silently said, "Oops."

Sex and the Single Fireman

A Bachelor Firemen Novel

JENNIFER BERNARD

Chapter One

Revenge, decided Sabina Jones, was a dish best served on the side of the road to the tune of a police siren.

It had all started with Sabina doing what she always did on Thanksgiving—hitting the road and blasting the radio to drown out the lack of a phone call from her mother. Thirteen years of no Thanksgiving calls, and it still bothered her. Even though she now had her life pretty much exactly how she wanted it, holidays were tough. When things got tough, Sabina, like any normal, red-blooded American woman, turned up the volume.

In her metallic blue El Camino, at a red light in Reno, Nevada, she let the high decibel sound of Kylie Minogue dynamite any stray regrets out of her head. She danced her fingers on the steering wheel and bopped her head, enjoying the desert-warm breeze from the half-open window.

So what if she had her own way to celebrate Thanksgiving? This was America. Land of the

Free. If she wanted to spend Thanksgiving in Reno letting off steam, the Founding Fathers ought to cheer along and say, "You go, girl."

The honk of a car horn interrupted Kylie in mid–"la-la-la-la." She glanced to her left. In the lane next to her, a black-haired, black-eyed giant of a man in a black Jeep aimed a ferocious scowl her way. He pointed to the cell phone at his ear and then at her radio, then back and forth a few times.

"Excuse me?" Sabina said sweetly, though he had no chance of hearing her over the blaring radio. "If you think I'm going to turn my radio down so you can talk on your cell phone while driving, forget it. That's illegal, you know. Not to mention dangerous."

The man gave an impatient gesture. This time Sabina noticed that his eyebrows were also black, that they slashed across his face like marauding Horsemen of the Apocalypse, that his eyes were actually one shade removed from black, with maybe a hint of midnight blue, and that his shoulders and chest were packed with muscle.

She rolled her window all the way down, pasted a charming smile on her face, and leaned out. With her window wide open, the noise from her radio had to be even louder. "Excuse me? I can't hear you."

He yelled, "Can you please turn that down!" in a deep, gravelly voice like that of a battlefield commander sending his troops into the line of fire.

Despite his use of the word "please," it was most definitely not a request. Sabina guessed that most people jumped to obey him. An air of authority clung to him like sexy aftershave. But she'd never responded well to orders off the job. At the station she didn't have a choice, but here in her own car, no one was going to boss her around, not even a gigantic, sexy stranger. She reached over and turned up the volume even higher.

"Is that better?" she yelled through her window, with the same sweet smile. With one part of her brain, she wondered how strict the Reno PD was about noise ordinances.

She couldn't hear his answer, but she could practically guarantee it included profanity.

For the first time this miserable Thanksgiving, her mood lifted. Her childhood holidays had always been spent fighting with her mother. In her mother's absence, she'd have to make do with bickering with the guy in the next car over. As someone who prided herself on never complaining, she'd much rather fight than feel sorry for herself.

It occurred to her that he might be talking to a family member. Some people had normal families and celebrated holidays in a normal fashion—or so she'd heard. She moved her hand toward the volume dial, ready to cave in and turn it down.

The man rolled his window all the way up, stuck one finger—a very particular finger—in one ear, and yelled into his phone.

Sabina snatched her hand away from the dial. If he yelled at his family like that, and had the nerve to give her the finger, he deserved no mercy. Besides, the light was about to change and she was going to make him eat her El Camino's dust.

She stared at the red light, tensing her body in anticipation. The light for the cars going the other direction had turned yellow. The cars were slowing for the stoplight, and the last Toyota still in the intersection had nearly passed through. She poised her foot over the accelerator.

Then something black and speedy caught the corner of her eye. The Jeep cruised through the intersection. The big jerk hadn't even waited for the light to change. It finally turned green when he was halfway through the intersection.

Indignant, she slammed her foot onto the accelerator. Her car surged into the intersection. He wasn't too far ahead . . . she could still catch him . . . pass him . . .

A flash in her rearview mirror made her yank her foot off the accelerator. A Reno PD cruiser passed her, lights flashing, siren blaring. It crowded close to the Jeep, which put on its right-turn signal and veered toward the curb. She slowed to let both vehicles pass in front of her. As the policeman pulled up behind the Jeep, she cruised past, offering the black-haired man her most sparkling smile.

In exchange, he sent her a look of pure black fire.

Sweet, sweet revenge.

Sabina's cell phone rang, flashing an unfamiliar number. For a wild moment, she wondered if it was the man in the Jeep, calling to yell at her again. Of course that was impossible, but who would be calling from a strange number? She'd already wished the crew at the firehouse Happy Thanksgiving. She'd already called Carly, her "Little Sister" from the Big Brothers Big Sisters program.

Was her mother finally calling, after thirteen missed Thanksgivings? Annabelle wasn't even in the U.S., according to the latest tabloid reports. But still, what if . . .

Her heart racing, she picked up the phone and held it to her ear. "Hello."

Clucking chicken noises greeted her. She let out a long breath. Of course it wasn't her mother. What had she been thinking?

"I can't talk right now, Anu. I'm in Reno."

"Yes, skipping Thanksgiving. That's precisely what I want to talk to you about."

"I'm not skipping it. I'm celebrating in my own way."

"I located a potential partner for you. A very obliging guest here at the restaurant. He's letting me use his phone so you can install his number in your contacts." Anu, who was from India, claimed pushy matchmaking was in her blood.

"Seriously. Can't talk." Especially about that.

"Very well. You go to your soulless casino filled

with strangers, drink your pink gin fizzes, and pretend you're celebrating Thanksgiving."

In the midst of rolling her eyes, Sabina spotted the police cruiser in her rearview mirror.

"Gotta go." She dropped the phone to the floorboards just as the police car passed her. The cop cruised past, turning blank sunglasses on her.

A sunny smile, a little wave, and the officer left her alone. A few moments later, the black Jeep caught up to her. The gigantic black-haired man looked straight ahead, either ignoring her or oblivious to her. For some reason she didn't like either of those possibilities. Or maybe she just wanted another fight.

She reached for her volume control and turned the radio up full blast. The man didn't react, other than to drum his fingers on his steering wheel. Fine. She rolled her window down to make it even louder, knowing how ridiculously childish she was being.

Thanksgiving brought out the worst in her, she'd be the first to admit.

The corner of the man's mouth quivered. Good. She was getting to him. The sounds of Kylie filled the El Camino, high notes careening around the interior, bass line vibrating the steering wheel. Adding her own voice to the din, she sang along at the top of her lungs. She might as well be inside a jukebox, especially with that gaudy light flashing in the rearview mirror . . .

Oh, *crap.*

One hundred and twenty dollars later, she pulled up in front of the Starlight Motel and Casino. Why couldn't she experience, just once, a peaceful Thanksgiving filled with love, harmony, and mushroom-walnut stuffing? Her mother had always dragged her to some producer's house where she'd be stuck with kids she didn't know, rich, spoiled, jealous kids who mocked her crazy red hair and baby fat. She'd always ended the evening in tears, with her mother scolding her. *This is what we do in this business, kiddo. Would it kill you to make a few friends? Those kids could be getting you work someday.*

Her mother had gotten that part wrong. Sabina had found her own work, thank you very much. And it meant everything to her.

The setting sun beamed golden light directly into her eyes, mocking her with its cheerful glory. Thanksgiving always messed with her, always bit her in the ass. On a few Thanksgivings, she'd tried calling her mother, only to get the run-around from her assistant. But now Annabelle was in France and none of her numbers worked anymore.

Damn. Why hadn't she just signed up for the holiday shift at the station and spent the day putting out oven fires?

She grabbed her bag and marched through the double front doors, only to stop short, blocked by a giant figure looming in her path. Even though she couldn't see clearly in the dimmer light of the lobby, she knew exactly who it was. A shocking thrill went through her; she should have guessed the man in the Jeep would turn up again.

"Well, this is a lucky coincidence," the man said in a voice like tarred gravel. "The way I figure it, you owe me three hundred and sixty-eight dollars. Cash will be fine."

"Excuse me?" She peered up at him, his black hair and eyes coming quickly into focus. Her stomach fluttered at the sheer impact of his physical presence. He was absolutely huge, well over six feet tall, a column of hard muscle contained within jeans and a black T-shirt. "If you're referring to your well-deserved spanking from the Reno PD, don't even start. No one made you run that red light."

"Sorry, did you say something? I can barely hear you over the ringing in my ears."

Sabina lifted her chin. If he thought he could intimidate her, he didn't realize who he was dealing with. She worked with firefighters all day long, not one of them a pushover. "Maybe you should try not yelling at your family for a change."

"Excuse me?" He glowered down at her, looking mortally offended. "What the hell are you talking about?"

Realizing she'd probably crossed a line, Sabina scrambled to recover. "Anyway, you already got your revenge. They gave me a ticket too. We're square."

"I wouldn't have had to yell if you'd had the

common decency to respond to a perfectly reasonable request."

Sabina felt her temperature rise. He wasn't making it easy to make peace with him. "Request? Something tells me you never make requests. Orders, sure. Requests, dream on."

"You think you know me?"

"Why should I want to know you when all you do is scowl and shout at me?"

"Shout?" He shook his head slowly, with a stupefied look. "They told me the people were different out here. I had no idea that meant insane."

Sabina tried to sidestep around him and end this crazy downward spiral of a conversation. "I wish the police gave tickets for rudeness, you'd have about three more by now."

He blocked her path again, so she found herself nose-to-chest with him. Sabina imagined him as a Scottish laird or a medieval warrior hacking at enemies on the battlefield. The man was fierce, but annoyingly attractive. He even smelled nice, like sunshine on leather seats.

"How about drowning out a man's first phone call with his son in two thousand miles? How's that for rudeness?"

He had a point. But a surge of resentment swamped her momentary pang of conscience. So some people *did* talk to their children on Thanksgiving. Normal people, irritatingly, aggravatingly, unreachably normal people. People who were not her or her mother.

"Fine," she snapped. "Here." She dug in her pocket and took out a handful of change. "We're at a casino, right? Play your cards right and you'll get your precious three hundred and sixty-eight dollars. Good luck."

She lifted one of his hands—so big and warm—and plopped her small pile of change into his palm. With the air of an offended duchess, she swept past him, deeply appreciating the way his black-stubbled jaw dropped open.

So maybe she'd been wrong before. Maybe revenge was a dish best served in a hotel lobby with a side of loose change.